THE LAST GUNFIGHTER
HELL TOWN

THE LAST GUNFIGHTER
HELL TOWN

WILLIAM W. JOHNSTONE
WITH J. A. JOHNSTONE

PINNACLE BOOKS
Kensington Publishing Corp.

www.kensingtonbooks.com

PINNACLE BOOKS are published by

Kensington Publishing Corp.
850 Third Avenue
New York, NY 10022

PUBLISHER'S NOTE
Following the death of William W. Johnstone, the Johnstone family is working with a carefully selected writer to organize and complete Mr. Johnstone's outlines and many unfinished manuscripts to create additional novels in all of his series like The Last Gunfighter, Mountain Man, and Eagles, among others. This novel was inspired by Mr. Johnstone's superb storytelling.

All Kensington titles, imprints, and distributed lines are available at special quantity discounts for bulk purchases for sales promotions, premiums, fund-raising, educational, or institutional use. Special book excerpts or customized printings can also be created to fit specific needs. For details, write or phone the office of the Kensington special sales manager: Kensington Publishing Corp., 850 Third Avenue, New York, NY 10022, attn: Special Sales Department; phone 1-800-221-2647.

PINNACLE BOOKS and the Pinnacle logo are Reg. U.S. Pat. & TM Off.

ISBN-13: 978-0-7860-1738-6
ISBN-10: 0-7860-1738-4

First printing: October 2007

10 9 8 7 6 5 4 3 2 1

Printed in the United States of America

Chapter 1

The kid was obstreperous. That was the way Johnny Collyer thought of him anyway, since Johnny had once been snowed in for the winter with nothing but a dictionary to read and he had gone through that sucker from cover to cover and memorized a lot of it.

But it would have been just as easy to say that the kid was an asshole, because that was true too.

Johnny moved the bar rag in circles over the mahogany, even though the wood already shone in the light from the oil chandeliers in the Silver Baron Saloon, and listened to the kid's braying laughter. He'd been drunk already when he came into the Silver Baron half an hour earlier, and he hadn't done anything since then except get drunker and more obnoxious. His friends, a couple of hard-faced hombres in range clothes, had tried to persuade him to control himself, but the kid wasn't having any of it.

Now he stood over the table where Professor Burton had been nursing a drink and demanded in a loud, arrogant voice, "What the hell are you dressed up for, mister? Goin' to a weddin'—or a funeral?"

The professor, who was always dapper in a suit, vest,

and bowler hat, replied in his fluid, cultured voice, "This is my normal attire, sir."

The kid laughed again. "Then you must be one o' them strange fellas who don't like women. That what you are, mister?"

Burton's middle-aged face, usually tranquil, flushed with anger. "Even if that were the case—which it's not, by the way—it would be none of your business. Now, if you wouldn't mind taking your questions elsewhere . . ."

The kid drew himself up as straight as he could, not an easy task considering how drunk he was. "Are you tellin' me to get the hell away from you?"

"In a more polite fashion . . . yes," Burton snapped. Most of the time he was the mildest of souls, but even he could be riled and he was well on his way to that point now.

Behind the bar, Johnny Collyer hoped that the professor wouldn't say anything else to annoy the kid. The youngster wore two guns, both in low-slung holsters, and clearly thought of himself as a badman. He might not be all that much of a shootist really, but he was more dangerous than the professor, that was for sure.

Johnny didn't want to see Burton get hurt, and he didn't want any gunfights in here. He hated scrubbing blood-stains off the floor, something he'd had to do several times in the past month, since the word had gotten out that the Lucky Lizard Mine had reopened. People started flooding into the former ghost town of Buckskin once they heard about the silver strike, eager as always to try to grab some of those riches for themselves.

And as always, more people meant more trouble.

The batwings swung open and Thomas Woodford stepped into the saloon. A thick-bodied man in overalls, flannel shirt, and battered old hat, Tip, as he was known to his friends, looked like a down-on-his-luck prospector.

Nobody would guess from his appearance that he owned not only the Lucky Lizard, but also the Silver Baron Saloon. Tip had started the saloon with some of the money from his first strike, later sold it, then took it over again when the man he sold it to left town. Nearly everybody had deserted Buckskin at that point, because the silver veins had petered out and the boom was over.

Not long ago, though, Tip had found the vein again, and Buckskin had once again become a boomtown, with all the progress—and problems—that came with such a development, including this drunk, hotheaded, kid gunslinger who pounded a fist down on Professor Burton's table and yelled, "Who the hell do you think I am, talkin' to me like that?"

"An imbecile who doesn't understand when a man wants to be left alone?" Burton responded in a cool voice that just infuriated the kid even more.

Tip Woodford backed out through the door and vanished into the night. Johnny muttered a curse. Looked like his boss was leaving him here to handle this mess alone.

Or maybe Tip was going for help. Johnny clung to that hope as he started to reach under the bar, to the shelf where he kept a sawed-off Greener. He couldn't actually fire the scattergun in here—too many innocent people might be hurt if he did—but the threat of it might settle the kid down.

Before Johnny could touch the shotgun's smooth stock, one of the kid's pards shook his head and said, "Leave it be, drink juggler."

Johnny swallowed hard. The kid's companions were older and more experienced. They had the lean, cold look of true gunmen about them, and Johnny knew he would be committing suicide to cross them.

He had already narrowly avoided one death sentence in his life. He took his hand away from the Greener.

"Conwell's just blowing off steam," the other gunman said. "He won't really hurt that old gent."

Johnny wasn't convinced of that.

The kid—Conwell—glowered at the professor and said, "On your feet, Fancy Pants. You and me are gonna settle this with lead."

He backed away, his hands hovering over his holstered guns, ready to hook and draw.

Burton shook his head. "I'm unarmed, and even if I wasn't, I don't make it a practice to engage in duels."

"This ain't gonna be no duel," Conwell said. "It'll be a killin', plain and simple. But you'll have a fair chance." He drew his left-hand gun and placed it on the table in front of the professor. "There you go. I'll let you reach for it. Hell, I'll even let you pick it up before I draw. What do you say to that, you—"

He unleashed a stream of vile invective that made Burton turn pale with rage. The professor's hands were lying on the table. Johnny held his breath as he saw the right one twitch a little, like Burton was struggling not to grab at the butt of that gun.

"Don't touch it, Professor."

The deep, powerful, commanding voice spoke from the saloon's entrance as another newcomer pushed through the batwings. He was medium height, maybe a hair above, and powerfully built without being muscle-bound. His face was a little too rugged to be called handsome. His clothes were nothing special: well-worn boots, denim trousers, a buckskin shirt, and a broad-brimmed brown hat that sat on thick dark hair touched with gray. The high crown of the hat was pinched in a little on the sides.

Two things *were* impressive about the newcomer—the holstered Colt Peacemaker on his right hip, and the badge pinned to his shirt.

"Leave the gun alone, Professor," the newcomer went on. "In fact, it might be a good idea if you got up and found another place to sit."

Burton nodded and started to scrape his chair back, but Conwell snapped, "Keep your seat, you son of a bitch. I ain't through with you yet."

"Oh, you're through all right, kid," the lawman said. "You're through in Buckskin. You're leaving town tonight."

Conwell faced him and sneered. "Who in blazes are you to be tellin' me what to do?" he asked. "You think I'm gonna pay any attention to what some broke-down old geezer of a star-packer tells me to do?"

Conwell's two companions were studying the newcomer more closely than Conwell was, and signs of recognition and surprise appeared on their faces. As their eyes widened, one of the men said, "Hold on, Conwell. You don't know who that fella is."

A harsh laugh came from the kid. "I don't know and I don't care! Nobody threatens to throw me out of town and gets away with it!" He stepped away from the table, giving Burton the opportunity to stand up and hurry out of the line of fire. In a gunfighter's crouch, Conwell went on, "I'm gonna kill me a marshal!"

"You damn fool," the other gunman said in a tight voice, "that's Frank Morgan!"

It was Conwell's turn to let his eyes go wide with shock. Even in his drunken, troublemaking state, he recognized the name. "Morgan?" he repeated. "The Drifter? What the hell's Frank Morgan doin' totin' a badge?"

"I'm the marshal of Buckskin now," Morgan said. Without taking his eyes off Conwell, he asked the kid's two companions, "You boys want any part of this?"

"Not hardly," one of them said without hesitation. "If the kid wants to push it, then it's his fight, not ours."

"Damn right," the other man agreed.

Conwell glanced over at them. "Fine pair o' partners you two are," he said in disgust.

"Shoot, kid, we'll back your play in most anything, you know that. But not *this*."

A faint smile touched Morgan's lips. "That puts it up to you," he told Conwell. "You're leaving one way or the other. But either way, you'll leave quiet."

His message was unmistakable.

For a long moment, the youngster stood there, nostrils flaring, breathing heavily. Then he muttered a curse and said, "All right. I don't feel like dyin' today."

"Always a wise decision," Morgan said.

The fancy spurs on his high-heeled boots clinking, Conwell stalked toward the door. Morgan moved aside to let him past. Conwell said over his shoulder, "You two bastards just steer clear o' me from now on. We ain't ridin' together no more." His ire was directed toward the two men at the bar.

One of them grunted and said, "That's fine with us. We're tired of pullin' your chestnuts out of the fire, anyway."

Sneering, Conwell slapped the batwings aside and went out into the night. Everyone in the saloon heard his boots stomping on the boardwalk outside as he walked off.

Frank Morgan came over to the bar and gave the kid's former companions a curt nod. "Appreciate you not taking a hand," he told them.

"We got no quarrel with you, Morgan. You the town marshal?"

Morgan nodded. "That's right."

"Well, we ain't broke any laws in your town and don't plan to, so you don't have any reason to worry about us."

Morgan's smile was genuine. "I'm glad to hear that."

Johnny Collyer noticed that the men didn't claim not to have broken any laws elsewhere, but Frank Morgan only had jurisdiction here in Buckskin, although he might stretch a point every now and then and deal with problems in the heavily wooded foothills around the reborn ghost town.

Morgan continued. "I think I know you boys. Hap Mitchell and Lonnie Beeman, right?"

The men nodded. "Yeah, that's us," one of them said. "But like we told you, we're not hunting trouble."

"Fact of the matter is," the other one said, "once we finish our drinks, we'll probably be movin' on."

Morgan nodded. "That sounds like a good idea to me."

Now that the trouble was over, Johnny said, "You want a drink, Marshal?"

"No, thanks," Morgan said. "But if there's any hot coffee left, I'd admire to have a cup."

Johnny smiled. The lawman's response didn't surprise him. Morgan took a shot of whiskey or a cold beer every now and then, but for the most part he preferred coffee.

"I reckon we can manage that," Johnny said as he started down the bar toward the cast-iron stove at the far end. The weather was mild these days, but he kept a fire banked in the stove anyway so the coffeepot would stay warm on it.

He was just reaching for the pot when something crashed on the boardwalk outside and then an instant later, a man riding a horse burst through the doors, knocking the batwings off their hinges. The horse didn't want to come inside the building and was fighting against its rider, but the man raked his spurs against the animal's flanks, making it whinny in pain as it lunged forward. The man in the saddle let out an animal-like howl of his own as he sent his mount plunging toward the bar and the men who stood there. The guns in his hands spouted lead and flame.

Chapter 2

Frank Morgan had only a second to recognize the rider as the kid called Conwell. Then he threw himself across the bar, rolling over it and grabbing Johnny Collyer. He hauled the bartender to the floor behind the bar as Conwell's shots shattered several bottles sitting on the backbar.

Frightened, angry shouts filled the air as the saloon's customers scattered. Some of them turned over tables and dived behind them, seeking cover as the kid's Colts blasted wildly and sent bullets flying around the room.

Gun in hand, Frank surged up behind the bar. He fired, but Conwell pulled his mount into a tight turn at the same instant. The panicky horse reared up and pawed at the air with its front hooves. Frank's slug plowed a furrow in the horse's shoulder instead of knocking Conwell out of the saddle. The horse screamed in pain, twisted and bucked, and came down hard. Floorboards cracked under its weight. The horse arched its back, sunfishing madly.

With a startled yell, Conwell flew out of the saddle. He came crashing down on a table, busting it to kindling. His left-hand gun slipped out of his fingers and skittered away across the floor.

He managed to hang on to his other Colt, however, and as he clambered up out of the debris of the broken table, he swung the weapon toward Frank.

Before Conwell could fire again, the Peacemaker in Frank's hand roared a second time. This shot didn't miss. It caught Conwell in the chest and threw the youngster backward. His finger tightened on the trigger and the gun in his hand exploded, but the barrel was angled upward by now and the bullet went into the ceiling without hurting anything. Conwell landed on the splintered tabletop. He gasped in pain, his back arched, and his boot heels beat a tattoo on the floor as death spasms wracked him.

Then with a rattling sigh, the life went out of him and his body relaxed.

The horse, still spooked half out of its mind with pain and fear, headed for the big window, rather than the open doors. It lifted off its feet in a leap and smashed through the glass, shattering the window into a million pieces and sending shards and splinters spraying over the boardwalk. The horse cleared the window, clattered across the boardwalk, jumped into the street, and bolted away.

"Somebody go after that horse!" Frank shouted. "It's bound to be cut up from the glass, and it'll need some attention."

A couple of the men who had been drinking in the saloon before the trouble erupted ran outside, and a moment later the swift rataplan of hoofbeats testified that they were giving chase to the runaway animal.

Frank helped a shaken Johnny Collyer to his feet and asked, "You all right, Johnny?" He knew the bartender had had health problems in the past.

Johnny nodded and said, "Yeah . . . yeah, I'm fine." He gazed around the room with a dismayed expression. "But look what's happened to the place!"

There was plenty of damage all right, and all of it could be laid at the feet of Conwell, who must have decided that he couldn't live with backing down, even to the famous gunfighter known as The Drifter. He had gone outside, gotten his horse, given in to his anger, and charged back into the saloon, guns blazing.

The tactic might have worked. Most men would have been too shocked to see a man on horseback bursting through the batwings to react in time to save themselves.

But not Frank Morgan. His reactions were lightning-swift, and years of living a danger-filled life had honed his instincts to a razor-sharp keenness.

He came out from behind the bar and went to check on Conwell. Frank was confident that the reckless youngster was dead, but it never hurt to be sure. More than one man had been gunned down by a "corpse" that wasn't really dead yet.

Conwell was, though. Frank looked over at Mitchell and Beeman, who had ridden into Buckskin with the kid. They had dived to the floor when the shooting started, and they were just now picking themselves up.

"Sorry I had to kill him," Frank told the two men.

"I'm not," Hap Mitchell said with a snort of disgust. "He was a hotheaded fool who nearly ruined lots of jobs for us—"

He stopped short, as if realizing that he might be saying too much. Frank knew good and well that the "jobs" Mitchell referred to were robberies of some sort, probably bank or train holdups. He and Beeman were known to ride the hoot owl trail. But those crimes hadn't taken place here in Buckskin, and Frank didn't have any wanted posters on the two men, so he didn't have any call to arrest them.

"Anyway," Mitchell went on after a second, "you

won't hear any complaints from us about you killin' that idiot, Morgan."

"He had it comin'," Beeman added. "Hell, the way he was throwin' lead around, some of those shots could've hit *us*!"

Still kneeling beside Conwell, Frank felt inside the dead man's pockets. He found a roll of bills and a leather poke with several double eagles inside it. He straightened and set the money on the bar.

"Reckon this should go to repair the damage he caused here in the saloon, and anything that's left over can go toward the cost of burying him."

Mitchell shrugged. "Fine with us. We got no call on that money."

Frank figured it was loot from some robbery, but he couldn't prove that. He pointed to the money and told Johnny Collyer, "Give that to Tip when he gets back here."

"He's the one who fetched you, right?" Johnny asked.

Frank nodded. "Yes, I was in the jail. Tip went on down to Jack's cabin to roust him out too, in case I needed some help. Must've had some trouble waking him up, because I expected them to be here before now."

As if they had been waiting for him to say that, a couple of men hurried along the boardwalk and then turned in at the saloon, stepping through the opening where the batwings used to be. With a stricken look on his face, Thomas "Tip" Woodford gazed around at the destruction and groaned.

"Lord, it looks like a tornado hit this place!"

"That's what happens when a fella rides his horse around inside," Frank said.

Catamount Jack walked over to Conwell's corpse and nudged it with a booted foot. "If this is the varmint what done it, I don't reckon he'll be ridin' again any time soon.

Leastways, not unless the Devil's got some saddle mounts in hell."

The tall, lean old-timer had a tuft of beard like a billy goat, and had sometimes been accused of smelling like a billy goat too. His buckskins were old and grease-stained. A shapeless felt hat was crammed down on his head. He had been a mountain man, prospector, buffalo hunter, scout, wagon train guide. . . . You name it and Jack had done it, as long as it was west of the Mississippi. Frank didn't know what the old-timer's real name was; he was just Catamount Jack. He had been working part-time as Buckskin's deputy marshal since Frank had taken the job of marshal a month earlier.

Professor Howard Burton came over to Frank and said, "I owe you a debt of gratitude, Marshal. I was fully aware that that insolent young pup was trying to goad me into a fight, but I almost let him do it anyway."

"Yeah, you looked like you were about to make a grab for that Colt when I came in," Frank said. "I'm glad you didn't, Professor. I'm afraid Conwell would have killed you before I was able to stop him."

Burton hooked his thumbs in his vest. "I'm a peaceful man by nature, of course, but sometimes my temper gets the best of me anyway."

Frank wondered if it had been an outbreak of Burton's temper that had led him to resign from his teaching position at a university back East and come West, winding up in the nearly abandoned ghost town of Buckskin, Nevada. When Frank had gotten here, Burton was one of a mere handful of inhabitants in the town. He didn't do anything for a living as far as Frank had been able to tell, but seemed to have plenty of money, which meant he had brought it with him. A few times, Burton had made cryptic comments that Frank took to mean the professor was writing a book, but he had no idea what the volume was about or if Burton would ever finish it. The professor could be a mite stuffy at times, but Frank liked him.

Tip Woodford, who was also the mayor of Buckskin, looked at the shattered front window and shook his head. "I'll have to have another pane o' glass freighted out here from Virginia City," he said. "Won't be cheap."

Johnny said, "We've got the money here that kid had in his pockets. Marshal Morgan said we could use it to fix up the place, right, Marshal?"

Frank nodded. "That's right, Tip. Whatever's left over goes to Claude Langley."

Tip nodded. Claude Langley was a newcomer to Buckskin, and a welcome one because he provided an important service.

He was an undertaker.

Before Langley's arrival in town, whenever somebody needed buryin', it was up to the citizens to take care of the chore. They had a small cemetery at the edge of town, and now they had somebody who specialized in putting people in it.

Although some might say that Buckskin had *two* people who specialized in putting people in graves, if you included the marshal.

Frank didn't want to think about that, though. These days he was trying to live down his reputation as a killer, not expand it.

Mitchell and Beeman had finished their drinks and now declined Johnny Collyer's offer of refills. "We'll be ridin' along," Mitchell said. "Just so you know we're leavin' town, Morgan."

"I don't suppose you want to take the kid with you?" Frank asked. "I've been assuming we'd have to bury him here, but if you want—"

"No, thanks," Beeman cut in. "You plugged him, you plant him."

Frank nodded, and the two gunmen walked out of the saloon. "Tough hombres, looks like," Catamount Jack observed when they were gone.

"Tough enough," Frank agreed. "I guess somebody needs to go fetch Langley, so he can bring his wagon up here and collect the body. I'm surprised he didn't hear the shots and come to see what happened."

"No need to make Langley come all the way up here." Jack stooped, caught hold of Conwell under the arms, and lifted him. His wiry muscles handled the deadweight as if it didn't amount to much. Jack slung the body over his shoulder and started toward the door.

"Good Lord," Tip said. "You plan on carryin' him all the way down to the undertaker's place?"

"Won't be the first time I've lugged a dead body around," Jack said.

Frank wondered what the stories behind the other times might be, but he decided it might be better not to ask. He followed the old-timer out of the saloon as Jack toted the grisly burden toward Langley's place at the other end of town.

Frank stopped at the marshal's office. He had been alert and careful during the walk, just in case Mitchell and Beeman had been lying to him and had come back to settle the score for their former partner with an ambush. Nothing of the sort took place, though. The night seemed quiet and peaceful again after the earlier disturbance.

The marshal's office and jail were located in a sturdy log building that had been constructed during Buckskin's first heyday as a silver mining town. Like many of the other buildings, it had fallen into disrepair during the decade it sat there empty and abandoned. With help from Tip and Jack, Frank had fixed the place up, patching the roof and the walls, rehanging the thick door that led into the cell block, and moving in a small stove, a table that functioned as his desk, and several chairs. Either he or Jack spent most nights here, and a cot in one corner gave them a place to sleep. Frank had a room in the boardinghouse run by Leo Benjamin and his wife Trudy. Leo also owned and operated one of Buckskin's general mercantile emporiums, and was probably the wealthiest man in town who *didn't* have a successful silver claim.

Frank hadn't gotten that cup of coffee in the saloon, so he checked the pot on his stove. What was left in there had turned to sludge, so he set it aside and told himself that he didn't need any coffee anyway. He'd been about to turn in for the night when Tip came in, huffing and puffing from the run, to tell him that there was trouble in the Silver Baron. So now Frank hung his hat on the nail by the door, took off his gunbelt, coiled it and placed it on the table, and sat down on the cot to remove his boots.

Footsteps outside told him someone was coming. A knock sounded on the door. He glanced toward the holstered Colt lying on the table and wondered if he ought to get it before he answered. Never hurt to be careful, he reminded himself as he stood up and grasped the gun's walnut grips. As he slid the iron from leather, he called, "Who is it?"

A woman's voice answered, "Diana."

Chapter 3

She didn't have to give her full name. Frank knew perfectly well who she was.

Diana Woodford was Tip's daughter. She was blond, beautiful, and had lived back East with her mother until the older woman had passed away a couple of years earlier. After that, she had come West to live with her father in Buckskin. Tip had still been married to Diana's mother even though they hadn't lived together for many years. She hadn't been able to stand life on the frontier, and Tip couldn't abide the thought of moving back East. He'd had plenty of money at the time, so they had set up separate households and he had supported them both. After the silver played out, Diana and her mother had been forced to take care of themselves. If Diana resented her father because of that, though, Frank had never seen any sign of it.

Diana had surprised her father, and probably herself too, by the way she took to living in the West. She was a good rider and could most often be found wearing boots, denim trousers, and a man's shirt. She could handle a rifle with a considerable amount of skill.

She was also twenty-four years old, which meant Frank

Morgan was a good fifteen or twenty years too old for her. That wouldn't have been a problem if not for the fact that in the time Frank had been here, Diana had demonstrated a definite interest in him.

Even if there hadn't been the age difference, Frank would have been cautious about developing any relationship with Diana. He had been married twice in his life, and both of his wives had met violent deaths. That tended to make a man leery of getting romantically involved, at least on any kind of serious basis.

And he respected Diana too much, not to mention his liking for her father, to consider anything that wasn't serious with her.

But he couldn't just send her away now that she knew he was here and awake, so he called, "Come in."

She opened the door and stepped into the office with a worried look on her face. "I heard there was trouble at the saloon."

Frank holstered the gun and put it back on the desk. "Quite a ruckus all right," he said. "A young fella took it in his head to ride his horse into the Silver Baron."

"What happened to him?"

She would find out soon enough, whether he told her or not, so he said, "I had to kill him."

Her blue eyes widened. "For riding a horse into a saloon?"

"For trying to kill me and anybody else unlucky enough to get in the way of all the bullets he was throwing around."

"Oh." Diana nodded. "Well, that's different, I suppose. Are you all right?"

"Fine. Not a scratch."

"Was anyone else hurt?"

"Not that I know of," Frank said. "Well, the horse got

grazed by a bullet and jumped through one of those plate-glass windows your pa's so proud of. I don't know how badly it was hurt. A couple of fellas went after it, but they didn't come back while I was around."

"Poor horse," Diana said. "And I suppose I should feel sympathetic toward its rider too."

Frank grunted. "I wouldn't waste too much time worrying about him. He was an owlhoot, and before that he was trying to goad Professor Burton into a gunfight. I'm pretty sure he would have killed the professor."

"That's terrible! Professor Burton is such a kind, gentle man. . . . Anyway, Frank, I'm just glad that you're all right." She moved a step closer to him. "I . . . I'd be very upset if anything bad happened to you." She reached out and laid a hand on his arm.

Frank had always liked it when women touched him like that, and with Diana it was no exception. She had somehow gotten even closer to him, so that she was standing no more than a foot away from him. Her head was tilted back a little so she could look up into his face, and it would have been easy as pie just to lean down and press his lips to hers in a kiss.

Instead, he turned away and said, "I'd offer you some coffee, but what's left in the pot is so stout, I'm afraid it'd jump out of the cup and run off under its own power if I tried to pour it."

She laughed, but he thought she sounded a little disappointed. "No, that's all right. Thank you anyway. It's late, so I suppose I should get home."

Frank reached for his gunbelt. "I'll walk you—"

"Nonsense. I'll be perfectly fine. I walked over here by myself, didn't I?"

"Yeah, and that probably wasn't a very good idea." Frank buckled on the belt and then took his hat from the nail. "Buckskin is a boomtown now. You've never seen it like this before. I've seen plenty of places like it, though, and there's always trouble just waiting to happen in a boomtown."

"All right, if you insist."

Frank took a Winchester from the rack on the wall and tucked it under his arm; then they left the office and stepped out into the street. Despite the late hour, a lot of lights still burned in Buckskin. During the past month, three saloons had opened to give the Silver Baron some competition, and a couple of the stores were still open, including Benjamin's Emporium. A wagon rolled along the street, and a few men on horseback were leaving the settlement. Music and laughter came from the saloons, the sounds drifting on the warm night air. Several pedestrians walked along the street, all of them male. There were only a handful of women in Buckskin—Diana, Leo's wife Trudy, and Lauren Stillman, Ginnie Carlson, and Becky Humphries, the three retired soiled doves who now ran what had been the settlement's only café. Their eatery had some competition now too, as a Chinaman had shown up and opened a hash house, and the newly reopened hotel also served meals in its dining room.

There were a few things Buckskin didn't have yet: a school, a church, and a whorehouse. A silver mining boomtown could probably get along all right without the first two, but Frank knew it was only a matter of time before some madam showed up with a wagonload of girls and set up in business. Lauren, Ginnie, and Becky could have already gone back to their old profession—they'd had plenty of offers from prospectors lonely for female companionship—but so far they were being stubborn about maintaining their retired status.

"The town's really growing fast, isn't it?" Diana said as

they walked along the street toward the house she shared with her father. They passed the offices of the Lucky Lizard Mining Company, where Tip handled his business affairs.

"Too fast," Frank said as he nodded in agreement. "Boom-towns have a habit of getting too big for their britches."

"Progress is good, though, isn't it?"

"To somebody who grew up in civilization like you did, I reckon it is. I grew up in Texas when the place still had all the bark on it, and since leaving there I've traveled around to some other mighty wild places. Progress is a good thing for most folks, but there are some of us who miss the old days and hate to see them go away."

She slipped her arm through his. He didn't want to offend her by pulling away, and he enjoyed the warmth and the closeness too, even if he didn't want to admit it even to himself.

"You talk like you're a hundred years old," she said with a laugh. "You're not ancient, Frank. You're not even that much older than me."

"Old enough to be your pa," he said with a stern note in his voice.

"But you're *not* my father," she pointed out, and he certainly couldn't argue with that.

When they reached the Woodford house, Frank felt a sense of relief when he noticed Tip approaching the place from a different direction. The mayor's presence would help him avoid an awkward situation. Frank had been afraid that Diana might want a good-night kiss—and he had also been afraid that he would want to give her one.

"Blast it, Diana," Tip said as they all came together at the gate in the recently painted picket fence in front of the house. "What are you doin' out and about at this hour?"

"I heard that there was trouble and went to make sure

Marshal Morgan was all right," she replied with a note of defiance in her voice.

"The marshal can take care o' himself just fine. Been doin' it for a lot of years, haven't you, Frank?"

"That's true," Frank said. "I just thought it would be a good idea to walk Diana home. You never know who or what you'll run into when it's late like this."

"I appreciate it." Tip gestured toward the house. "Go on in, darlin'. I'll be there in a minute. Got something I need to talk to Frank about first."

Diana seemed reluctant to leave, but she nodded and said, "Good night, Marshal."

Frank returned the nod and tugged on the brim of his hat. "Miss Woodford."

Tip waited until Diana was in the house before he said, "That gal's turnin' into a reg'lar pest. Don't worry about hurtin' her feelin's if she starts to bother you, Frank. Just send her packin'."

"I doubt if it'll ever come to that," Frank said. "Did you really want to talk to me about something?"

"Oh, yeah. Jack got that kid's carcass down to Langley's all right, and I told Claude to fix up a coffin for him. Nothin' fancy. There was enough *dinero* in his pockets to pay for the damages to the Silver Baron and a pine box too." Tip rubbed his jaw and frowned. "Where do you reckon that money came from, Frank?"

"I think it was loot from some robbery," Frank answered without hesitation. "Those hombres the kid was riding with, Mitchell and Beeman, are outlaws. I'd seen them a time or two before, in various places."

He didn't elaborate on where he had seen them, and Tip didn't ask. Tip knew that Frank had a reputation as a gunfighter and had spent time in some rough places.

Nobody had ever accused Frank Morgan of being a common owlhoot, though.

"You reckon it was a good idea to let them go?"

Frank shrugged. "They hadn't caused any trouble here in Buckskin. If I'd had wanted posters on them, I could have held them for the law elsewhere, but no paper on them has crossed my desk. I don't have any way of knowing if they're actually wanted anywhere right now."

"Yeah, I guess that makes sense," Tip said. "I don't much cotton to the idea of owlhoots comin' into our town, though."

"Well, you'd better get used to it," Frank advised him. "The word is out all over the territory that you've found the old Lucky Lizard vein again, and there have been a couple of other strikes in the area. People of all sorts come flooding into a place when there's a gold or silver strike, and that includes outlaws. Might as well try to stop the sun from coming up in the morning. We're actually lucky we haven't had even more trouble."

"Yeah." Tip sighed. "I know you're right, but I don't have to like it. I'm just damned glad that you showed up in Buckskin when you did, Frank."

It was violence that had brought Frank to the settlement in the first place. He had pursued an old enemy here, a man who had tried to have him killed. Once that matter was settled, Frank had stayed around for a few days because he liked the area and liked the people. At that time, he hadn't known that Tip had rediscovered the vein of silver that everyone thought had played out ten years earlier. When Tip had told him about that and asked him to take on the job of marshal in the town that was bound to grow again, Frank had hesitated. . . .

But not for long. He had been feeling some vague stirrings, a notion that it might be time for him to settle down at last after a lifetime of drifting. Buckskin was as good a place as any to put that notion to the test.

"One more thing," Tip said. "Those fellas who went after the kid's horse caught it and brought it back to Hillman's livery stable. It's down there now. Amos said he'd dope up that bullet graze and the cuts from the broken window. Since the kid's partners've already left town and didn't take the horse with them, I was thinkin' maybe you ought to claim him, Frank."

"Me?" Frank was surprised by the offer. "I've got a horse."

A damned good horse, in fact. The big, rangy Appaloosa called Stormy had been with Frank for several years. They made a good team, along with the wolflike cur known only as Dog.

"Yeah, but a fella can't have too many good horses. Think about it, anyway. Maybe in the mornin' you can go down to Hillman's and take a look at it."

"I suppose I can do that," Frank agreed.

He lifted a hand in farewell as Tip turned and went through the gate and up the walk to the house. As Frank glanced in that direction, he thought he saw the curtain over a window move a little. A lamp was burning in the room, and the yellow glow revealed a distinctively female silhouette against the curtain. A smile tugged at Frank's mouth as he turned and started walking back toward the marshal's office.

Figuring out what to do about Diana Woodford was a problem all right, but woman trouble had one advantage over the sort of problems Frank usually ran into.

Diana just wanted to kiss him, not shoot him!

At least, not yet. . . .

Chapter 4

The next morning, Frank walked down to Amos Hillman's livery stable to take a look at Conwell's horse. By all rights, the animal ought to belong to the kid's relatives, if he had any, but Frank's check of the kid's pockets hadn't turned up any letters or other items with a name or address on them. Even if Conwell had any family left, Frank didn't see any way to get in touch with them. And since Conwell had had enough cash on him to pay for his burying and the damages to the saloon, there was no need to sell the horse to pay for those expenses.

So as Mayor Woodford had said, there was no reason why Frank couldn't claim the horse as his own . . . other than the fact that Frank felt a mite uncomfortable about killing a man and then taking his mount. Felt a little too much like horse thievery to him.

But when Frank walked into Hillman's stable, the lanky, one-eyed liveryman greeted him by saying, "Mornin', Marshal. I'm damned glad you shot that son of a bitch last night. He had it comin'."

"Why's that?" Frank wanted to know. He thought it was reason enough that Conwell had been trying to kill him and anybody else in the saloon unlucky enough to get in the way of a bullet, but he was curious why Hillman had made that statement.

"Anybody who'd treat a hoss like that hombre did deserves to get ventilated."

"Riding him into the saloon that way, you mean?"

Hillman shook his head. He was a tall, grizzled man in overalls, with a thatch of gray hair sticking out from under an old hat and a black patch over his left eye. He said, "I mean mistreatin' the poor critter for months, from the looks of the scars on him."

"The horse had a bullet graze, and some cuts from broken glass," Frank pointed out.

"I ain't talkin' about those wounds. Hoss has got scars that tell me somebody beat him reg'larlike, probably with a quirt or somethin' like that. Didn't take care o' the cuts, neither. Just let 'em scab up and heal over as best they could."

A frown creased Frank's forehead. He had no proof that Conwell was responsible for beating the animal. Conwell could have bought—or more likely stolen—the horse any time, including recently.

But having seen the cruelty and viciousness in the kid firsthand, Frank had no doubt that Conwell had been capable of whipping the horse until it bled. His gut told him that was exactly what had happened.

"Let's take a look at him," Frank said, his voice edged with concern.

Hillman led him along the center aisle of the barn. Dog was lying in front of Stormy's stall, but he got up to trot over to Frank and get his ears rubbed. The big cur and the Appaloosa were pals, so Dog hung around the stable most of the time while Frank was in town.

Things had been too hectic in the saloon the night

before for Frank to pay too much attention to the horse Conwell rode into the saloon. Now, as he and Hillman came up to the stall where the animal stood, he saw that it was a big, strong-looking gelding whose hide had an odd sheen to it.

"I don't know that I've ever seen a gold-colored horse like that," Frank commented.

Hillman shook his head. "Me neither, and I been runnin' livery stables for nigh on to forty years now. Mighty strikin'-lookin' critter, ain't it?"

"He certainly is," Frank agreed. The horse came to the gate at the front of the stall and stuck his head over it. Frank reached up and scratched the horse's nose. "Sorry about shooting you, big fella. I wasn't aiming to."

The horse tossed his head, then butted his nose against Frank's shoulder as if to tell him that it was all right.

As Frank laughed, Amos Hillman said, "You just creased him a mite, Marshal. I daubed some ointment on there and on the cuts he got from the broken window, and I reckon he'll be fine. Tip come by earlier this mornin' and said you might want him."

"I've already got a horse," Frank said, pointing with his left thumb toward Stormy's stall across the aisle.

"Man can't have too many good horses."

Frank chuckled. "Tip said the same thing. I suppose somebody's got to claim this fella."

"Might as well be you," Hillman said.

"All right, we'll see how it goes," Frank said with a nod as he reached his decision. He took a coin out of his pocket and handed it to Hillman. "That'll pay for his keep for a while."

"Aw, Marshal, you know you don't have to pay for nothin' here in Buckskin less'n you just want to."

"I want to," Frank insisted. "I'm new at this law business, but I've seen too many star-packers turn crooked once they started taking favors from the townspeople. I intend to pay my way."

Hillman pocketed the coin and said, "Folks sure was way off when they claimed you was nothin' but a no-account gunslinger." He added, "Not that anybody here in Buckskin ever thought that, 'cause we knowed better right off. I'm talkin' about in other places I been."

"Yes, I've got a reputation I never really wanted," Frank agreed. "Unfortunately, once you get a rep like that, it tends to stick to you like glue."

"Well, you're sure provin' it wrong here." Hillman reached over the stall gate and patted the horse on the shoulder. "Don't worry about ol' Goldy here. I'll take good care of him."

"Goldy, eh?" Frank said with a smile. "The name suits him. I guess it'll stick too."

Later that morning, Frank and Catamount Jack were both in the marshal's office when Claude Langley came in and said, "I suppose we're ready to take care of the bury-ing, Marshal, in case you want to be there."

Frank heaved himself out of his chair and reached for his hat, which he had placed on the table earlier. "I reckon I ought to be, since I'm the one who killed the young fella. You'll hold down the fort, Jack?"

"Sure," the old-timer replied. "Go on and have . . . well, I guess have a good time ain't somethin' you'd say to somebody on their way to a buryin', is it?"

"No," Frank said as he settled his hat on his head. "It's not. But I'm not going as a mourner either, so I'm not sure what you'd say in a situation like that."

He and Langley left Jack there pondering on the question

and walked along the street toward the edge of the settlement. The cemetery on the outskirts of Buckskin held quite a few graves from the town's previous silver boom. Even when Buckskin was largely a ghost town, Tip Woodford had continued to care for the burial ground, keeping the weeds out and the low stone fence around it in good repair. Not long ago, Buckskin's cemetery had been in better shape than many of the buildings in town.

Claude Langley was a small, dapper man with a goatee and a soft accent that revealed his Virginia origins. He had driven into town at the reins of an actual hearse drawn by six black horses. He also had a wagon, though, and it was the vehicle that carried Conwell's plain pine coffin to the cemetery, pulled by a pair of mules. The wagon, with Langley's helper at the reins, arrived at the cemetery at the same time as Frank and the undertaker.

A couple of prospectors who hadn't had any luck yet in finding silver worked part-time as gravediggers. They had the hole ready for the coffin. Together with Frank and Langley's helper, they unloaded the pine box from the wagon and lowered it into the grave with ropes. Buckskin didn't have a preacher yet, so Langley usually said a few words at burials. Today, he turned to Frank and asked, "Would you like to say anything, Marshal?"

Frank took his hat off, stood beside the open grave, and said, "I didn't know this young fella, don't even know his full name. I wish he hadn't made me shoot him. If he'd had any sense, he'd still be alive this morning. But I suppose things happen for a reason, and I suppose that sometime in his life he had somebody who cared for him. If that's so, I hope that somehow they'll rest a little easier because we gave him a decent burial." Frank stepped back, shrugged, and put his hat back on. "That's not much, but I reckon it's all I've got to say."

Langley nodded and gestured to the gravediggers, who picked up their shovels and started throwing dirt from the pile into the hole. Frank turned and started to walk away. The grim, hollow sound of dirt hitting the coffin lid followed him.

He had seen too much death over the years to lose any sleep over the likes of Conwell, but he wasn't so hardened and calloused that he felt nothing at all. Frank had always been a reader, carrying a book or two in his saddlebags during all those long years of drifting, and he recalled a line written by the poet John Donne: "Any man's death diminishes me."

Probably not the best thing for a gunfighter to be thinking about, Frank mused, but the idea was with him anyway.

Deep in thought like that, he almost didn't hear the hoofbeats of the approaching rider. But then he realized someone was coming and glanced up.

The man approaching on a roan stallion was dressed mostly in black. A red bandanna tied around his neck was the only splash of color about him. Gray hair fell from under the flat-crowned black hat to hang around his shoulders. The deep tan and high cheekbones of his hawklike face told Frank that he might have some Indian blood, but he couldn't be sure if the man was a 'breed.

The stranger's thonged-down holster told a story of its own, though, and it was one that Frank didn't like.

The man reined in about twenty feet away and swung down from the saddle. He said in a raspy voice, "You'd be Frank Morgan?"

"I would," Frank agreed.

"My name is Harry Clevenger."

Frank nodded. "I thought I recognized you, but it's been a long time."

Clevenger frowned as he asked, "We've met?"

"No, but you were pointed out to me one night down in Taos, about fifteen years ago. You were in Don Robusto's cantina."

Clevenger's eyes narrowed. "You were that close to me and I didn't know you were there?"

"That's right."

"If I'd known, we'd have had this showdown then."

Frank shook his head. "I didn't have any call to want a showdown with you, mister. Still don't, as far as I know."

"You don't want to know who's faster?"

Frank sighed. "To tell you the God's honest truth, I don't give a damn. I stopped worrying about things like that a long time ago."

"But you're still here," Clevenger insisted. "You're still alive. You've outdrawn everybody who ever went up against you. You must care about that."

"I care about staying alive. Whether or not that means I'm faster on the draw than some other fella . . ." Frank shook his head. "I haven't lost a minute of sleep worrying about that for years now."

Clevenger stared at him for a long moment in silence, then finally grunted in surprise. "Huh. That ain't what I expected out of you, Morgan, but it don't change anything. I heard you'd taken to toting a badge, but that don't mean anything either. I'm still here to kill you."

"Clevenger," Frank said, "right back there behind me is a brand-new grave. The young fella lying in it thought he was a dangerous man, fast on the draw. He'll be a long time dead because he felt that way. You and I have both lived longer than we had any right to expect, the sort of lives we've led. Why don't you climb back on that horse and live a while longer?"

Face set in stubborn lines, Clevenger shook his head.

"No, sir," he said. "Not while the famous Frank Morgan is still drawing breath. One of us has got to go down, Morgan."

Frank sighed, knowing that Clevenger wouldn't be talked out of this. The man had been a gunfighter almost as long as Frank had, with plenty of kills to his name. He fought fair, but he had a reputation as being a cold-blooded bastard too, who had been known to finish off a man once he was wounded and down. There was not an ounce of mercy in him.

"All right," Frank said. "It's your play. You want to dance, you start the ball."

Clevenger sneered, and less than the blink of an eye later, his hand flashed with blinding speed toward the gun on his hip.

It came as no surprise to Frank that Clevenger was fast. The gunman wouldn't have lived this long if he hadn't been. Their guns came out of leather at the same time, but the barrel of Frank's Colt leveled out just a hair ahead of Clevenger's. Smoke and flame geysered from the Peacemaker's muzzle. Clevenger fired half a heartbeat later, but that was too late for him. His gun had already dropped toward the ground as he was driven backward by the slug from Frank's gun that smashed into his chest.

Clevenger landed on his back. He struggled to rise for a second, then sagged down into death. His hat had fallen off, and the breeze tugged at the long gray hair and moved it around in front of his face.

Frank took a fresh cartridge from one of the loops on his shell belt and replaced the spent one in the Colt's cylinder, then pouched the iron. Behind him, he heard Claude Langley call to the gravediggers, "Better get started on another one, boys."

Chapter 5

Catamount Jack met Frank about halfway back to the marshal's office. He had a shotgun in his hands.

"I got to thinkin' maybe I shouldn't'a sent that feller out to the graveyard when he come by the office lookin' for you," Jack said. "Figured I'd go out there and make sure ever'thin' was all right, but then I heard a couple o' shots. Reckon he must've found you all right."

"He did," Frank said.

"Hombre plan on stayin' around Buckskin for long?"

"He didn't plan on it, but I reckon now he won't be leaving."

Jack let out a cackle of laughter; then as Frank frowned, the old-timer said, "Sorry, Marshal. I know killin' a man is serious business. But Good Lord, didn't he know who he was goin' up against?"

"He knew," Frank said. "That's why he came looking for me. His name was Harry Clevenger, and he had a reputation as a fast gun."

"Not fast enough." Jack was still grinning. His attempt at being more solemn hadn't been successful.

"Do me a favor, would you, Jack?"

"Sure."

"Find Mayor Woodford and ask him if he'd come over to the office, would you?"

"All right, but Tip's liable to already be up at his diggin's. I'll check the Lucky Lizard office and his house, though."

Frank went on to the marshal's office while Jack went in search of the mayor. Earlier that morning, Frank had made some fresh coffee, and he was halfway through a cup of it when Tip Woodford came through the door of the office. He wore his usual overalls and slouch hat.

"Jack said you wanted to see me, Frank?"

"That's right. Coffee?"

"No, thanks. I got to get up to the mine in a little while. What can I do for you?"

Frank sat down behind the table. "I guess you heard what happened out at the cemetery a while ago."

"Jack told me," Tip said with a casual nod. "Are you all right? That hombre didn't wing you?"

Frank shook his head and said, "I'm fine. His bullet didn't come anywhere near me. You don't seem too bothered by this, Tip."

The mayor shrugged his heavy shoulders. "Why should I be bothered? It wasn't me the fella wanted to kill. And you said yourself that you're fine, so I don't have to go huntin' another marshal. . . ."

"It's going to happen again," Frank said.

Tip frowned. "Somebody comin' here to draw against you, you mean?"

"That's right. Harry Clevenger was only the first. To tell you the truth, I expected it to happen before now. The word's getting around that I've settled down in Buckskin, so now every would-be shootist in these parts knows where to look for me."

"There can't be *that* many gunfighters left. I mean—"

"I know what you mean. Smoke Jensen and Matt Bodine are settled down with families and spend most of their time on their ranches. Nobody messes with them. But there are still a handful of old-timers, like this hombre Clevenger who showed up today, and more importantly, there'll always be green kids who think they're fast on the draw and want to prove it. Dime novels have been around long enough now so that some of them have grown up reading the blasted things. They think the West is nothing but shoot-outs and showdowns, and they want to get in on the action. I'm a prime target for youngsters like that, Tip."

"I don't doubt any of what you say, but I'm not sure what you're gettin' at, Frank."

"I'm saying that as long as I'm the marshal here, you're going to have men riding into Buckskin for no reason other than to try their hand at killing me. That can't be good for the town."

Tip's eyes widened. "You want to quit?"

"I don't *want* to. I like it here. But I don't want to be the cause of bringing trouble down on the town."

Tip scratched at his jaw with a blunt finger and frowned in thought. "Listen here, Frank. When Dutton's gang rode in here and took over, you were the one who came along and saved us. They might have killed all of us before they were through. Might've done even worse."

Frank knew what he meant. The hired killers who had worked for Charles Dutton would have gotten around to raping Diana and the other women in town sooner or later, before murdering all the inhabitants and burning Buckskin to the ground.

"Buckskin's just now turnin' into a real town again," Tip went on, "but it can't do it without you. The folks who come here know that you'll keep 'em safe. Without a good marshal to keep the lid on, you know how fast a boomtown can boil over. That's no good for anybody."

Tip was right about that too, but it didn't ease Frank's mind completely. He said, "You're sure you've thought this over enough?"

"I don't have to think it over for very long to know that I damn sure want Frank Morgan to be the marshal o' my town," the mayor declared. "Buckskin just wouldn't be the same without you."

Frank took a deep breath and then nodded. "All right, if that's the way you want it. I felt like I ought to warn you, though, that the violence is liable to get worse before it gets better."

"Shoot, that's gonna be true whether you're here or not," Tip said with a smile. "Why do you reckon I asked you to pin on that badge in the first place?"

Several days of relative peace and quiet went by. Frank had to break up a few drunken fights in the Silver Baron and the other saloons, and once one of the combatants was so determined to keep the brawl going that Frank had to tap him on the head with the butt of his Colt and drag the fella down to the jail to sleep it off. That was the biggest ruckus that occurred.

Harry Clevenger had been dead broke when he got to Buckskin, so Amos Hillman sold the gunfighter's horse to pay for his burial. Clevenger's saddlebags contained a letter, from a woman in St. Louis named Ida Skillery. Frank felt uncomfortable reading the letter, but glanced over it enough to discover that she was Clevenger's sister. He wrote her a letter telling her that her brother had passed away from a sudden illness and expressing his sympathy.

In this case, he didn't think it would do any harm to fudge the truth a little.

Nobody else showed up gunning for him, but in the middle of a bright Nevada afternoon, a dusty buggy rolled into the settlement carrying a man who *was* looking for Frank.

At that moment, Frank happened to be standing on the boardwalk in front of the marshal's office with his left shoulder leaning against one of the posts holding up the awning over it. His right thumb was hooked in his gunbelt, near the butt of the Colt.

He straightened from that casual pose as the buggy veered toward him. The man handling the reins brought the single horse to a halt in front of the boardwalk.

"Frank Morgan?" he called.

"That's right," Frank said.

The man looped the reins around the brake lever and climbed out of the buggy. He was in his thirties, short and stocky, wearing a town suit. A soup-strainer mustache drooped over his mouth, and a pair of rimless spectacles perched halfway down his long nose like a bird on a fence.

"I'm Garrett Claiborne," he said, introducing himself as he stepped up onto the boardwalk. The way he said his name seemed to indicate that he expected Frank to recognize it.

Frank stuck out his hand and shook with the newcomer. "Welcome to Buckskin, Mr. Claiborne. What brings you here?"

"You didn't get the wire about me coming out?" Claiborne asked with a frown.

"I haven't gotten any wire," Frank said. "Don't know if you've noticed or not, but the telegraph wires don't run all the way out here. We have to ride up to Virginia City to send telegrams or get any replies, and I don't think anybody's been that way lately."

"Well, this is distressing," Claiborne said, "but I don't suppose it really matters. I can just tell you now."

"Tell me what?"

"Mr. Browning sent me to take over the Crown Royal Mine."

That came as a shock to Frank. "You mean Conrad Browning?"

"That's right. I'm a mining engineer and superintendent. I've managed several mines that are part of the Browning holdings."

Frank had to take a minute to digest that. Conrad Browning was his son, but Frank hadn't seen him or been in touch with him in over a year. For a long time, they had been estranged, and it hadn't helped matters when Frank had reconciled with Vivian Browning, his first love and Conrad's mother, only to have her gunned down by outlaws not long afterward. In his grief, Conrad had blamed Frank for that.

The gulf between them had shrunk over time, though, and they had even managed to work together when gun trouble plagued a railroad Conrad was building down in New Mexico Territory. Vivian Browning had been a canny businesswoman, building a fortune in holdings that included banking, railroads, mining, freighting, and even a stagecoach line or two. She had left part of those holdings to Frank, and as a result he was a very wealthy man, but he had little interest in such things and was more than content to allow Conrad to run the business however he saw fit. That was good judgment, because Conrad had made it even more successful and lucrative than before.

One of the Browning holdings in years past had been the Crown Royal Mine, in the hills near Buckskin. It had closed down about the same time as the Lucky Lizard, and hadn't been worked in more than ten years. But Frank and

Conrad still owned it, so when Frank had learned that the silver vein in the Lucky Lizard wasn't played out after all, he had ridden into Virginia City and sent a wire to Conrad informing him of that fact. He hadn't really considered the possibility that Conrad would send someone to reopen the mine.

That was what had happened, though, because the hombre was standing right in front of Frank, waiting for him to respond to the surprising news.

"Come on in the office," Frank said. "I reckon we've got things to talk about."

"Indeed we do," Claiborne agreed.

When they were settled down in chairs, the mining man went on. "Mr. Browning has given me carte blanche to operate the mine as I see fit, assuming that's all right with you, Mr. Morgan."

Frank chuckled. "I have a hard time believing that Conrad put it quite that way. More than likely, he told you to run things and to hell with whatever I thought."

"Mr. Browning *does* place a great deal of trust in my abilities," Claiborne replied, but Frank thought he heard a hint of amusement lurking behind the formal words. "He said that you might be of help in acclimating me to the area and securing laborers to work in the mine."

"You shouldn't have any trouble finding fellas to swing picks and shovels. A lot of men have come to try their hands at prospecting since word of the new strike got out, but most of them haven't had any luck. Some of them will be glad to work for wages again. I don't know that you'll find anything in the old Crown Royal, though."

"I intend to do a thorough exploration and assessment of the mine," Claiborne said. "Not to brag, but I'm pretty good at finding ore if it's there to find."

"Well, I wish you luck. I'll introduce you to the mayor

and some of the other folks around town and help you find a place to stay. There might be an empty room over at the Benjamins' boardinghouse."

"I plan to stay at the mine. All I need is a tent and a cot, and I have both packed in the rear of my buggy."

Frank shrugged. "All right. You can probably manage that fine at this time of year. Might get a little chilly at night, but not too bad."

"This mayor you mentioned . . . that's Thomas Woodford, correct?"

"Right," Frank nodded.

"One of our competitors." Now there was a note of disapproval in Claiborne's voice.

"Tip Woodford's a fine man," Frank said, and his tone was brisk and businesslike now. "I won't stand for any cutthroat tactics just because he owns a mine too."

"You don't have to worry about such behavior from me, Mr. Morgan," Claiborne said. "I'm sure Mr. Woodford and I will get along just fine. You'd be better advised to be concerned about Hamish Munro."

"Who the hell is Hamish Munro?"

"The man who now owns the Alhambra Mine, not far from the Crown Royal and the Lucky Lizard." Claiborne pushed his spectacles up on his nose. "And a man for whom, if I'm not mistaken, the word *cutthroat* was invented."

Chapter 6

The canyon was located up in the Nevada high country, way the hell and gone from anywhere. That was the way the men who were camped here liked it. Isolation was their first line of defense. The way the mountains folded in on themselves, nobody would even know the canyon was here just to look at it. You had to be aware of its existence, and even then, you'd have a hard time finding the trails in and out without a guide.

And if you did, chances are you'd be shot out of the saddle before you got within a mile of the place.

Half-a-dozen log cabins were scattered around the floor of the narrow canyon, which was watered by a tiny stream that sprang from the cliffs where they narrowed back down to a solid wall. A couple of sturdy pole corrals had been erected nearby. Plenty of game still roamed the area, so the smell of roasting venison usually filled the air.

Several members of the gang had wives—at least they called themselves that, whether the unions were strictly legal or not—and they stayed here at the hideout all the time, along with a couple of old-timers who were too stove-up to go out on jobs anymore, plus any of the other men who were recuperating from bullet wounds and needed more time to get better before they resumed their careers of outlawry.

The gang's numbers varied. At its core was a group of six men who had ridden together for years, but other owlhoots came and went. There might be twenty or thirty men in the hidden canyon at times.

Today there were fifteen, and they were bored, so they gathered in front of one of the cabins to watch Gates Tucker and Dagnabbit Dabney try to cut each other to pieces with bowie knives.

The trouble started over a woman, but it could have just as easily been a disagreement over cards, or a spilled drink, or any other excuse to break the monotony of waiting for the next job to come along. Tucker's woman had taken up with Dabney behind Tucker's back, and Tucker might not have found out about it if he hadn't passed by Dabney's cabin and overheard him saying, "Dagnabbit! Dagnabbit!" as he had the habit of doing while he was in the throes of passion. Tucker knew that Dabney didn't have a woman in the canyon at the moment, and curious as to who it was Dabney was screwing, he'd peeked in the window and seen his own sweet Hannah bouncing her hips on a corn-shuck mattress with Dabney on top of her.

Tucker didn't bother going around to the door. He just climbed in the window and roared, "I'll make you think dagnabbit, you son of a bitch!"

In the resulting fracas, he had pitched a still-stark-naked Dabney out the window, and probably would have killed him if several other members of the gang who'd been attracted by the commotion hadn't grabbed him and held him back. In order to liven things up around the hideout, and to make the fight more fair since Tucker was a head taller and fifty pounds heavier than Dabney, they had suggested that the two men settle their dispute with cold steel. The old saying was that God created all men equal but that Sam Colt made them more equal. A bowie wasn't quite the same as a Peacemaker, but it went quite a ways toward evening things up.

So Dabney got dressed, Hannah wrapped a sheet around her, and most of the outlaws gathered to watch the fight. It went without saying that the fight would be to the death.

Tucker had the longer reach, but Dabney was quicker. They circled each other, darted in and out, thrust and parried and cut. Blade rang against blade, and sparks flew as the steel clashed. Tucker drew first blood, but Dabney returned the favor a heartbeat later. After ten minutes, both men had several bleeding cuts.

The door of one of the other cabins opened and a tall, powerful man in a fringed buckskin shirt stepped out onto its rickety porch. A blond beard covered his jaw, and fair hair hung from under a hat with a pushed-up brim. He wore a scowl on his face as he stared toward the two men slashing at each other with knives. "What the hell?" he muttered.

He went down the steps to the ground and stalked toward the group of spectators, who were yelling encouragement to the two fighters and making bets with each other over which one would survive the fight.

"What's goin' on here?" the newcomer demanded of one of the outlaws.

The man looked around and said, "Oh, howdy, Jory. You ain't heard?"

"I heard all hell breakin' loose, sounded like," the man called Jory snapped. "Before that I was tryin' to get some shut-eye."

"Well, Gates and Dagnabbit is fightin'—"

"I can see that. What started it?"

"Gates found out that Dagnabbit's been beddin' his woman."

Jory frowned. "Is there anybody in camp who *ain't* bedded Hannah at one time or another?"

"No, I reckon not, but Gates told ever'body to steer clear of her. He's done gone sweet on her."

"Lord have mercy," Jory muttered. "Nothin' makes a man stupider'n a woman. You're bettin' on which one's gonna win?"

"That's right. You want some of the action?"

Jory scratched at his beard and thought about it for a moment, then said, "Anybody betting that neither one of them live through it?"

The other outlaw shook his head. "Nope. Ever'body's bettin' on one or the other."

"Then I'll bet that neither one of them makes it through this fight alive," Jory said.

"Hell, I'll take that bet!"

Several of the other outlaws joined in and within minutes, Jory had a sizable amount of money wagered on the outcome. Meanwhile, Tucker and Dabney were bloodier than ever and were visibly tiring. It would only be a matter of minutes before one of the men made a fatal slip.

All the bets were down, so Jory shouted, "Hey! Gates! Dagnabbit!"

Both of the fighters paused, startled by the shout. As they looked around, Jory pulled his gun from its holster and shot them both, the pair of shots slamming out so close together, the reports sounded almost like one. Tucker and Dabney crashed to the ground, their brains blown out.

Jory slid his gun back into leather, smiled at the shocked outlaws, and said, "Neither one of 'em lived through the fight. Pay up, boys."

A few jaws clenched in anger, but nobody said anything, and after a second the men began paying off on their bets.

Because this was the infamous Jory Pool they were dealing with, their leader, the fastest on the draw and the most vicious member of the bunch, and nobody wanted to cross him.

A hail from one of the lookouts posted up on the canyon wall told Pool that riders were coming in. The newcomers had to be members of the gang; otherwise they would have been gunned down out of hand if they approached the hideout. Pool collected his winnings, then walked out to meet the two riders.

He recognized Hap Mitchell and Lonnie Beeman, both of whom had ridden with the gang on several jobs in the past. They hadn't been here to the hideout for quite a while, so as they reined in and raised their hands in greeting, Pool said, "Howdy, boys. Where you been lately?"

"Oh, here and there," Mitchell answered, being deliberately vague about it. Pool wouldn't have expected any less.

"You didn't lead no posse back here, did you?" Pool asked with a scowl.

Beeman laughed and said, "You know us better'n that, Jory. No bunch of lawdogs could follow us less'n we wanted them to."

"We came across something a few days ago we thought you might be interested in," Mitchell said. "You heard of a place called Buckskin?"

"Ghost town, ain't it?" Pool asked with a grunt.

"It used to be, but it's not anymore. They found silver there again. One of the mines has opened back up, and it wouldn't surprise me if some of the others did too. And there are prospectors roamin' all over those hills looking for other veins. Buckskin's a boomtown again, and I expect it'll just get bigger."

An avaricious grin spread across Pool's bearded face. "Lots of *dinero* there for the takin' in a boomtown," he commented.

"Yeah, but that's not all," Beeman said. "They got themselves a marshal."

Pool gave a contemptuous snort. "I'm not worried about some two-bit tin badge."

In a quiet voice, Mitchell said, "The fella packing the star in Buckskin is Frank Morgan."

Pool's eyes widened in surprise. "Morgan? The one they call The Drifter?"

"His own self," Mitchell confirmed.

"Never thought anybody as fiddle-footed as Morgan would ever settle down and take a marshal's job. I've wanted to cross trails with him for a long time." Pool grinned again. "You're right, that is interestin'. Mighty interestin'."

He started to laugh. It wasn't a pretty sound.

Behind him, the rest of the gang had finished emptying the pockets of Gates Tucker and Dagnabbit Dabney. Now, some of them picked up the bodies and started to carry them toward the ravine, where they would be tossed in to await the scavengers.

"What's goin' on over there?" Mitchell asked as he looked past Pool.

"Never mind about that," Pool said. "Tell me more about this place called Buckskin."

Garrett Claiborne wanted to go out and have a look at the Crown Royal Mine the same afternoon he arrived in Buckskin, but Frank convinced him it was too late in the day for that. Although Frank had a good general idea of the mine's location and was sure he could find it, he hadn't been out there himself since coming to Buckskin, even though he knew he was a part-owner of the property.

Instead, Frank took Claiborne around town and introduced him to people, explaining that Claiborne had come to reopen the Crown Royal. That created quite a bit of interest among Buckskin's merchants, especially Leo Benjamin. Another working mine meant more miners with money to spend.

When they went into the offices of the Lucky Lizard Mining Company, Tip Woodford wasn't there, but Diana was. She was seated at a desk, going over columns of figures entered in a ledger. Frank knew that Diana did some of the bookkeeping work for her father, but he had never seen her actually engaged in that chore. Nor had he seen her wearing spectacles, as she was now.

To tell the truth, they didn't look bad on her.

She seemed embarrassed, though, and reached up to remove the spectacles as soon as she saw Frank coming in to the office. She put a smile on her face and said, "Hello, Marshal. What are you doing here?"

"Thought I'd stop by and introduce Garrett Claiborne here to your father," Frank said.

"I'm sorry, he's still out at the mine. But I'm glad to meet you, Mr. . . . . Claiborne, was it?"

"That's right," the mining engineer said. "I take it you're Miss Woodford?" He stepped forward and extended his hand. "The pleasure is all mine, I assure you."

Diana stood up and took his hand. "Why, Mr. Claiborne, how gallant of you. With a name like that, I assume you're Southern?"

"From Georgia, ma'am," Claiborne said, although to Frank's ear he didn't have much of a Southern accent, certainly not one like Claude Langley's. Frank supposed that since Claiborne was a mining engineer, he had lived all over, which had a way of diminishing an accent.

"What brings you to Buckskin?" Diana asked.

"I work for the Browning Mining Syndicate. I've come to take charge of the Crown Royal Mine and put it back into operation."

Diana's eyebrows rose, and her voice was a little cooler as she said, "Really? I wasn't aware that there were any plans to do that."

"Yes, indeed. Once we found out about your father's rediscovery of the Lucky Lizard vein, we decided it would be worthwhile to do some further explorations in the Crown Royal."

"I suppose the word was bound to get out."

"Yes, when we heard from—"

Frank broke into the conversation, saying, "I reckon most folks in Nevada have heard about the new strike by now." No one in Buckskin knew that he had any stake in the Crown Royal, and he wanted to keep it that way. Folks had a way of treating wealthy people differently. He preferred to remain just plain old Frank Morgan. The reputation as a gunfighter that he carried with him was bad enough without people knowing he was rich too.

Evidently, Claiborne was smart enough to pick up on what Frank's interruption meant, because he said, "Yes, the word's spread far and wide by now. In fact, the Alhambra Mine will be opening again too. It was bought not long ago from the original owner, Milton Jernigan, by a man named Hamish Munro."

Frank was curious about that. After Claiborne's earlier comment about Munro, not much more had been said about the man. Now Frank asked, "Did Munro know about the strike before he bought the Alhambra?"

"My understanding is that he did not. Munro makes a

habit of buying old mines and claims, on the chance that he can make something of them where the original owners failed. More often than not, he's right." Claiborne smiled. "But he had a real stroke of luck with the Alhambra, even more so than usual. That's why, according to the rumors I've heard, he's coming to Buckskin to supervise the mine's operation personally."

"You don't know that he's going to be lucky," Diana pointed out. "No offense, Mr. Claiborne, but most of the prospectors who have come here looking for silver haven't found any yet. My father is the only one who's been really successful."

Claiborne shrugged. "It's possible that the Crown Royal vein really *is* played out. But mining methods have improved in the past decade, Miss Woodford. We can find and remove ore with greater ease and efficiency now than we could then. So there's really only one way to find out."

"Well, I wish you luck." Diana laughed. "At any rate, it's good to have such a handsome, intelligent man as yourself in Buckskin. I hope we'll be seeing a lot of each other, even though we're competitors."

Claiborne's face turned a little pink at the flattery. "Ah, yes," he managed to say. "Indeed."

Frank put a hand on Claiborne's shoulder to steer him toward the door of the office. "Tell Tip we came by," he said to Diana.

"I certainly will," she replied, giving him a cool, challenging look. Then she gave Claiborne another smile and added, "Stop in to see me any time you like, Garrett."

"Yes, of course," he said as he tipped his hat to her.

Frank knew good and well what Diana was doing. She was playing up to Claiborne in an attempt to make him jealous. That was just fine with him, because it wasn't going to work. In fact, he hoped the tactic backfired on her and she really did get interested in Claiborne. That would solve Frank's problem of figuring out what to do about her. And even though Claiborne was considerably older than Diana, the age difference wasn't nearly as much as it was between her and Frank.

Yeah, he thought, a romance between the two of them would suit him just fine.

He might even have to play cupid, just to nudge things along.

Chapter 7

After taking Claiborne's buggy down to Amos Hillman's livery stable, Frank talked the mining engineer into spending the night at his house, since he planned to sleep on the cot in the marshal's office anyway.

Early the next morning, with Catamount Jack taking over as deputy, Frank saddled up Goldy and got ready to ride out to the Crown Royal with Claiborne. In the stall across the aisle, Stormy tossed his head angrily when he saw Frank leading out the other horse.

"Don't worry, fella," Frank said to the Appaloosa. "You're not being replaced. I just want to see how Goldy here acts on the trail."

Goldy's injuries were mostly healed, and the gelding acted eager to stretch his legs. Dog came along too, trotting alongside the horse as Frank rode over to the café, where he had arranged to meet Garrett Claiborne. As he got there, Claiborne came out of the building, followed by Becky Humphries, who was wiping her hands on her apron. Pretty, redheaded Becky was the youngest of the three women who ran the café, and she was smiling as she said, "Y'all come back to see us any time, Mr. Claiborne."

He tugged on the brim of his hat. "I'll do that, Miss Humphries. I must say, those biscuits were some of the best I've ever eaten."

Becky blushed. "Go on with you, you flatterer," she said with a little laugh.

Looking a little embarrassed, Claiborne said to Frank, "Ready to go, Marshal?"

"Yep. Amos has got your buggy horse harnessed up and waiting for you."

Claiborne nodded. "I'll be right back then." He headed toward the livery stable, his stride brisk.

"Mornin', Marshal," Becky said. "I like that new friend of yours."

"He seems like a decent sort," Frank agreed. "I didn't know you were a Southern girl."

Becky's accent became more pronounced as she said, "Why, Ah suspect there's a whole heap o' things you don't know about li'l ol' me, Marshal."

"Uh-huh," Frank said with a dry grin. Becky was used to playing up to men; it was sort of an occupational habit with her. She had probably gotten Claiborne to admit that he was from Georgia, and that was all it took for Becky to transform herself into a Southern belle.

The thing of it was, Frank didn't know if he wanted Becky flirting with Claiborne or not. He had hoped to distract Diana Woodford with the mining man, and if Claiborne got mixed up with Becky, then Frank would be right back where he started with Diana.

He supposed he could let it drop to Claiborne that Becky used to be a whore . . . but as soon as the thought crossed his mind, Frank discarded it and scolded himself for even thinking such a thing. He liked Becky—and her partners Lauren and Ginnie too, for that matter—and didn't want to embarrass them.

A man his age shouldn't still have to be worrying about romance and suchlike, he told himself. He ought to be past all that. Dealing with gunmen and outlaws and killers was a mite easier, most of the time.

Claiborne rattled up in the buggy. Becky waved good-bye as Frank and Claiborne headed out of town.

As they left the settlement behind, Claiborne said, "You, ah, seem to have an abundance of attractive young women in Buckskin, Marshal. Miss Humphries and the other two ladies in the café, and of course Miss Woodford . . ."

Frank chuckled. "I hate to break it to you, Mr. Claiborne, but with those four, you've already met all the eligible females in Buckskin. Trudy Benjamin, who runs the boardinghouse, is married. You met her husband Leo at the general store yesterday."

"Oh, yes, of course."

"They're the only women in town, for now anyway. I'd be surprised if more don't show up soon, though. You've been around boomtowns before, so you know what I mean."

"Ah, yes. I certainly do." Claiborne sounded like he didn't approve.

A decade earlier, when the Crown Royal was still operating, a decent road had run between the mine and the settlement. Over the years, nature had reclaimed some of the road, until it was now just a narrow trail. Claiborne had trouble negotiating some of it in the buggy.

"We're going to have to improve this route," he said between bumps and jolts. "We'll be bringing wagonloads of ore over this trail."

"Assuming there are wagonloads of ore still to be found," Frank pointed out.

"Yes, of course. But I have a feeling there will be."

Frank hoped Claiborne was right, not so much for his own sake, but for Conrad's and also for the town's. With several successful mines operating in the vicinity, Buckskin might grow into a fine city.

"This is beautiful country," Claiborne said a short time later as they rounded a bend in the trail and the landscape sprawled out in front of them in an impressive panorama of wooded hills, lush valleys, and stark, snowcapped mountains looming over all of it. "Quite rugged and uncivilized, of course, but still beautiful."

"It's not as uncivilized as you might think," Frank said. "If it was, we'd have to be worrying about Paiutes lifting our hair right now. Wasn't all that many years ago such things were still going on. Now, though, all the Indians have been pacified. The grizzly bears and the cougars have retreated up higher in the mountains, and even the diamondback rattlers aren't as common as they used to be." Frank shook his head. "No, the only real danger you're liable to run into now comes from outlaws."

"There are still outlaws in this area?"

"There are outlaws anywhere you go, if there are people there," Frank said. "It's human nature for some folks to be downright ornery and crooked."

"I suppose." Claiborne let go of the reins with one hand and pointed. "There! Is that the mine?"

"I believe it is," Frank said.

They arrived at the Crown Royal a few minutes later. Frank was surprised to see that several buildings were still standing, including a large one where the narrow-gauge railroad tracks that emerged from the hole in the side of the hill terminated. That was the stamp mill, where the ore brought out of the mine in carts was pulverized so the silver could be separated out from the worthless rock. The mine superintendent had probably had his office in there too. Nearby was a long, low building that must have served as the barracks for the miners. There was also a cookshack, a mess hall, and several storage sheds. Frank guessed that was what those buildings had been used for, anyway.

Claiborne brought the buggy to a halt, looked around, and said, "Well, this is quite impressive. Everything appears to be in better shape than I thought it would be. I'll have to take a closer look to be sure, of course."

Frank swung down from the saddle and looped Goldy's reins around the trunk of a sapling. "Let's go take that look," he suggested.

Claiborne climbed out of the buggy and headed straight for the mine entrance. "I want to check the shoring timbers in the shaft," he said over his shoulder as Frank and Dog followed him. After a second, Dog bounded ahead and darted toward the black opening in the hillside.

"Probably smelled a rabbit in there," Frank said.

Claiborne stopped short and cast a nervous look in Frank's direction. "What if it's one of those grizzly bears or mountain lions you mentioned?"

"Dog's got more sense than to charge into a hole that's got a grizz or a cougar in it," Frank assured him. The big, wolflike cur disappeared into the shaft. Loud barks echoed as Dog gave chase to whatever prey had lured him in there.

Frank and Claiborne both stopped short as they heard a low rumble from inside the mine. "Damn it!" Frank said. "Dog! Dog! Get out of there!"

"Good lord!" Claiborne said. "The noise must have set off a cave-in!"

Frank started forward at a run. He and Dog had been trail partners for a long time, had endured a lot of hardship and danger together. The idea of the big cur being trapped in a cave-in horrified him.

To his great relief, Dog darted back into sight at the mine entrance, racing out of the black shaft as a cloud of dust boiled from the opening behind him. Claiborne groaned as the rumble of falling rock died away.

"The timbers must have been practically rotted away," he said. "There's no telling how much damage was done."

"Sorry," Frank said as Dog came trotting up to them. "To tell you the truth, I never even thought about the old fella causing a cave-in."

Claiborne sighed. "It's all right. I suppose in a way it's a blessing. The most unstable parts of the shaft will have already collapsed, and now it won't be quite as dangerous when we go in there to dig it out and shore up the rest of the tunnels."

"You hear that, boy?" Frank said with a grin as he scratched Dog's ears. "Good job."

"I wouldn't go quite *that* far," Claiborne said, "but this is certainly not an insurmountable obstacle."

They spent the next hour examining the shaft and the buildings. Frank felt a twinge of nervousness when he stepped in to the hole in the hillside, but Claiborne looked at the thick timbers supporting the roof and told him it was safe enough. Still, Frank was glad to be back in the open air.

Most of the machinery in the stamp mill had been dismantled and hauled away when the mine was closed down before, but as Claiborne said, "That's all right. We'll bring in more modern equipment and do an even better job now. There have been great improvements in the pulverization and amalgamation processes in the past ten years."

"That's good to hear," Frank said, "even though I don't really know what you're talking about. But if Conrad Browning has faith in you, Garrett, then so do I."

"I won't let you and Mr. Browning down, Marshal."

When they had finished looking around, Claiborne nodded and said, "I don't see why we can't have this mine up and running in a month, maybe less, depending on how many workers we're able to hire. The initial expenditure will be fairly high, but the Browning Mining Syndicate can afford it. I've seen the assay reports on the ore coming out of the Lucky Lizard now, and if we can approach the same quality here, the Crown Royal should be a lucrative venture once again."

"Well, whatever I can do to help you, just let me know. Most of my time is spent keeping the peace in town, of course, but I'll be glad to lend a hand out here as much as I can."

Claiborne smiled. "Marshal, can I be blunt?"

"Sure," Frank said.

"What I really need is for you to just stand back and let me get to work."

Frank laughed and clapped a hand on his shoulder. "I reckon I can do that!"

On their way back to Buckskin, Frank and Garrett Claiborne had to pass fairly close to the Alhambra Mine, and when Frank asked if Claiborne wanted to take a look at the place, he shrugged and said, "We might as well. Just a quick look, though. I'm not sure it would be ethical to do too thorough an inspection of it, since it's owned by a competitor."

"That's a good point," Frank agreed. "Shouldn't hurt anything to have a glance around, though."

Frank found the trail that veered off toward the other mine, and he and Claiborne followed it for the next quarter of an hour as it ran around rugged hills and along spiny ridges. They came to a shelf of land that jutted out from a gray cliff that rose almost straight up for a couple of hundred feet. Several squarish towers of rock stuck up from the top of the cliff, like battlements on a castle or fortress.

They were natural formations, but they had a striking, man-made look about them.

"I can see how the mine got its name," Claiborne commented as he and Frank approached. "The original owner must have been a world traveler. That cliff bears a distinct resemblance to the Spanish palace known as the Alhambra."

"I wouldn't know about that, since I've never been there myself," Frank said, "but I'll take your word for it, Garrett."

He reined in when they were still about fifty yards from a group of ramshackle buildings and the black mouth of a mine shaft in the hillside. From the looks of things, the Alhambra was in worse shape than the Crown Royal. Claiborne brought the buggy to a halt beside Frank.

"I don't see any signs of life," the engineer said. "Munro's men must not have gotten here yet."

"You're sure this fella Munro's going to open up this mine again?"

Claiborne smiled. "The mining industry is like any other business, Marshal. It's full of rumors, and everyone tries to keep up with everyone else's activities. From everything I've heard, Hamish Munro has high hopes for this—"

Before Claiborne could go on, Frank shouted, "Get down!" He had seen a telltale glint of sunlight on metal just inside at one of the windows in the old mill building.

Claiborne just looked confused and wasn't budging, so Frank kicked his feet from the stirrups, leaped from the saddle, and landed in the buggy. He grabbed Claiborne and dived out the other side of the vehicle, dragging the startled engineer with him.

If that reflection he had seen didn't mean anything, Frank was going to feel mighty silly when they hit the ground.

As they sprawled on the rocky earth, however, a rifle

cracked and sent a bullet whistling through the space where Claiborne had been a few seconds earlier. Frank's instincts had been right again—there was a bushwhacker lurking in the old stamp mill.

But as more shots slammed out and slugs began to kick up dust around them, Frank figured this was one time when it might have been better to be wrong!

Chapter 8

Frank surged to his feet with one hand hooked in Claiborne's collar. He hauled the smaller man upright and hustled him around to the rear of the buggy. The vehicle wouldn't provide much cover, but it was better than nothing. As they ran, Frank heard the wind-rip of another bullet close beside his ear. It was a sound he had heard all too many times in his eventful life.

They ducked behind the buggy as another shot ricocheted off some of the brass trim on it. The horse hitched to the front of the buggy snorted in fear and moved around skittishly. If the horse bolted, they would be left out in the open, exposed to the bushwhacker's fire.

"My God!" Claiborne exclaimed in a shaken voice. "Why are they shooting at us?"

"Your guess is as good as mine," Frank said. He drew his Colt as he crouched there. The range was a little far for a handgun, but his Winchester was in the saddle boot strapped to Goldy. The gelding had trotted off a few yards and then stopped. Frank could have tried to whistle him over, but since Goldy seemed to be out of the line of fire, Frank wanted him to stay there.

As the shots paused for a moment, probably so the bushwhacker could reload, Frank shouted, "Hey, you in the mill! Hold your fire, blast it! We don't mean you any harm!"

The only reply was a resumption of the shooting. Bullets tore through the canvas canopy over the buggy's seat.

Frank glanced over at the big cur and snapped, "Dog! Go get him!"

Dog took off running toward the mill. His powerful muscles bunched under his shaggy hide as he raced over the ground. Bullets plowed into the dirt around him, but he darted from side to side so that, as fast as he was moving, he was an almost impossible target to hit.

Dog disappeared around the back of the mill. His instincts and animal cunning told him to come at the bushwhacker from the rear.

Frank just hoped the rifleman was the only one in the old mill; otherwise Dog might be in for a hot lead welcome.

Sure enough, a moment later he heard shots from inside the building. With a grimace, he told Claiborne, "Stay here and keep your head down!"

Then he burst out from behind the buggy and sprinted toward the mill, weaving in his approach as Dog had done.

Riding boots weren't made for running, but Frank managed to get up some pretty good speed as he ran toward the mill. No more shots were coming in his direction. If nothing else, Dog had provided a good distraction for the would-be killer.

Frank hoped that wasn't going to cost his shaggy trail partner his life, though.

When he got close to the door, he lifted his foot and slammed his boot heel into the wood just below the knob. The door crashed open. Frank went through it in a crouch, the Colt up and ready. His keen eyes took in the scene instantly. Four men were in the room, which at one time must have been an office. One of the men was down on the floor, rolling around trying to keep a snarling, snapping Dog from ripping his throat out. The other men held guns, but couldn't fire at the big cur for fear of hitting their friend instead.

Frank's noisy entrance drew the attention of the others away from the struggle between man and dog on the floor. One of them yelled, "Look out, Gunther!"

A tall, burly man holding a rifle swung toward Frank, but found himself staring down the barrel of The Drifter's Peacemaker. That was the last sight a great many men had seen in their lives.

This time, instead of shooting, Frank gave the man in front of his gun a chance to surrender. "Drop it," he said. *"Now!"*

The man called Gunther was bald except for a pair of dark, bushy eyebrows. He scowled in anger, but with Frank's gun on him, he had no choice but to bend and place the rifle on the floor at his feet.

"Slide it over here," Frank ordered. "You other men, I want your guns too."

"Somebody help me!" the man wrestling with Dog screamed. He was already gashed and bloody, his shirt in ribbons from the big cur's sharp, rending teeth.

"Dog!" Frank snapped. Instantly, Dog backed off, still growling as his hackles stood up menacingly.

The other men had pistols in their hands. Since the bushwhacker's shots had come from a rifle, Frank had no doubt that Gunther had been the one firing them. As Frank gave them a cold, level stare, the men put their guns on the floor and kicked them across the room.

"You're gonna be damn sorry about this, mister," Gunther

blustered. "Threatenin' us and siccin' that damn wolf on us . . . we'll have the law on you!"

"He's a dog, not a wolf," Frank said, "and I *am* the law. Besides, you were the one who came close to killing me and my friend, remember?"

Gunther didn't back down. He said, "I had a right to shoot at you! You're on private property, mister."

"That's Marshal to you."

Gunther sneered. "Marshal o' Buckskin?"

"That's right."

"You got no authority out here. Your jurisdiction ends at the edge of the settlement."

Technically, he was right. But as the only star-packer in this area, Frank figured that as a practical matter, his authority extended a little farther than Buckskin itself.

The man Dog had savaged was helped to his feet by his friends. His injuries looked worse than they really were, Frank knew.

"That . . . that varmint's loco!" the man said as he pointed a shaking hand at Dog. "Came at me like a hydrophobia skunk!" He let out a groan of dismay. "Is he mad, mister? Am I gonna start foamin' at the mouth from them bites?"

"I'm more worried about Dog coming down with something," Frank said. "Who are you men?"

Gunther thumped his chest with a malletlike fist. "We work for Hamish Munro . . . and in case you don't know, mister, Hamish Munro is the owner of the Alhambra Mine! That means we belong here, and you're nothin' but a damn trespasser! We've got a right to shoot trespassers."

From just outside the door, a tentative voice asked, "Marshal Morgan, are you all right?"

Gunther's eyes widened in surprise. "Claiborne!" he bellowed. "Is that you?"

Garrett Claiborne appeared in the doorway. "Good lord," he muttered. "You."

"You fellas know each other?" Frank asked.

A look of stern disapproval appeared on Claiborne's normally mild face. "Yes, I know this man, Marshal. He's Gunther Hammersmith. We've encountered each other before. He's also a mining engineer."

An ugly smile twisted Gunther's mouth. "And a helluva lot better one than you'll ever be, Claiborne."

Frank was surprised to hear that the big, bald man was any sort of engineer. He had the look of a bruiser and a brawler, the sort of brutal hired hardcase who followed orders instead of giving them.

Gunther looked at Frank and went on. "Mr. Munro hired me and my boys to get this mine open and working again. Like I said, we've got a right to be here, and you don't."

"Haven't seen you around Buckskin," Frank said.

Gunther snorted in disgust. "Why would we bother going into your two-bit town? We brought our own supplies with us. We've been inspecting the mine and shorin' up what needs to be shored up. We won't need to go to Buckskin until we're ready to hire miners, and that won't be for a few days yet."

Frank had to admit that the man sounded like he was telling the truth. He wasn't completely convinced, though.

"You got any proof of what you're telling me?" he asked.

"I don't have to show you any proof of anything!"

"No," Frank said, "but I'm the one holding the gun, and I'm still a mite riled up about those shots you took at us."

"All right, all right," Gunther said. He reached into a hip pocket and took out a folded envelope. He removed a sheet of paper from it, unfolded it, and held it out. "This is a letter from Mr. Munro authorizin' us to be here."

Without taking his eyes off the four men, Frank asked Claiborne, "Would you recognize Munro's signature, Garrett?"

"Yes, I think so. I've seen it on quite a few documents."

"Take a look then."

Claiborne took the sheet of paper from Hammersmith, being careful not to get in Frank's line of fire. He read the letter and then said, "It's what he said it was, and Mr. Munro's signature appears to be genuine."

"All right." Frank lowered the Colt but didn't holster it. "Mr. Claiborne and I will be leaving now. We're going to take your guns with us, though."

"You can't do that!" Hammersmith protested.

"We'll leave 'em a half mile down the trail," Frank went on as if he hadn't heard the objection. "That way, we'll already be gone by the time you get them back, and you won't be tempted to take any more shots at us."

"This ain't right. It ain't legal."

"If you want to file a formal complaint, you can ride into Buckskin and do so."

Hammersmith glared but didn't say anything else. Claiborne gathered up the guns and, staggering a little under the weight of all the hardware, carried them back to the buggy. Frank backed out of the office, keeping his Colt trained on the open door. He whistled for Goldy, and he was thankful when the horse came trotting up to him. Obviously, one of his prior owners had trained the horse.

With practiced ease, Frank swung up into the saddle using only his left hand to grip the horn. His right was still filled with the butt of the Peacemaker. He waited until Claiborne had climbed into the buggy, turned it around, and sent it rolling along the trail at a quick pace before he turned Goldy around and rode away as well. Dog loped alongside, tongue lolling from his mouth, obviously pleased with himself.

Frank glanced over his shoulder several times, just in case Hammersmith and the others had more guns hidden somewhere in the mill, but by the time he and Claiborne were out of sight of the mine, they hadn't emerged from the building.

He called a halt half a mile down the trail, and Claiborne dumped the guns out of the buggy as Frank had promised. As they set off toward Buckskin again, Frank said, "I got the feeling you and that fella Gunther don't like each other very much."

"Gunther Hammersmith is a brute," Claiborne said with more genuine anger in his voice than Frank had heard from him so far. "He's the sort of man who thinks he has to enforce his will on the men working for him by means of fear and violence. He's beaten a couple of men to death when they stood up to him. The last time was at a mine in Colorado. He was fired as superintendent, and I was brought in to take his place. He's hated me ever since. I think he believes that I was responsible for him being discharged from the job."

"If he beat a man to death, why wasn't he put in jail instead of being fired?"

Claiborne shrugged. "The man who owned the mine had a considerable amount of influence. And some of the other miners swore that the man Hammersmith killed attacked him first. Hammersmith claimed he was just defending himself. Everyone was too afraid of him to contradict his story."

"Sounds like the sort of gent this Hamish Munro would hire, if he's as ruthless as you say he is," Frank commented.

"Yes, Munro and Hammersmith certainly make a good match. Hammersmith has worked for Munro before, and

I'm not surprised to see that he's the one Munro picked up to supervise the Alhambra's operation. This is going to complicate the situation, especially for you, Marshal."

"You're saying that I'm going to have trouble with him when he comes into Buckskin?"

"After today, with the grudge that he's bound to hold against you . . . I'd say you can count on it."

Chapter 9

Frank and Claiborne didn't run into any more trouble on their way back to the settlement. By the time they reached Buckskin, it was early afternoon. Claiborne still hadn't met Tip Woodford, so when they passed the rotund, overall-clad mayor on the street, Frank reined in, hailed him, and motioned him over.

"Tip, I'd like for you to meet Garrett Claiborne."

"Yeah, you're the minin' engineer, come to take over the Crown Royal," Tip said as he stuck out his hand. "My gal told me about you comin' into the office. Put 'er there, Claiborne. I'm glad to meet you."

Claiborne smiled as he shook hands with Tip. "I must say, that's a friendly greeting considering that we're competitors, Mr. Woodford. The pleasure is mine."

"I don't see us as competitors," Tip explained. "I got my claim, and the folks who own the Crown Royal got theirs. I'm hopin' there's plenty o' silver in the hills to go around for all of us."

"That's my hope as well."

"Diana said for me to invite you to supper tonight if I

happened to run into you." Tip glanced toward Frank. "And you too, Marshal."

"That's very considerate of you and your daughter, sir, but—"

"We'll be there," Frank said. He still had hopes of getting Claiborne and Diana together.

After Tip had moved on, Claiborne frowned at Frank and said, "I had hoped to get started lining up workers for the mine."

"You'll still have time this afternoon to do that. Start at the Silver Baron Saloon. It's Tip's place, but all the prospectors show up there sooner or later, and Tip won't mind you doing a little recruiting in there."

Claiborne looked a little dubious, but he said, "All right. I'll take your advice, Marshal."

Frank gave Claiborne directions for finding the Woodford house, in case they didn't run into each other again before it was time to go there for supper, then headed for the marshal's office after putting up his horse at Hillman's livery. He wondered if he ought to tell Claiborne that he was part-owner of the Crown Royal. Obviously, Conrad hadn't seen fit to share that information with the mining engineer, so Frank decided he would follow his son's lead.

The door to the marshal's office was jerked open just before Frank got there, and Catamount Jack came out carrying a shotgun. A grim look was on the old-timer's face, and Frank knew right away there was trouble.

"Marshal!" Jack said. "Glad you're back."

"What's going on, Jack?"

"Fella came by just a minute ago and said a bad ruckus was about to break out down at one o' them new whiskey palaces. Kelley's Top-Notch, I think he said. I was about to go see about it."

"I'll take care of it," Frank said.

Jack extended the shotgun. "Want the Greener?"

"No, that's all right. If I need a gun, I've always got my Colt."

Jack grunted and said, "I reckon that's usually been plenty for you, ain't it, Marshal?"

Frank didn't reply to that. His reputation as a gunfighter dogged him enough already without him talking about it.

As he strode away from the marshal's office, he recalled that Kelley's Top-Notch Saloon, which had been in operation for a little over a week, was a hole-in-the-wall place around a corner, facing one of Buckskin's side streets instead of the main street. Hardly a palace, as Jack had described it. As Frank's long legs carried him around that corner, he heard a sudden crash from inside the saloon. He broke into a run and slapped the batwings aside.

The Top-Notch was a long, narrow room with the bar on the right, a scattering of tables on the left, and a big pot-bellied stove that was cold at the moment in the rear of the room. One of the tables had been knocked over and the chairs around it upset. Playing cards were strewn around on the floor, along with some bills and coins. That was enough to convince Frank that the fight now going on had its origins in a poker game gone bad.

A burly hombre wearing work boots, overalls, and a flannel shirt was trading punches with a slightly smaller man whose suit and fancy cravat marked him as a gambler. The professional cardplayer was no effete fop, though. He was standing toe to toe with the miner and slugging it out. Both men had bruises on their faces already.

A bartender with a turkey neck and no chin stood behind the hardwood, watching the battle with a worried, pop-eyed expression. Three other men, all dressed like prospectors, stood back on the other side of the room, also intent spectators to the fisticuffs.

Frank thought about drawing his gun and firing a shot into the ceiling. That would probably put a stop to the fracas, but it would also needlessly damage the roof. Rain leaked through bullet holes just as easily as through any other opening.

Instead, he bellowed at the top of his lungs, "Hey! Break it up, you two!"

The battlers ignored him and continued to swing wild, looping punches. Most of the blows missed, which was a good thing. If they had all connected, the men might have done some serious damage to themselves by now.

With a disgusted sigh, Frank moved toward the two men. As the tides of battle made them sway closer to him, he reached out and caught hold of the miner's collar. He hauled back hard and flung the surprised man toward the bar. The gambler had just thrown a punch that missed because Frank pulled the miner out of its path. He stumbled forward, off balance because of the missed punch, and Frank caught hold of his arm to keep him from falling.

The gambler glared at Frank, his bruised and battered face twisting with anger. "What the hell do you think—" he started to demand, but then he looked over Frank's shoulder and his eyes widened with surprise. "Look out!"

Frank let go of the gambler and twisted around to see the miner lunging at him and swinging a bottle of whiskey he had snatched up off the bar. In his blind rage, he was now attacking the man who had interfered in his fight with the gambler.

Frank jerked his head to the side, knowing the bottle might crush his skull if it connected. It slammed into his left shoulder instead and sent pain shooting through Frank's body. Not the left arm, though. It went numb.

Hunching over a little against the pain, Frank hooked a hard right into the miner's belly. It was almost like punching a slab of wood. The blow had enough power behind it to knock the man back a step, though. Still using his right fist because his left arm was useless for the moment, Frank clubbed the miner on the left side of the head, just above the ear.

That staggered the man but didn't put him down. He dropped the bottle, caught himself, and roared in furious defiance as he lunged forward, tackling Frank around the waist.

The miner was heavier than Frank and bore him backward. Frank tripped on some of the debris from the broken table and fell backward. He crashed to the floor, and the miner's weight came down on him with stunning force. The breath was knocked out of his lungs, and the room flashed red and black around him as his head bounced off the rough floor.

Hamlike hands fastened around his neck, the fingers digging in with cruel force as they cut off his air. Since the hard landing had already knocked the breath out of him, Frank didn't have any air in reserve. He knew he would pass out in a matter of seconds, so he had to do something fast. He clawed at his holster, intending to draw the Colt and slam it against his attacker's head.

But the holster was empty. The gun had fallen out sometime during the struggle, probably when Frank was knocked off his feet.

He tried to heave himself up off the floor, but the miner weighed too much. Consciousness began to slip away from him. He heard his own blood pounding in his head like the frantic beat of a drum.

Even over that racket, he heard the loud thud that sounded somewhere close by, followed by a second one. The terrible pressure on Frank's throat eased and then went away entirely as the miner's fingers loosened. He slumped to the side, falling off Frank. With the weight gone, Frank's chest heaved as he dragged life-giving breaths of air into his lungs again.

He looked over and saw the miner sprawled on the floor beside him, out cold. Blood trickled from a cut in the man's thick brown hair and ran down the side of his face. Somebody had clouted him a couple of good ones—it had taken two blows to knock him out—and when Frank glanced up he wasn't surprised to see the gambler standing there with a broken table leg clutched in his hand.

The man reached down with his other hand and said, "Let me help you up, Marshal."

Frank and the gambler clasped wrists, and the man lifted Frank with seemingly little effort. When he was back on his feet, Frank gave a shake of his head to clear the lingering cobwebs out of his brain. He nodded toward the unconscious miner and said, "You could have killed him, you know, hitting him with a table leg like that."

The gambler laughed. "Not very damned likely. Bastard's got a skull made out of iron, and it's thick too. Anyway, if somebody had to die, I figured he was a better choice than Buckskin's marshal."

"Can't argue with that," Frank said. He flexed the fingers of his left hand. Feeling had begun to return to that hand and arm. "I'm obliged to you."

The gambler shrugged. "Hell, the only reason you got mixed up in this fracas was because you tried to keep him from busting up me and my place any worse than he already had." He held out his hand again. "I'm Ed Kelley, with two *e*'s. I own this saloon."

Frank shook hands with him. He had seen Kelley around town but hadn't met the man yet. Kelley was about thirty-five, with broad shoulders, thick dark hair, and a narrow mustache. He was disheveled from fighting at the moment, but he had the look of a man who would usually be pretty dapper.

Frank's hat had come off during the fight. He picked it up, slapped it against his leg to get the sawdust from the floor off it, then settled it on his head.

"What started this ruckus?"

Kelley shrugged. "The usual misunderstanding. Rogan thought I was cheating because I won a big pot from him."

"Were you?"

Kelley's eyes narrowed for a second, as if he were thinking about taking offense at that question, but then he chuckled and shook his head.

"I guess being a lawman you have to ask that question, eh?"

"I like to know what's going on in my town," Frank admitted.

It was amazing how quickly he had come to think of Buckskin as *his* town.

"Well, in the interests of full disclosure . . . no, I wasn't cheating, Marshal. I don't have to cheat to win. Rogan is a reckless, impulsive player. I could clean him out any day of the week without half trying."

Frank nodded. "All right. That's pretty much the answer I was expecting, so I'll take your word for it, Kelley. Just make sure you continue to run clean games here."

"That's what I've done every other place I've been."

Frank turned to the other three miners and said, "This fella Rogan a friend of yours?"

"We work together at the Lucky Lizard," one of them replied. "I wouldn't say we were his friends."

"Well, pick him up anyway and haul him down to the jail for me."

Another of the men scowled. "We ain't deputies that you can boss around, Marshal."

"No, but you work for me," Tip Woodford said from the doorway, "and if you want to keep on workin' for me, you'll do what the marshal asked."

Some grumbling went on, but the three men did as they were told and lifted the still-unconscious Rogan. As they carried him out of the saloon, Frank called after them, "Tell my deputy to lock him up and keep him there until tomorrow morning." Then he turned to Woodford and said, "I'm obliged for the helping hand, Tip."

The owner of the Lucky Lizard frowned. "I heard that Rogan was in here raisin' hell and got over here as soon as I could. Feel like it's sort of my fault, since he works for me."

"Just because you pay a man wages doesn't make you his keeper," Frank pointed out.

"Maybe not, but Rogan ain't gonna be gamblin' away any more money I pay him, because as soon as he comes to, I'm firin' him. He's been a troublemaker from the start, always complainin' and tryin' to stir up the men against me. I pay 'em decent wages and treat 'em decent too. I don't need somebody like Dave Rogan around causin' an uproar for no good reason."

"I hope you don't attach any blame to me for what happened, Mr. Woodford," the saloon keeper said. "We haven't met. I'm Ed Kelley."

Tip shook hands with him and said, "No, I don't blame you, Kelley. Ain't your fault that Rogan's an ornery bastard."

"You own the Silver Baron Saloon as well as that mine, don't you?"

"That's right."

Kelley slid a cigar from his vest pocket and put it in his mouth, leaving it unlit as he clamped his teeth on it. "Biggest saloon in Buckskin, or so I've heard. I haven't checked it out for myself yet."

"Stop by any time and have a drink on me," Tip offered.

Kelley nodded. "I'll do that." He took a neatly folded handkerchief from the breast pocket of his coat and touched it to a cut on his forehead. "Now if you'll excuse me, gentlemen, I'd like to go clean up." He gave Frank and Tip a pleasant nod and turned toward a door in the rear of the room. As an afterthought, he said to the bartender, "Get this mess straightened up in here."

"Right away, Boss," the man responded.

Frank and Tip left the saloon. "You've had a mighty busy day," the mayor commented. "Trouble every which way you look, seems like."

Frank nodded. "That's what life is like in a boomtown," he said.

Chapter 10

Back at the jail, Catamount Jack jerked his thumb over his shoulder when Frank came in and said, "I got that fella locked up back yonder in one o' the cells."

Frank nodded. "That's fine. You can let him out in the morning if you're here. If not, I'll take care of it."

"Gonna fine him for tryin' to kill you?"

Frank touched his throat, which was a little sore from Rogan trying to strangle him. "I probably ought to, but he lost all his money to Ed Kelley at the Top-Notch. That's what he was so upset about. I reckon spending a night in jail will have to be punishment enough for him. That and losing his job, because Tip's going to fire him for causing another ruckus."

"Serves him right. We don't have to feed him, do we? Can't we at least let him go hungry tonight?"

"That wouldn't be humane," Frank said with a chuckle. "I'll talk to the ladies over at the café and see if they'll bring a tray over to him."

Jack scowled in disapproval.

"And one for you too," Frank added.

The old-timer perked right up at that. "See if that gal

Ginnie can bring it over," he suggested. "I think she likes me a mite."

Frank tried not to grin. Plump, blond Ginnie Carlson liked most men; it was in her nature. It was a wonder that being a soiled dove for several years and dealing with them on a regular basis hadn't soured her on the entire male population, but it hadn't.

"I'll see what I can do," he promised.

A groan from the small cell block prompted him to step over to the door and look through it. Rogan stirred on the bunk where he had been placed, but he wasn't fully conscious yet. Frank wondered if he ought to have Professor Burton take a look at Rogan, since the professor was the closest thing Buckskin had to a doctor. Frank hoped that Ed Kelley hadn't cracked Rogan's skull with that table leg.

A couple of minutes later, though, Rogan sat up, swung his legs off the bunk, and began cursing in a low, monotonous voice. Frank decided he was all right after all, probably just had one hell of a headache. Maybe a night in jail would help cure Rogan of that.

Frank lifted a hand in farewell as he left the office. "See you later," he said to Jack.

He went over to the café, which wasn't busy at the moment because the midday rush was over and it wasn't time for supper yet. In fact, Lauren Stillman was the only person there. Older than Becky and Ginnie, she was in her early thirties. Rather than being classically beautiful, she was what some people called a handsome woman. The thick brown hair that fell around her shoulders softened her looks somewhat. She smiled at Frank and said, "Hello, Marshal. What can I do for you?"

He explained about wanting a couple of meals for Catamount Jack and the prisoner, and Lauren promised to take care of it, even down to agreeing to have Ginnie deliver the food to the jail.

"I heard about that fight you had with Dave Rogan," she said.

"Word's gotten around already?"

"Buckskin is a small town. Everybody knows everybody else's business." Lauren paused. "For example, I know that you're having dinner with Diana Woodford tonight."

"Well, not just with Diana," Frank said. "Her pa will be there too, as well as that new mining engineer, Garrett Claiborne."

"Yes, but the only one Diana is really interested in is you."

Frank started to get uncomfortable. Lauren must have seen that, because she laughed.

"Surely I'm not telling you anything you don't already know, Frank," she said with a hint of familiarity in her voice. The two of them had taken an easy, instinctive liking to each other as soon as the women arrived in Buckskin a few weeks earlier. "Like I said, in a small town everybody knows everybody else's business."

"There's no business involving me and Diana Woodford," Frank insisted.

"But that's not because she wouldn't like for there to be."

Frank just shrugged. "Diana's wasting her time. A young woman like her needs to find herself a more suitable fella. Somebody a whole lot younger than me."

"With people like us, it's not the years so much as it is the miles."

"That's the truth," Frank said.

Lauren waited, as if halfway expecting him to say something else, but after a minute he just went on. "If you'll see that those meals get sent over to the jail . . ."

"Of course," she replied, her tone brisk and businesslike now. "Don't worry about it, Marshal."

"I'll pay you for them—"

"No need. I'll bill the mayor. It's the town's responsibility to feed prisoners, not yours."

"You're sure?"

"Positive."

"All right then." Frank gave the brim of his hat a tug. "Be seeing you."

As he turned and left the café, he thought he heard a sigh escape from Lauren Stillman. But he couldn't be sure, so he just closed the door and kept walking.

Jack had been stuck in the office most of the day, so Frank relieved him for a while, giving the old-timer a chance to go back to his cabin and check on Eldorado, the rangy mule that had accompanied Jack on numerous prospecting trips. Eldorado was semiretired now, as was Jack himself. A man never really got the lure of gold and silver out of his veins, but some of them learned to live with it. Jack had, and he didn't want to go prospecting anymore. At least, that was what he claimed.

When Jack got back to the office, Frank walked over to the small cabin the town was providing for his residence. Claiborne was inside, shaving and cleaning up. "Just thought I should make myself presentable," he said.

"Good idea," Frank agreed. Since Claiborne had a fire going in the stove, he heated some water for himself and got his razor out.

As dusk settled down over the rugged Nevada countryside, the two men walked toward the Woodford house, both of them freshly shaven and smelling of bay rum. Tip and Diana lived in the largest house in town, built with the proceeds from the first strike at the Lucky Lizard Mine more than a decade earlier. During the years Tip had lived there alone, after his wife left him and moved back East, taking Diana with her, he had allowed the house to deteriorate quite a bit. When Diana returned, she had taken one look at the place, rolled up her sleeves, and started in on the task of cleaning it up and fixing it up.

She had done a good job. The Woodford place was once again the nicest home in town. The picket fence in front had a fresh coat of whitewash on it, as did the walls of the two-story house itself. The flower beds had all the weeds pulled out of them, and flagstones had been carefully placed to make a walk leading to the front porch steps. The windows were all clean and glowed with warm yellow light from the lamps inside filtering through the curtains Diana had hung over them.

"What a lovely home," Claiborne said as he and Frank went up the walk to the porch.

"You can give Diana credit for that," Frank said. "An old pelican like Tip would just as soon live in a tent or a shack. Diana's the one who fixed the place up. Yes, sir, she'll make some lucky man a fine wife one of these days."

"Indeed."

They climbed to the porch and Frank knocked on the door. It opened a moment later. Diana greeted them with a smile and said, "Hello, gentlemen. Come right in."

She wore a pale blue dress that went well with her blue eyes, fair skin, and blond hair, Frank thought. This was one of the few times he had seen her when she wasn't wearing boots and jeans and a man's shirt. This evening she looked utterly feminine—and so lovely she'd almost take a fella's breath away.

She seemed to have that effect on Claiborne too, because he was having trouble finding his tongue. Finally, he said,

"Ah . . . thank you, Miss Woodford. And thank you for inviting us to dinner."

"We want to make you feel welcome in Buckskin, Mr. Claiborne." She turned to Frank. "Let me take your hat, Marshal."

Frank handed her his high-crowned Stetson. She took Claiborne's bowler hat too, but seemingly as an afterthought.

Tip came down the stairs and joined them in the foyer. He wore a dusty brown tweed suit. His shirt had a stiff collar and there was a tie around his neck. He dug a finger under his collar and tugged on it as he grunted and said, "Howdy."

Diana gave his hand a light slap and scolded, "Father, I told you to stop messing with your collar. It's not going to kill you to dress like a civilized person for a change."

"It might," Tip said. "This here collar's liable to choke me to death."

"Look at how nicely Mr. Claiborne's dressed, and he doesn't seem to mind."

"Reckon he's more used to it than I am. Come on in the parlor, boys, and we'll have a snort before dinner."

Diana rolled her eyes but didn't object. She said, "I'll go check on the food."

Tip led Frank and Claiborne into a comfortably furnished parlor and poured drinks for all three of them from a crystal decanter. As they sipped the smooth whiskey, Claiborne said, "You have a lovely home here, Mr. Woodford, and your daughter is quite lovely too."

"Yeah, well, most o' the time she's pretty down to earth, but she likes to put on airs ever' now and then. I reckon the way she was brought up had somethin' to do with that. No offense to Diana's ma, God rest her poor soul, but my wife could be a mite prissy when she wanted to. Diana's been a lot happier here in Buckskin than I thought she'd be when she came out here to live with me."

"It must have been difficult for her, losing her mother like that. I find her strength quite admirable."

Frank said, "So do I. She's a fine young woman."

"We can stand here gabbin' about Diana all night," Tip said, "or we can talk about the mines. How'd the Crown Royal look to you, Claiborne?"

"Well . . ." Claiborne hesitated, and Frank figured he was naturally wary about discussing the operation with a rival mine owner.

Tip waved a blunt-fingered hand. "Oh, hell, don't worry, I ain't plannin' on tryin' to jump your claim. It'll be fine with me if the Crown Royal's a success again, because that'll be good for the town."

"In that case," Claiborne said, "I don't mind telling you that I think opening the mine again won't pose too much of a problem. There'll be plenty of hard work that needs to be done, of course, but if I can hire some good men, we can meet the challenge."

"I know of one man you can hire. Name of Rogan."

Frank caught Claiborne's eye and shook his head. "Wouldn't be a good idea," he said. "The hombre's a trouble-maker."

"Oh, hell, I was just joshin'," Tip said. "I wouldn't have let the young fella hire Rogan. But I sure as shootin' fired him. Went by the jail and talked to him just a little while ago, told him he was through at the Lucky Lizard."

"How'd he take it?" Frank asked.

"Not good. Grabbed the bars and rattled 'em while he was cussin' at me. He didn't settle down until ol' Cata-mount Jack stuck a Greener in his face and warned him he wouldn't get no supper unless he stopped carryin' on so."

"He *does* sound like a troublemaker," Claiborne said. "I hope all the men in Buckskin aren't like that."

"Not hardly," Frank assured him. "I'll give you a hand finding some fellas who want to work."

Before they could discuss any more business, Diana appeared in the doorway of the parlor and announced, "Dinner is ready."

It was good too. Fried chicken, greens and potatoes out of the garden patch behind the house, and biscuits and gravy. Frank praised the food, which made Diana blush with pleasure, but the words were more for Claiborne's benefit. He wanted to make sure the mining engineer understood just what a fine catch Diana would be.

Claiborne was shy, and even though he could be glib enough when he did speak, he kept his mouth shut most of the time, no matter how much Frank tried to get him and Diana to talking. Still, she seemed to like Claiborne well enough, so Frank was a little encouraged.

When it came time for them to go, though, after the men retreated to the parlor for some brandy and cigars, Diana was waiting on the porch to bid them good night. She lingered the longest on her farewell to Frank, putting her hand on his arm and saying, "Please come back anytime, Marshal."

"Yes, ma'am," he said in a gruff voice. He put a hand on Claiborne's shoulder and practically shoved him forward.

"It was a wonderful evening, Miss Woodford," he said. "The food was delicious and, well, no man could complain about the company."

"How sweet of you. Good evening, Mr. Claiborne."

As they walked away, once they were out of earshot, Claiborne said, "Miss Woodford really is a fine young woman. You're a fortunate man, Marshal."

"Me? Why me?"

"Obviously, she's fond of you. I believe she's set her cap for you."

"I'm old enough to be her father, blast it!" Frank turned and poked a finger against Claiborne's shoulder. "She needs somebody younger, like you."

"Me? Why, I would never dream of interfering with someone else's romance."

"There's no romance to interfere with," Frank insisted.

"Perhaps not in your mind, but in the young lady's, who knows?" Claiborne laughed. "And when it comes to matters of the heart, Marshal, we both know that as men, we don't really have all that much say in the matter, now do we?"

That was true, unfortunately, Frank thought with a frown.

But he had planted a seed anyway, he hoped, and maybe someday it would grow into something.

Chapter 11

Frank let Dave Rogan out of the jail cell early the next morning. The miner, whose heavy-jawed, beard-stubbled face seemed to be set in a permanent scowl, said, "You're gonna be sorry for lockin' me up, Marshal. And that bastard Kelley's gonna wish I'd never set foot in his place."

"I'd say there's a good chance Kelley already feels that way," Frank said. He took a step closer to Rogan and his voice turned cold and hard as he went on. "Listen to me, mister. If you start any more trouble in Buckskin, you're liable to get a lot worse than you got this time. I won't stand for it, you hear me?"

Rogan met Frank's level gaze with a defiant stare, but after a moment he glanced away and muttered, "Yeah, yeah, I hear you."

"Then you'd better remember what I said."

Rogan turned and stomped toward the door. Frank stopped him by saying, "Rogan! Since you don't have a job anymore, maybe it'd be a good thing for you to move on and find something somewhere else."

Looking back over his shoulder, Rogan asked, "Are you runnin' me out of town?"

"I'm just saying that it might be wise to move on."

"I like it here." Rogan jerked the door open and stomped out.

With a sigh, Frank watched him go. He had a feeling that he hadn't seen the last of Rogan—nor the last of any trouble caused by the man.

As the days passed, though, Rogan didn't show his face in Buckskin, and for the most part, things in the settlement were quiet and peaceful. With the help of Frank and Tip Woodford, Claiborne found half-a-dozen men who were tired of prospecting and not finding any silver and willing to go to work for the Crown Royal. When Frank rode out to the mine to check on how they were doing, he found the air full of the ring of picks and shovels, the rasp of saws, and the biting *chunks!* of axes, as the men worked to clean out, shore up, and extend the shaft. They were hard workers, Claiborne reported, and the job of reopening the mine was progressing on schedule, or maybe even a little ahead of schedule.

Frank didn't see anything of Gunther Hammersmith, although he heard that the superintendent of the Alhambra had been in town looking for workers too. That was Hammersmith's right, Frank supposed. After their run-in at the mine, he didn't like the man, but as long as Hammersmith didn't break any laws, Frank was prepared to tolerate him.

New settlers continued to show up in Buckskin just about every day. Some came on horseback, some in buggies or wagons, some even walked in, carrying all their belongings on their backs. As Frank had been expecting, a madam showed up, bringing four girls with her. They moved in to one of the empty houses and set up for business right away, and they certainly didn't lack for customers. Prospectors who hadn't been with a woman for months flocked to the place. Some of the more respectable citizens, like Leo and Trudy Benjamin and Professor Burton, disapproved, but Frank knew there was nothing he could do about it. In their own way, the prostitutes provided a valuable service and a civilizing influence. A man who wasn't boiling over with repressed lust was less likely to start trouble in other ways.

As a precaution, Frank paid a visit to the madam, who introduced herself as Rosie, and told her that he expected her and her girls to conduct their business in a quiet manner, without any problems.

Rosie laughed and said, "Believe you me, Marshal, nobody wants things to stay peaceful more than we do. Ruckuses are bad for business. Now, before you go, how'd you like to spend some time with one of the gals? On the house, of course."

Frank declined. He had seen too many corrupt starpackers who accepted favors and collected graft from the townspeople they were supposed to be serving. He might still be relatively new to the law business, but he was determined to do it the right way.

A week after Claiborne's arrival in town, the encounter with Hammersmith, and the trouble with Rogan, Frank was lounging in front of the marshal's office, sitting in a chair that was tipped back against the wall, balancing himself with a booted foot propped against the railing along the front of the boardwalk, when he saw a couple of men riding into town. The front legs of his chair hit the boardwalk with a thump as he recognized one of them. He stood up and stepped to the edge of the walk.

The two men saw him and angled their horses in his direction. As they reined in, the smaller of the two nodded and said, "Howdy, Frank. It's been a while."

"Ten years at least, Farnum," Frank replied. "How are you?"

The man shrugged. He had a broad, friendly face and

curly, graying hair under a thumbed-back Stetson. With his
sly grin and small stature, Clint Farnum had always reminded Frank a little of a gnome or some sort of creature
like that from a children's fairy tale book. Despite his size,
he was fast on the draw and a lethal gunman.

"I'm all right," Farnum said in reply to Frank's question.
"I'm a mite surprised you didn't say something about how
you figured I was dead by now."

"I hadn't heard anything about you getting killed,"
Frank said with a shrug. "I assumed you were still around."
He inclined his head toward Farnum's companion, who
was at least a head taller than the affable little gunslinger.
"Who's your friend?"

"This is Charlie Hampton. Wouldn't say that we're friends,
but we're riding together for the time being, anyway."

"You're Frank Morgan?" Hampton asked in a heavy, unfriendly voice.

Frank nodded. "That's right."

"You don't look like much. Hell, you're supposed to be
as fast on the draw as Smoke Jensen or Matt Bodine.
Maybe even faster."

Farnum laughed. "The Drifter's fast enough to have
stayed alive this long, Charlie. How much faster'n that
does a man have to be?"

"He won't be alive much longer," Hampton said. He
started to dismount.

Frank waited until the man was halfway out of the
saddle, with his right foot out of the stirrup and his right
leg lifted over the horse's back. Then he palmed out his
Colt, leveled it at Hampton, and said, "Hold it right there."

Hampton froze in that awkward position and said,
"What the hell!"

"That ain't hardly fair, Frank, gettin' the drop on a man

like that," Farnum said, grinning so that he looked more like a gnome than ever.

"I don't give a damn about fair," Frank said. "I knew as soon as I saw you fellas ride in that one or both of you were looking for a gunfight—"

"Not me," Farnum said. He held up both hands, palms out toward Frank. "I've been in my share of showdowns, but I'm not a big enough fool to go up against The Drifter. Charlie here was the one who wanted to test his rep. I'd heard you had pinned on a badge here in Buckskin, so we moseyed on over to see you."

"Damn it, Morgan," Hampton said, his voice showing the strain of maintaining his uncomfortable position. "How long you expect me to stay here like this?"

"Until I tell you to move," Frank snapped. "Nobody asked you to come here and cause trouble."

Even in the position he was in, Hampton managed to sneer. "Looks to me like you're afraid of me, Morgan," he said. "Afraid to face me man-to-man."

Farnum *tsk-tsked* and shook his head. "Charlie, Charlie," he said. "That wasn't a smart move. But then, nobody's ever accused you of being too smart, now have they?"

"What's going on here, Farnum?" Frank asked. "You get tired of riding with Hampton or something, so you brought him here to have me kill him for you?"

Before Farnum could answer, Hampton said, "You're the only one who's gonna die, old man!"

"You might as well get it over with, Frank," Farnum advised. "Charlie here is a stubborn one. He's not going to give up or go away until he gets what he wants—a crack at you."

By now, the confrontation had begun to draw some attention from the citizens of Buckskin. Hampton's awkward pose and the gun in Frank's hand caused a murmur of conversation as some of the townspeople started gathering nearby.

Frank turned his head to say in a sharp, commanding tone, "You folks move along." He hoped to avoid any gunplay, but if lead started to fly, he didn't want any stray bullets cutting down innocent bystanders.

That second when his attention wasn't on Hampton anymore was the break the would-be gunfighter had been waiting for. He dived the rest of the way out of the saddle, jerking his revolver from its holster as he tumbled to the street. He rolled over and came up shooting.

Frank had already dropped into a crouch and pivoted toward Hampton before the gunslinger could squeeze the trigger, so Hampton's first shot whined harmlessly past his head to thud into the thick, log wall of the marshal's office. That was Hampton's first shot—and only shot, because in the next heartbeat Frank's Colt blasted twice and flame geysered from the mouth of the Peacemaker's barrel.

The heavy .45-caliber slugs slammed into Hampton's chest and threw him backward in the street. Frank twisted again, back toward Farnum, in case the little man was going to make a try for him. Farnum hadn't moved, though, except to lift his hands and hold them in plain sight, so that Frank could see right away they were empty.

"Don't shoot, Morgan," Farnum said. "This was all Charlie's play, not mine. I told him he was a fool to try to take you."

Frank's instincts told him that Farnum spoke the truth. He stepped down off the boardwalk and walked over to where Hampton lay. The gunfighter was on his back, arms and legs splayed out, his revolver lying beside his hand where it had slipped from his nerveless fingers. Frank kicked the gun out of reach, just as a precaution, then toed

Hampton's shoulder. The man's head lolled loosely on his shoulders. The glassy look in Hampton's eyes had already told Frank that he was dead, but it never hurt to make sure of these things.

The sudden blast of gunshots had made the gathering crowd scurry for cover, but now as silence reigned in Buckskin's main street, their curiosity drove them from their hiding places. A murmur of questions grew in volume.

Frank replaced the two rounds he had fired with fresh cartridges from the loops on his shell belt, then pouched the iron. A bitter taste filled his mouth. He turned his head toward the bystanders and said, "Somebody fetch Langley."

One man hurried off to let the undertaker know what had happened. The others stayed where they were and stared at Hampton's corpse.

"Is it all right if I get down off this horse?" Farnum asked.

Frank made a curt gesture with his hand indicating that Farnum could dismount. He swung down from the saddle and looped the reins around the hitch rack in front of the boardwalk.

"I'm sorry about this, Frank," Farnum said, and he sounded sincere. "I know you and I have never been what you'd call friends—"

Frank grunted to show his agreement with that statement.

"But I tried to talk him out of it," Farnum went on. "He was bound and determined to give it a try, though. He said you were the last really famous gunfighter who's left, and if he ever wanted to make his rep, he'd have to go through you to do it."

"Why would a man want a reputation as a gunfighter in this day and age?" Frank said. "Men like us are relics,

Clint. The West the way we knew it as youngsters is getting farther and farther away with each passing day."

Farnum shrugged. "True enough. But as long as folks still remember what it used to be like, it's not going to go away completely. There'll always be somebody who wants to try to recapture it." Farnum nodded toward Hampton's body. "Like him."

"Yeah, I reckon you're right." Frank looked along the street, and saw Claude Langley's wagon rolling toward the scene of the shoot-out. He looked back at Farnum and asked, "You plan to stay in Buckskin for long?"

"Haven't decided yet. I might. Seems like a nice enough little town." That sly smile stole across Farnum's face again. "And it's got a good marshal to enforce law and order."

Frank jerked his head toward the Silver Baron. "Come on down to the saloon with me. Least I can do is buy you a drink, for old time's sake."

"I'm much obliged for your hospitality."

Farnum fell in step beside Frank as they started toward the saloon. Farnum had to take three steps for every two strides that Frank's longer legs made, but Frank didn't slow down to make it easier for him to keep up.

They hadn't reached the Silver Baron yet when Frank saw dust boiling up from the trail leading into town. He stopped and frowned as he heard pounding hoofbeats and the rattle of wheels. "What the devil?" he muttered.

A moment later, a stagecoach came into view, pulled by a good-looking six-horse hitch. Rather than the red and yellow of a typical Concord coach, this vehicle was painted a dark blue. The side curtains were pulled over the windows to keep the dust out, so Frank couldn't see who was inside as the stagecoach rolled past.

"I didn't know Buckskin was on one of the stage lines," Farnum commented.

"It's not."

"Then where'd that coach come from, and what's it doing here?"

Frank shook his head. "I have no idea, but I reckon I'd better find out." He started back up the street, adding over his shoulder, "We'll have that drink later."

"I'll be around," Farnum said.

The stagecoach came to a stop in front of a building that had once been a hotel. Prospectors had moved into the place, taking it over and using it as a rooming house. Frank crossed the street at an angle toward the place, walking past the spot where Claude Langley and his helper were loading Hampton's body into the back of the undertaker's wagon. Frank didn't even glance in that direction. That violent incident was over, and now his attention was focused on the newcomers to Buckskin.

The man handling the stagecoach's reins was accompanied on the driver's box by another tough-looking hombre holding a Winchester. Both of them climbed down from the box as Frank approached. The driver headed for the back of the coach while the guard stepped over to the door on the side closest to the boardwalk and opened it.

Then he turned toward Frank and brought the rifle's muzzle up. He watched Frank in a somewhat threatening manner.

"Take it easy, mister," Frank said. "I'm the law in these parts."

A man climbed out of the coach and stepped down to the street. He wore a dark, expensive suit, and a diamond stickpin sparkled on his cravat. A derby hat perched on his head. He wasn't overly big, but he appeared to have a wiry strength to him. He looked at Frank with cold blue eyes and said, "You're the marshal?"

"That's right," Frank replied with a nod. "Name's Frank Morgan."

The man in the suit didn't offer to shake hands. He nodded toward the old hotel instead and said, "I *own* this building. I'll expect you to immediately evict anyone who's living here illegally."

That demand took Frank by surprise. "You got proof of that, mister?"

"Of course," the man snapped. "My secretary will provide you with any documentation you need. Right now, I expect you to do your duty, though, and carry out my request so that my companions and I can move in without being disturbed."

The stranger's arrogant attitude rubbed Frank the wrong way, so he didn't really care whether or not he gave any offense as he asked, "And just who the hell are you, anyway?"

"Hamish Munro. Now hop to it, Marshal."

Without waiting to see what Frank was going to do, Munro turned toward the open door of the coach and extended a hand. A woman's arm reached out of the vehicle, and Munro took her hand.

One of the loveliest women Frank had seen in a long time stepped out of the coach, looked around, and said, "So this is Buckskin."

Chapter 12

Somehow, Frank wasn't surprised to learn Hamish Munro's identity. Everything he'd heard from Garrett Claiborne had indicated that the mining magnate was a thoroughly unpleasant individual, and this dapper stranger certainly fit the bill. Frank had halfway expected Munro to show up in Buckskin sooner or later.

He was a little startled that Munro would bring such a stunning woman to a rugged Nevada boomtown, though.

The woman was young, no more than twenty-five. She wore a dark blue traveling outfit, the color of which pretty well matched that of the stagecoach. It was an Abbott & Downing coach, Frank noted, the same sort used by most of the stagecoach lines, but Munro must have purchased it from the company for his personal use and had it repainted and fitted out with lots of fancy silver trim. The horses pulling the coach had that same silver trim on their harness.

Frank turned his attention back to the young woman. Thick masses of blond hair so pale as to be almost white were piled atop her head, under a neat little blue hat. The dress she wore was tight enough that it clung to the lines of a slender but well-curved body. Her lips were full and red, her eyes gray. She managed to be sensuous and reserved at the same time, not an easy feat.

Munro didn't offer to introduce her. Instead, he took her arm in a smug, possessive manner and said, "Come along, my dear."

They started toward the doors of the old hotel.

"Hold on a minute," Frank said. "There are folks who have been living here, and they're liable to not take kindly to being tossed out on their ears."

Munro looked back at him and said, "As you can well imagine, Marshal, I don't care whether they take kindly to it or not, to use your phrase. This is *my* building. I intend to use it as my residence and also the local office of my company. Anyone who has been staying here had been doing so unlawfully. I won't press charges against them, since they weren't aware of the situation, but I want them out. *Now!*"

Having orders barked at him like that was more than Frank was going to stand. He moved a step closer to Munro and said in a low, dangerous voice, "Listen here, mister. I don't give a damn who you are or what you own or how much money you have. You talk to me with some respect, or we won't have just gotten off on the wrong foot. We'll stay that way."

Munro met Frank's gaze without flinching, but didn't say anything for a long moment. Then he gave an abrupt nod. "All right, then, we understand each other. As the legal owner of this building, I request that you remove the people who have no right to be living in it."

Frank thought it over and then said, "I reckon you have the right to make that request. This is going to be done in an orderly fashion, though. I'm not going to drive people out at gunpoint."

"Handle the matter however you see fit, Marshal, just as

long as that official, *legal* request that I made is carried out with a reasonable amount of promptness."

Munro had adopted a formal attitude, but Frank could still see the anger seething inside him. He was accustomed to getting whatever he wanted, whenever he wanted it, and it made him furious when anyone defied him. Munro had enough money to get away with acting like that—most of the time.

But not here. Not with Frank Morgan.

"Most of the men who have been staying here won't be in their rooms right now. They're out prospecting, or working at one of the mines. I'll get my deputy and we'll go through the place. All the gear in the rooms can be moved over to the marshal's office for now, and its owners can claim it later. Shouldn't take more than an hour or so. That suit you?"

"Where do you suggest my wife and I wait in the meantime?" Munro asked. "We've had a long ride, and she's tired."

So the blonde was Munro's wife. Frank had wondered if she was married to the mining magnate, or if she was his daughter, because she was only half of Munro's age.

Obviously, the stagecoach wasn't the only thing he had bought for his personal use.

Frank pointed across the street. "There's a nice little café over there, and I'm sure the ladies who run it would be glad to serve you some coffee and maybe something to eat, if you're hungry."

The blonde said, "It *has* been a long time since we stopped to eat, Hamish."

Munro jerked his head in a nod. "Very well. Would you mind letting us know when you have the hotel ready for us to occupy, Marshal?"

"Not at all," Frank said.

He thought he might send Jack to deliver that message

when the time came. He wasn't sure he wanted to deal with Hamish Munro again so soon.

As Munro and his wife walked toward the café, another man got out of the stagecoach. He wore a suit similar to Munro's, although not as expensive, and a brown hat. About thirty, he was handsome in a pale, bland sort of way. He offered a soft hand to Frank and said, "I'm Nathan Evers, Marshal. Mr. Munro's confidential secretary. I heard the two of you discussing this hotel, and if you'd like, I can show you the legal documents proving that Mr. Munro purchased it from the previous owner."

Frank shook his head. "I don't reckon that's necessary. You wouldn't offer to show me the papers unless you really had 'em." A thought occurred to him. "I wonder just how much real estate Munro's managed to buy here in Buckskin by tracking down the folks who used to own it."

Evers smiled and said, "As I mentioned, Marshal, I'm a *confidential* secretary. I'm afraid I can't discuss such business matters with anyone except Mr. Munro."

"What about his wife?" Frank asked.

"Mrs. Munro doesn't concern herself with her husband's financial affairs."

No, Frank thought, as long as Munro had plenty of money, the blonde wouldn't care about anything else.

Evers turned to the driver and the guard and said, "Why don't you unload the bags here on the porch, and I'll let you know when you can bring them on into the hotel."

The men nodded. The driver had already opened the canvas-covered boot at the rear of the coach, so they began taking carpetbags and trunks from it and stacking them on the hotel porch.

Frank crossed over to the marshal's office, where the crowd had broken up and folks had gone on about their business once Hampton's corpse had been carted off. Jack had come up while Frank was over at the hotel, and as he leaned on the boardwalk railing, the old-timer asked, "What's goin' on over there at the old hotel? I never seen a stagecoach painted that color before."

"And you probably never will again," Frank said. He explained about Hamish Munro's arrival in Buckskin, and added that the mining magnate wanted the squatters cleared out of the hotel. "Come along and give me a hand with that."

"Sure. I heard you had to kill another fella who showed up to try and make a name for himself as a fast gun."

"Who told you that?"

"Hombre name of Farnum, down to the Silver Baron."

Frank nodded. "Keep an eye on him if you happen to run into him again."

"Farnum, you mean? He seems to be a likable, harmless little fella."

"That's what he wants you to think. He's slick on the draw, and he's never been overly particular about who he works for or who he rides with. He's spent more time on the wrong side of the law than on the right side."

Jack let out a whistle of surprise. "You don't say! I damn sure will keep an eye on him then."

They walked over to the hotel and went inside. Nathan Evers came with them, and Frank didn't object. He figured that Evers probably had a right to be here. He also had no doubt that Evers would tell Munro everything that Frank and Jack said and did.

Let the fella spy to his heart's content, Frank told himself. He and his deputy didn't have anything to hide.

Only three of the men who had moved into the hotel were there at the moment. All of them lodged bitter protests when Frank told them they would have to move out.

"Sorry," he said. "I don't have any choice in the matter.

The building's legal owner showed up, and he wants every-body out."

"We didn't know who owned the place and didn't figure anybody would care if we stayed here for a spell," one of the men said.

"Nobody cared until now."

"We ain't gonna get in trouble for trespassin' or anything like that, are we?"

"Not as long as you gather up your gear and move out right away," Frank said.

A lot of angry muttering went on in the process, but the men did as they were told. Meanwhile, Frank and Jack went through the other rooms and carried out clothes, war bags, and other belongings.

"Take all this stuff over to the office," Frank told Jack. "The men who own it can come by there later and get it."

"Seems like we're goin' to a heap o' trouble for this Munro hombre," Jack groused.

"He's within his legal rights."

"There are legal rights . . . and then there's what's *right*," Jack said.

Frank felt pretty much the same way, but when he had pinned on the marshal's badge, he had agreed to abide by the law, whether he always liked it or not.

In less than an hour, the hotel had been cleaned out of squatters. Most of the building's original furnishings were still intact. It wouldn't take a lot of time and effort to clean the place up, and Frank was sure that Munro had the money to pay someone for that time and effort. If Munro was willing to invest even more, he could turn the hotel into a showplace again. That wouldn't surprise Frank either.

When they were finished, Evers volunteered to go to the café and let his employer know that the hotel was ready for their occupancy. Frank was more than willing to let Evers handle that chore. He nodded his thanks and said, "Come on, Jack. Let's get back to the office."

As they walked away, Jack rumbled, "If you ask me, havin' that fella here in town is gonna be nothin' but trouble."

"I didn't ask you," Frank said, but then he gave a grim chuckle and added, "But I reckon I agree with you anyway."

By evening, word of Hamish Munro's arrival in Buckskin had spread all over the settlement, eclipsing even the story of Frank's gunfight with the ill-fated Charlie Hampton. The fact that Munro himself had come here meant that he was serious about making the Alhambra a going concern again, and that meant more jobs for the prospectors who hadn't had any luck of their own in finding silver, as well as more business for the stores and saloons in town.

Garrett Claiborne came into the marshal's office shortly after sundown. He had traded in his suit for work boots, corduroy trousers, and a flannel shirt, since he'd been spending most of his time at the Crown Royal in recent days. A fine layer of dust on the engineer's clothing told Frank that Claiborne had just ridden in from the mine.

"What can I do for you, Garrett?" Frank asked as he sat behind the desk. "Help yourself to a cup of coffee, if you'd like."

"Thanks," Claiborne replied. "I'd like that very much." He poured himself a cup from the pot on the stove, took a grateful sip, and then said, "I've come to report some trouble at the mine, Marshal."

Frank sat up, his interest quickening. "What sort of trouble?"

"Sometime last night, someone pried up some of the

rails leading from the shaft to the stamp mill, so that we can't use the ore carts. They scattered the ties as well, so we're having to practically rebuild the line."

"Who would do a thing like that?" Frank asked with a frown.

"I have no idea." Claiborne took another sip of the coffee, then added, "Actually, I *do*. I suspect Gunther Hammersmith and his men of being behind the damage."

"Why would Hammersmith do that?"

"It's the sort of mischief he's capable of. Just yesterday, we finished the repair work inside the shaft and brought out our first carts of ore. I think Hammersmith had someone spying on us, watching the mine through field glasses or something like that, and he knew we were about to start production in earnest again. By sabotaging the rail line, he's slowed us down. It'll take several days to repair the damage that was done."

Frank shook his head. "He's got his own mine to operate. Well, I guess it's Hamish Munro's mine, but you know what I mean."

"And if the Alhambra can outproduce the Crown Royal, that will make Hammersmith look better in Munro's eyes," Claiborne pointed out.

"I don't know," Frank said with a dubious shake of his head. "Seems like a stretch to me."

"*Someone* damaged those rails. Who else would have a reason to do such a thing, even a far-fetched reason? Our only other real competition is the Lucky Lizard, and I can't imagine Mr. Woodford doing anything like that, or employing someone who would."

"No, that's not Tip's way of working," Frank agreed.

Claiborne went on. "And I heard when I rode into town that Munro himself arrived today. Is that true?"

Frank nodded. "It is. He brought his wife and his confidential secretary with him."

"The fact that Munro is on hand is all the more reason for Hammersmith to try to make himself look better by making us look worse. I'm convinced he's behind what happened."

"What do you want me to do about it?"

Claiborne shrugged and said, "I'm not sure. I know you don't have any jurisdiction out at the mines. I suppose you could confront Gunther Hammersmith the next time he comes into town. . . ."

"And he'd just deny having anything to do with it."

"Yes, you're probably right about that."

Frank sat back in his chair and frowned. As the marshal of Buckskin, he might not have any jurisdiction in this matter, but as a part-owner of the Crown Royal—even though Claiborne was unaware of that fact—he sure as hell had an interest in what happened out there.

"Let me think about it," he said to Claiborne. "And in the meantime, you'd better start posting guards at night. I reckon you didn't have any sentries out before, or whoever tore up those rails wouldn't have been able to do it without being discovered."

"That's true," Claiborne said with a rueful shake of his head. "I didn't think guards were necessary. I should have known better with Hammersmith in the vicinity."

"Just be careful," Frank advised. "Don't jump to conclusions. You don't want to get into a shooting war with Hammersmith without good reason."

"And if there *is* good reason? If he tries something else even worse?"

"Then leave it to somebody whose business is shooting," Frank said. "Like me."

Chapter 13

With Gates Tucker and Dagnabbit Dabney both dead, the woman called Hannah had moved in with Jory Pool. She had been with Pool at times before, and she figured that getting her back was one reason Pool had gunned down the other two men—besides sheer, cussed meanness, that is, which Pool had plenty of.

With the interest Pool had shown in hearing about Buckskin, Hap Mitchell and Lonnie Beeman had supposed that he intended on raiding the town right away. Considerable time had gone by since then, however, and the gang was still tucked away in its canyon hideout. They were starting to get restless, running short of supplies, cash, and patience. Everybody had a hankering to pull another job.

Nobody questioned Pool, though, because none of them had a hankering to die swiftly and violently. They grumbled about the delay amongst themselves, though.

When the boss outlaw sent for them one night, Mitchell and Beeman thought maybe he was getting ready to plan the attack on the town. They went to Pool's cabin, where Hannah opened the door to Mitchell's knock.

"Come on in, boys," Pool called from inside the cabin.

As they entered the room, they saw Pool sitting at a rough table with some greasy playing cards spread out in front of him in a solitaire hand. A half-empty bottle of whiskey sat close at hand. Pool waved his visitors over and told them to have a seat on the other side of the table.

Hannah came to stand beside him. He reached up and caressed her meaty rump, digging his fingers in. "Get the boys something to drink," he ordered.

She nodded and said, "Sure, Jory honey," then fetched another bottle and a couple of tin cups. She poured whiskey in the cups and slid them across the table to Mitchell and Beeman.

Each of the men sipped the fiery liquor, then Mitchell said, "You wanted to see us, Jory?"

"Yeah." Pool moved a red seven onto a black eight. "I been hearin' talk about how we need to go out on another job."

"The boys are anxious," Mitchell admitted with a shrug. "They're eager to get out there and show you what they can do."

"I know what they can do. And I know the time's not right yet. Buckskin's a boomtown. It's gonna keep growin' for a while yet. The more it grows, the more loot there'll be for the taking when we do hit it."

"That makes sense," Beeman said. "But the more people there are in the settlement, the more of a fight they'll be able to put up, ain't that right?"

Mitchell glanced with slitted eyes at his friend. What Beeman had just said was logical enough, but it might be taken as arguing with Jory Pool too, and that was never a wise thing to do.

"If we strike at just the right time, it won't make any difference how many people are in the settlement. They won't put up a fight. It's just a matter of waitin' for the proper moment."

"Well, I reckon you'd know better about that than we would,

Jory," Mitchell said, shooting another glance at Beeman and hoping he'd take the hint to keep his piehole shut.

"Damn right I know better." Pool picked up the bottle and downed a slug of whiskey. "I'll tell you what else I know," he went on as he thumped the bottle back down on the table. "I don't want to be hearin' a lot of whisperin' and complainin' behind my back because we haven't ridden out yet. That makes me think you fellas don't appreciate all I done to put this gang together and make sure it's run right."

Mitchell shook his head. "Now, Jory, it ain't like that at all—"

"Tell you what," Pool said as if Mitchell hadn't spoken. "If there's anybody who don't like the way I run things, he can speak up, right out in the open. If you boys want somebody else to be the boss, why, he can challenge me. I like to run things fair and square."

Despite the calm, rational words Pool spoke, Mitchell saw a crazy light flickering in the man's eyes. Pool was smart and cunning and one hell of a leader, but he was also a man it paid not to cross. They all knew that, so Mitchell started to say, "Nobody wants to—"

"There's just one thing," Pool broke in. "I don't take it too kindly when I feel like you boys don't appreciate me."

"I swear, Jory, that ain't the way—"

Pool looked up at Hannah as she stood beside him and said, "Kiss me, honey."

She smiled. "Why, sure, Jory." She bent down to kiss him, resting one hand on the table beside the cards to steady herself as she did so. She gave him a long, sensuous kiss, so passionate in its intensity that it made Mitchell and Beeman squirm a mite in their chairs.

With his lips still locked to hers, Pool brought his other hand out from under the table with his bowie knife clutched in it. Moving so fast that it took everyone by surprise, he brought the blade down and drove the razor-sharp steel through Hannah's hand so that it was pinned to the table like an insect on a display board. She jerked upright, threw her head back, and shrieked in agony.

Pool kept his hand on the knife, bearing down on it so that Hannah couldn't free her hand. As she slumped forward and collapsed onto the table, whimpering in pain, Pool said to Mitchell and Beeman, "I love this gal. She's mighty precious to me. So if I'd do this to somebody I love, what do you think I'd do to somebody who crossed me and tried to stir up hard feelin's against me over this Buckskin business?"

"N-nobody's gonna do that, Jory," Beeman said, his eyes wide with shock and horror.

"Damn right," Mitchell added. "You're the boss, Jory. What you say, goes. Always has and always will."

Pool nodded. "All right then. Go on back to the boys and tell 'em what you saw here tonight. Tell 'em I don't want to hear any more grumblin' behind my back. You've got my word, we'll hit Buckskin when the time's right. *When I'm damned good and ready.*"

The two men scraped their chairs back, nodded, and turned to hurry out of the cabin. Mitchell heard the sound of Pool pulling the bowie knife out of Hannah's hand. She let out another groan as the blade came free.

But neither Mitchell nor Beeman looked back, and as they closed the door behind them, they heard Pool saying in a tone of genuine affectionate concern, "That hand don't look so good, darlin'. You'd better tie a rag around it or somethin'."

Frank spotted Clint Farnum at the bar of the Silver Baron when he walked into the saloon that evening. Farnum was talking to the bartender, Johnny Collyer, and Johnny was laughing. Farnum had an easy way about him that made most folks feel like his friend, even though they might have known him for only a short time. He inspired trust.

Frank didn't trust him. He knew better. But Farnum had never double-crossed him, so he was willing to give the little gunfighter the benefit of the doubt—for now—although he was going to be wary about it.

Farnum grinned at Frank and said, "Ready to have that drink now, Marshal?"

Frank gestured toward Farnum's empty glass. "Give a refill on me, Johnny."

"You're not drinking, Frank?"

"I'll have a cup of coffee."

"Yeah," Farnum said, "I recollect now that you were never much of a whiskey man. That's probably why your nerves have stayed so steady over the years."

"Might have something to do with it," Frank allowed with a faint smile.

Farnum picked up the glass Johnny had filled with amber liquid again. He inclined his head toward the rear of the room, where there were several empty tables, and said, "Sit down with me for a minute, Frank? There's something I'd like to talk to you about."

Curious what Farnum could have to discuss, Frank took the coffee cup Johnny handed him and nodded. "All right, I reckon I've got a few minutes before I start my evening rounds."

They walked back to one of the tables and sat down. Keeping his voice pitched low so that no one could eavesdrop on the conversation, Farnum said, "This town of yours looks to be growing mighty fast."

Frank nodded. "It's like any other town where there's been a gold or silver strike. For a while, it tries to bust wide open at the seams. But in time, it'll settle down, and if the ore holds out, it'll grow into a mighty nice place one of these days."

"Right now, though, I'll bet you've got your hands full. A boomtown's nothing but trouble. And you've got to deal with other problems on top of it . . . namely young bucks like Charlie who want to gun you down and make a name for themselves. I've heard that hardly a week goes by without somebody like that showing up."

"Who told you that?" Frank asked, his jaw tightening. He knew he was probably the subject of gossip around town, but he didn't have to like it.

Farnum shook his head. "Doesn't matter who told me. The word's all over town. These folks like you, so they're willing to put up with it. Got to be hard on you, though, trying to keep the lid on and not get killed at the same time."

"That's the chore any lawman faces. I pinned the badge on. I'll do the job."

"Sure you will. But all you've got for a deputy is a broken-down old-timer."

Frank laughed. "Go and tangle with Catamount Jack and then come back and tell me how broken down he is. I think you'll find that he lives up to his name."

"Maybe so. It still seems to me like you could use another deputy. Somebody who knows how to handle trouble." Farnum smiled. "Maybe because he's started so blasted much of it in his time."

Frank stared at the other man in surprise. He couldn't help it. After a moment, he asked, "Are you saying that you want a job as my deputy, Clint?"

An uncharacteristically solemn expression appeared on Farnum's normally jovial face. He leaned forward and said, "I know I've spent a lot of time in my life riding some dark and lonely trails, Frank. I've heard the owl hoot many a night. But so have you."

Anger welled up inside Frank. "I've lived by the gun, and I've done plenty of things I'm not proud of. But I haven't spent one day of my life as an outlaw."

"Maybe not, but those are the stories people tell about you."

"'Stories' is right. There's not a lick of truth to most of them."

Farnum waved a hand. "I won't dispute that. Reckon you'd know about that better than anyone else. But my point is, you put all that behind you. You stopped drifting, settled down, pinned on a badge, of all things. You know of any reason I couldn't do that too?"

Frank knew of several, including some bank robberies and stagecoach holdups that Farnum had been in on.

But on the frontier, the line between lawman and outlaw was sometimes a mighty thin one, and Frank knew that quite a few respected star-packers had come from shady backgrounds. Of course, it sometimes went the other way too. More than one outlaw had started out carrying a badge before turning crooked. The Dalton brothers were prime examples, having served as deputy U.S. marshals in Indian Territory before taking up the owlhoot trail.

So maybe Farnum deserved a chance, but Frank would need some more convincing first.

"Why do you want to be a deputy?" he asked.

Farnum shrugged. "I'm not as young as I used to be. Hell, none of us are. I've spent too many nights on the cold, hard ground. I've got a hankering for a job where I can go home at night and climb into a real bed." He leaned back and toyed with his glass, turning it in circles. "And it wouldn't be so bad to have a job where people look at you with a little respect, like you're something better than a no-good owlhoot."

Frank knew that feeling. He had seen the fear in people's eyes when he was around. In other places, he had seen mothers grab their children and hustle them to the other side of the street when he came along, as if they thought a gunfight was going to break out any second. And there was some truth to that too. He never knew when somebody was going to force a showdown with him.

It was a little different in Buckskin. The townspeople knew of his reputation, of course, and they had seen for themselves that he attracted would-be killers like honey drew flies. But as Farnum had pointed out, they knew him and liked him, and they wanted him to be their marshal despite the baggage he brought with him. Hell, the town had fallen into disrepair and disrepute for a long time, and now it was taking on a new identity. By accepting the job as marshal, maybe he had been trying to do the same thing. Maybe Clint Farnum deserved that same chance.

Frank looked across the table at him and asked in a harsh voice, "Are you on the dodge?"

"You know damn well there's paper out on me in some places," Farnum replied without hesitation. "But I'm not wanted anywhere in Nevada, and that's the God's honest truth."

"So nobody's after you? You don't have trouble dogging your trail? You're not looking for a place to hide out for a while?"

"No to all those questions. I'm shooting straight with you, Frank. Maybe I'm a mite old for it, but what I really want is to settle down and make something of myself."

Frank didn't hear anything in Farnum's voice or see anything on his face except sincerity. He thought about it for a long moment, then said, "I don't know that the town could pay you much of a wage. We could probably come up with a place for you to stay, though, and maybe you could eat at the boardinghouse or the café."

"That'd be enough for now," Farnum said with an eager bob of his head.

"I suppose I could talk to the mayor about it and see what he says." Frank took a sip of his coffee, which had cooled off while he and Farnum were talking. "The way the town's growing, another deputy was going to be needed sooner or later."

Farnum grinned. "Might as well get me started while you've got the chance then."

"Yeah, I reckon. You'd better not be lying to me about this, though, Clint."

Farnum held up his hand like he was taking a pledge and said, "You've got my word on it—"

At that moment, a man slapped the batwings aside and hurried into the saloon, almost running. He went to the bar and asked Johnny Collyer if the marshal was there. Frank heard the question and looked around to see Johnny pointing him out. The man who had just come in was one of the prospectors who had flocked to Buckskin to search for silver. Frank had seen him around the settlement quite a few times, but didn't know his name.

The man came over to the table now and said, "Marshal, you'd better get down to Rosie's place. I think there's about to be a killin' there."

Frank glanced at Farnum and asked, "You ready to start earning your keep, such as it is?"

The little gunfighter pushed himself to his feet. "Let's go to work, Marshal," he said.

Chapter 14

Frank and his new deputy didn't waste any time getting down to Rosie's place. Again, Farnum had to hurry to keep up with Frank's longer strides, but he didn't complain.

Under normal circumstances, Frank would have either handled this problem by himself or gotten Catamount Jack to give him a hand. He hoped he wasn't making a mistake by trusting Farnum, but this would be a good test of the little gunfighter's true intentions. If he really wanted to reform and settle down, this was his chance.

Rosie and her girls had fixed the house up fairly nice, even though the men who came here didn't really give a damn about ambience or décor. They just wanted some warm, willing, female companionship for a spell. Rosie had traded her girls' favors for some carpentry work and a fresh coat of whitewash on the outside of the house, and she had hung up curtains inside and rolled out rugs on the floors.

Frank heard angry shouts from inside the parlor as he and Clint Farnum reached the front door. Without knocking, Frank opened it and went in. He found two men jawing at each other in loud voices. They were arguing over one of the soiled doves, a pretty Chinese girl in a thin shift who stood there with her arms crossed over her small breasts and a bored look on her face.

One of the men was a roughly dressed prospector with a bristly red beard. The identity of the other man surprised Frank. He was the distinguished-looking Professor Howard Burton, just about the last man Frank would have expected to be getting into a ruckus over a whore. But Frank supposed that no matter how educated or intellectual a gent might be, he'd still need to get laid every once in a while.

Frank raised his voice so he could be heard over the shouting and said, "Hold it! Both of you, just settle down, blast it!"

The two men hadn't seemed to notice until now that Frank had come in. They stopped arguing and turned to look at him. Professor Burton's face turned red, and he said, "Good Lord, Marshal, what are you doing here?"

"I could ask the same thing of you, Professor," Frank replied, and Burton's face flushed even more. "I'm here on official business. Somebody said there was about to be a killing down here."

"Nonsense," Burton snorted. "This is just a simple disagreement."

The prospector said, "Simple disagreement, hell! This fancy pants is tryin' to steal my gal away from me!"

"She's not *your* gal," Burton said. "If anything, she's mine, because I have a standing appointment with her—"

"Well, there you go! I plan on layin' down with her, not standin' up, so my *appointment's* more important than yours!"

Burton glared and muttered, "How can you argue with a man who doesn't understand the most fundamental rudiments of the English language?"

"Yeah? You can stick it up *your* fundament, mister!"

Red-faced and breathing hard, the two men squared off again, their jaws thrust out belligerently. Frank shouldered between them, being none too gentle about it, and used both thumbs to point over his shoulders.

"All right, that's it," he declared. "Nobody's sticking anything anywhere. Both of you get out of here. Now!"

Rosie had been watching the confrontation from the other side of the parlor. The stout, middle-aged woman protested, "Wait a minute, Marshal. You can't just kick those boys out like that. Neither of them have paid anything yet."

"They can come back tomorrow night," Frank said, "at different times. That way they won't be arguing over . . ."

"Linda," the Chinese girl supplied, in unaccented English. She had probably been born in the United States, to immigrants who had come from China to help build the Central Pacific Railroad.

"They won't have to argue over Linda here," Frank went on.

The prospector frowned and said, "But what about tonight? I still got me one hell of an itch."

"You should've thought of that before you started threatening people."

The man shook a finger at Burton. "That fancy pants threatened me first! Called me an uneducated lout, he did!"

Burton sniffed. "Simply stating a fact."

"Shut up, Professor," Frank snapped. "You're not making things any better." He jerked a thumb at the prospector again. "You. Out."

The man went, but not before muttering a lot of curses on his way to the door. He slammed it behind him with more force than necessary.

Professor Burton straightened his coat and hooked his

thumbs in his vest. "I greatly appreciate the assistance, Marshal," he said to Frank. "While I regret that you had to see me in a moment of mortal weakness, tempted by the lusts of the flesh, I'm glad you came along when you did and saved me from being forced to hand that recalcitrant buffoon the thrashing of a lifetime."

"Yeah, me too, Professor," Frank said, his voice dry with sarcasm. "Now move along."

Burton frowned. "Surely you don't mean that I have to leave? The altercation is over, and I assumed your decree was for that lout's benefit—"

"I said you were both leaving, and I meant it."

Burton looked like he wanted to argue, but the cold stare that Frank gave him seemed to make him think better of it. He turned to Linda and said, "I'm forced to bid you good evening, my dear, but I'll see you tomorrow evening—"

"I'll be here," she cut in, still speaking excellent English. She looked over at Frank and Clint and added with an inviting smile, "Either of you gents interested in a poke?"

Clint licked his lips and started to say something, then changed his mind and gave a regretful shake of his head. "I reckon I'm on duty," he said.

"That's right," Frank told him. "We'll make the evening rounds together, so you'll know the routine."

That caught Burton's attention. "You have a new deputy, Marshal?" the professor asked.

"Yep. This is Clint Farnum. Clint, meet Professor Burton."

The two men shook hands, with Burton saying, "I'm pleased to make your acquaintance, sir, though I wish it was in more decorous surroundings."

"Oh, don't worry about that," Clint told him. "I've met some of my best friends in whorehouses."

The three men left together, ignoring Rosie's questions about how a lady was supposed to make any money in this town. The hour was late enough now so that not as many people were on the streets, even though the saloons were still open and doing a good business.

"What brings you to Buckskin, Mr. Farnum?" Burton asked.

"Oh, the marshal and I are old friends," Clint answered. "I heard about him packing a badge here and thought maybe he could use a good man."

The part about them being old friends was stretching the truth a mite, Frank thought. He and Clint had known each other for a long time, but they had never been close. As for the rest of it . . . well, time would tell.

"I hope you enjoy your stay here," Burton went on.

"I'm sure I will, Professor."

Burton said good night and angled off toward his cabin. Frank and Clint continued along the street, and Frank began checking the doors of the businesses they passed, making sure each one was locked up tight for the night.

"I get the idea," Clint said. "Got to take care of the store-keepers. They pay your wages, after all."

"It's just part of the job—" Frank began.

He was interrupted by the sudden blast of gunshots from behind them.

Frank whirled around, drawing his Colt as he did so. Beside him, Clint Farnum's gun seemed to leap into his hand with blinding speed, although actually he was a fraction of a heartbeat behind Frank on the draw. As Frank crouched, ready to return the fire, he realized that the shots weren't directed at him and his new deputy. He spotted a dark form slumped in the street, in the area where Professor Burton had been walking.

"Professor!" Frank shouted as he broke into a run toward the sprawled shape. He heard Farnum pounding along behind him, but with his longer legs he outdistanced the smaller man in just a few strides.

The gunshots had stopped, leaving an echoing silence that filled the night. After a second, shouted questions began to come from the saloons. Everybody wanted to know what the shooting was all about.

Frank had a terrible feeling he knew the answer. That angry prospector had lain in wait for Professor Burton and then drygulched him. Frank hadn't seen a gun on the man and had figured he was unarmed. If he had been packing an iron, Frank would have taken it away from him to prevent just such an ambush from occurring.

The prospector had either had a hidden gun, or he had fetched a weapon from his saddlebags. The how didn't matter. What was important was that Burton was hit.

Frank dropped to a knee beside the professor. He was aware that he was making himself a target, but he wanted to know how badly Burton was hurt. The wounded man lay facedown in the street. Frank grasped his shoulder and rolled him onto his back. As he did, Burton's coat fell open and Frank saw the dark stain on the professor's vest. It was low on Burton's right side.

Burton let out a groan, telling Frank that he was still alive anyway. Clint ran up, a little out of breath, and said, "I heard the fella running down that alley over there. I'll go after him while you tend to the professor!"

Before Frank could countermand that decision, Clint dashed off again, toward the dark mouth of an alley where the bushwhacker must have been lurking, waiting for the professor to come along. Even though it annoyed Frank that Clint had acted on impulse that way, without waiting for orders, he knew that his new deputy could take care of himself. He ripped Burton's vest and shirt open to see just how bad the wound was.

The light was uncertain, just what came from the moon and stars and the reflected glow from some lamp-lit windows down the street, but when Frank probed the wound with the fingers of his left hand, he found that it was just a shallow furrow in Burton's side, a couple of inches above his waist. It had bled quite a bit, but was more messy than serious. The bullet hadn't penetrated and done any real damage. Once the wound was cleaned and bandaged, it ought to heal without much trouble. Burton would be stiff and sore—he wouldn't feel like visiting that Chinese girl Linda for a while, Frank thought—but in time he would be as good as new.

Claude Langley came hurrying along the street with a lantern in his hand. As the light washed over Frank and the professor, the undertaker asked, "More business for me, Marshal?"

"Not this time," Frank said. "This one's still alive. He needs to be patched up, though."

"I can do that," Langley offered. "I'll take him down to my place."

"Much obliged," Frank said as he straightened to his feet. He looked toward the dark alley where Clint Farnum had disappeared in search of the bushwhacker. He hadn't seen or heard anything of Clint since the deputy had run off.

As Frank stalked toward the alley, gun in hand, more shots suddenly shattered the night air, coming from somewhere behind the row of buildings. He broke into a run and dashed along the alley, stumbling a little over some of the trash that littered the ground. He heard two different guns, and figured Clint had caught up to the man who had shot the professor. As he reached the other end of the alley, he saw Colt flame bloom in the darkness to his right.

Pivoting in that direction, Frank spotted a dark shape as it darted behind some barrels stored at the rear of a building.

Spurts of gunfire came from a clump of trees nearby. Bullets tore into the barrels and splintered the wood as they punched all the way through the empty containers. The man who had taken cover behind them dashed into the open again as he realized that the barrels weren't providing any real shelter from the gunfire after all.

By the size of the running shape, Frank recognized the man as Clint Farnum. The deputy suddenly tripped and went down, right out in the open where he would be a perfect target for the gunman hidden in the trees.

Before the bushwhacker could draw a bead on the fallen deputy, Frank leveled his Colt and squeezed off four rounds as fast as he could, leaving one round in the cylinder in case he needed it. The range was fairly long for a handgun, and the light was bad, but this was far from the first time that Frank had risked his own life, or that of someone else, on his skill with a Colt.

He had aimed at the last spot he had seen muzzle flashes. Now, as Clint pushed himself up and seemed to be waiting for slugs to smash into him and drive the life from him, the bushwhacker's gun fell silent. Frank kept his gun trained on the trees. After a moment, a figure staggered out of the shadows. He tried to lift the gun that he still clutched in his hand, but he lacked the strength to do so. He pitched forward onto his face and lay still.

Frank covered the man as he started forward. Clint came to his feet and called, "Frank? That you?"

"Yeah," Frank replied. "Are you hit?"

"No, just shaken up a mite from that hard fall I took. But I'd be plumb full of holes right now if not for you."

Frank went straight to the man he had shot. He toed the body over onto its back. Clint came up and snapped a match to life with his thumbnail, and as the harsh glare spread over the face of the bushwhacker, Frank recognized the angry prospector from Rosie's place.

"He must've really been mad about not gettin' any," Clint said with a faint chuckle.

The front of the prospector's overalls were stained with blood in three places where Frank's bullets had struck him. His eyes were open and staring, and his chest rose and fell a couple of times before he shuddered and his final breath rattled in his throat. The staring eyes turned glassy.

Frank started reloading the gun in his hand. As the match burned down and Clint dropped it before it could scorch his fingers, he asked, "How's the professor?"

"Not hurt too bad," Frank replied as he thumbed fresh cartridges into the Colt's cylinder. "It's a good thing this hombre wasn't a better shot, or the professor would be dead now. As it is, all he's got is a bullet graze in his side."

"The professor's a lucky hombre," Clint said. "Like me. When I tripped and fell out there in plain sight, I figured I was a goner for sure." He paused. "Thanks, Frank. I reckon you saved my life."

Frank grunted. "I'd do the same for any of my deputies."

"Hey! Hey, Marshal, you back here?"

"Speaking of which . . ." Frank said as he turned to look toward the new voice. Catamount Jack hurried out of the alley carrying a lantern in one hand and a six-gun in the other. Frank called to him, "It's all right, Jack. The shooting's all over."

Jack came up and held the lantern high so that its light washed over all of them. "Sounded like a reg'lar war bustin' out for a minute there." He frowned at Clint Farnum. "Who's this?"

"My new deputy," Frank said.

"I'm bein' replaced?" Jack practically yelped as his bushy eyebrows shot up.

"Not at all," Frank hastened to assure him. "Clint's signing on as a second deputy, because the town is growing so fast . . . and trouble right along with it."

Jack grunted. "You can say that again." He nodded toward the corpse. "I reckon this fella was tryin' to grow some trouble of his own?"

"That's right. He had a run-in with Professor Burton earlier and then bushwhacked him."

"Yeah, I seen Claude Langley and some other fellas carryin' the professor down to the undertakin' parlor. Figured for sure he was dead, but Claude said he was just wounded and he was gonna patch him up, not plant him."

Frank slid his Colt back into the holster. "I guess I'd better go see about him. I'll tell Claude to come back here with his wagon for this fella too."

"I'll stay here and keep an eye on the carcass," Jack offered.

"And I'll finish making those evening rounds," Clint volunteered.

Frank thought it over and then nodded. "I'm obliged to both of you boys," he said. "Seems like Buckskin is in good hands."

Chapter 15

A shudder went through Jessica Munro as she listened to the guns going off somewhere else in town. Even though she was in no danger—at least, as far as she knew—the thought that men were out there killing each other made her question her wisdom in coming here to this wild, untamed town.

But Hamish was here, and he had insisted that she accompany him. As usual, what Hamish wanted, he got.

Wearing a dark blue dressing gown—Hamish's favorite color—Jessica thought about stepping over to the window and looking out. Perhaps she could see what was going on. At the same time, she didn't want to draw attention to herself, so she stayed where she was, seated in front of a dressing table with a flyspecked mirror. She ran a bone-handled brush through her long, fair hair, which she had unleashed from its elaborate arrangement of piled-up curls so that it tumbled around her shoulders and down her back.

She studied the bedroom's reflection in the mirror. It was part of the hotel's only suite, with a small sitting room adjacent to it where Hamish was going over some papers with his secretary, Nathan Evers. The place had been cleaned up considerably since their arrival that afternoon. Hamish had seen to it that the rooms he and Jessica would be using had been dusted and swept and mopped. Fresh linens that they had brought with them from San Francisco were on the bed. The furnishings in the room were comfortable enough, Jessica supposed. A tin bathtub sat in one corner, with the soapy water she had used to soak off the dust of their journey now cooling in it.

She set the brush on the dressing table and looked at herself more closely in the mirror. Only the faintest suggestions of lines were visible around the corners of her eyes and mouth . . . but faint though they might be, they were there. Another five years and she would start to look her age, she guessed. She had worked hard to delay that onslaught, but there was only so much a person could do to hold back the ravages of the years. Right now she was a stunningly beautiful woman, but in time she would be merely very attractive. Would Hamish still want her then?

She grasped the lapels of her robe and pulled them apart, revealing her breasts, turning back and forth in the chair to see if she could detect any signs of sagging. No, they were still as firm as they had been when she was a girl. She wondered how the straitlaced Nathan Evers would react if she were to step into the doorway between the bedroom and the sitting room and stand there with her robe open like this, so that he could see her breasts. She could always pretend it was an accident and claim that she thought he had left. She bet Nathan's eyes would nearly pop out of his head at the sight. She smiled at that thought.

Hamish would be angry, of course, but it wouldn't last long. To tell the truth, she knew that deep down he enjoyed the way other men looked at her. Jealous he might be, but proud too. What greater accomplishment could a man have than to possess a wife that every other man wanted to bed?

Well, a lot of money might be almost as good, she supposed . . . and Hamish Munro certainly had that. Otherwise, she wouldn't be sitting here in this god-forsaken hamlet of Buckskin, Nevada.

She pulled the robe tight around her as she heard a footstep at the door between the rooms. By the time the door opened, she had the brush in her hand again and was running it through her hair. Hamish came into the room.

Jessica met his eyes in the mirror and said, "Mr. Evers is gone?"

"That's right," Hamish replied. "We've finished our work for the evening."

He was a compact man, only an inch or so taller than his wife. A fringe of reddish-gray hair remained around his ears and the back of his head; otherwise he was bald. At first glance, he didn't look at all impressive, but he had a fire and a ruthless determination that made larger men do his bidding without question. He had made fortunes in both railroading and mining with the same basic tactic: If anyone presented an obstacle to what he wanted, he found a way to crush them. It was as simple as that.

Jessica set the brush down again. "How long do you think we'll be here?"

Hamish took his coat off and draped it over the back of a chair. "That's hard to say," he replied as he removed his cravat and his stiff collar. "I'll meet with Hammersmith tomorrow and get his report on the operation out at the Alhambra. I know that he's hired some men, but I don't think he has a full crew yet. Once the mine is producing ore at a suitable rate, I'll leave it in his hands and we can return to San Francisco."

"But you don't know how long that will be?"

Hamish shrugged. "How can I? These things take time."

"You don't even know for certain that there's any silver

left in the mine," she ventured, knowing that to cast any doubt on his ultimate success usually annoyed him.

"It's there," he snapped. "The Lucky Lizard is producing again, and the reports I've received indicate that the Crown Royal is too. So will the Alhambra."

"If that's true, why did those mines sit there abandoned for so long?"

"Our methods are better now," Hamish said. "We can find ore in places that we couldn't before."

Jessica didn't pretend to understand the mining business. She supposed Hamish knew what he was talking about.

He smiled as he came over to stand behind her. "You shouldn't be worrying about things like that," he said. He rested his hands on her shoulders. "Let me be concerned about the business. That's my job."

She knew his hands wouldn't stay on her shoulders for long. "And what's my business?" she asked with a coy smile on her face. The words and the expression were so instinctive, she didn't even have to think about them.

He slid his hands down her front and parted the robe, as she had done earlier, pulling it back even more so that her shoulders were bared too. Leaning over her, he pressed his lips to one smooth, sleek shoulder as he filled his palms with the firm globes of her breasts.

"Your business is to make your husband happy," he said as he caressed her.

She closed her eyes for a second. It was a job, all right—but thankfully, she was good at it.

Outside, the shooting had stopped. Jessica hadn't really noticed when that happened.

By the time Frank reached the undertaking parlor, Claude Langley had already cleaned and bandaged the bullet graze in Professor Burton's side. The professor had a hangdog expression on his face when Frank came in.

"I'm a fool, an utter fool," he announced. "Brawling over some doxie, then getting shot over her."

"Having woman trouble doesn't make you a fool, Professor," Frank assured him. "It just makes you a normal hombre."

"Oh? I'll wager *you* never had such bad luck with females, Marshal."

Frank's jaw tightened as he thought about the women in his life. His first love had been a girl back in Texas, where he'd grown up. Mercy, as beautiful as her name. But her father had forced them apart, and even though Frank had met her again years later, to this day he wasn't sure if Mercy's daughter Victoria was actually his child, although he liked to think that she was. And at least Mercy was still alive. . . .

Later, he had married Vivian, and again circumstances had kept them from being together. Without even knowing about it, he'd had a son with her, the young man known as Conrad Browning. Vivian hadn't survived her reconciliation with Frank; outlaws had gunned her down. The circumstances that had brought him to Buckskin in the first place had been related to that tragic incident.

Then there had been Dixie, sweet, courageous Dixie. She had married Frank only to die at the hands of lawless men, just like Vivian. That had been enough to make Frank wonder if he carried a curse with him. Maybe the vengeful spirits of all the men who had met death in front of the flaming barrel of his Colt were conspiring to insure that his every attempt at happiness ended in tragedy. In the past few years, the only woman he'd been close to who *hadn't* died was Roanne Williamson, in the town of Santa Rosa down along the border between Texas and Mexico.

Frank was enough of a pragmatist not to really believe in curses, though. Despite the settling influence of civilization, in many places the West was still wild. It was still a frontier—although that frontier was shrinking—and that meant plenty of danger for anyone brave enough to live there. Tragedy didn't dog his trail any more than it did those of lots of other men.

He became aware that Professor Burton was looking at him, waiting for a response to his comment. Frank shrugged and said, "You could be right, Professor." That was the easiest way out. Frank Morgan had never been one to seek the easiest trail, but in this case, it seemed like the right thing to do.

"You can be sure that I shall avoid that woman's establishment in the future," Burton said.

"Don't go making promises you can't keep, Professor," Langley said with a smile.

"But man should be the master of his own desires, don't you think?"

"Hasn't ever happened before on a consistent basis, going all the way back to the Garden of Eden," Langley replied. "Don't see any reason to think things are going to change now."

Frank said, "I'll leave you two to discuss philosophy, if you're of a mind to. I need to see if my deputies ran into any more trouble making the rounds."

Langley rubbed his hands together. "And I need to get to that corpse, I guess. Want to give me a hand, Professor?"

Burton paled even more than normal. "I think I've seen enough of the results of violence for one night, thank you."

Frank chuckled as he left the undertaking parlor. He walked back to the marshal's office, and by the time he got there, both Catamount Jack and Clint Farnum were there too.

"Get the rest of the rounds made all right?" Frank asked as he hung his hat on one of the nails beside the door.

Clint nodded. "Everything's locked up for the night, except for the saloons, of course. They're still going strong." The little gunfighter was perched on the edge of the table that served as Frank's desk. His legs were short enough that his booted feet didn't quite reach the floor.

"Claude's helper brung the wagon and we loaded that fella's body onto it," Jack put in. "I reckon he got back all right with it. I didn't go with him."

"Yeah, it got there, from the way Langley was acting when I left," Frank said with a nod.

Clint grinned and said, "There have been two killings since I got here. Is Buckskin always so exciting, Frank?"

"It's too exciting, if you ask me. But that's the way it is when a town is booming like this one, I reckon."

"Businesses doing well, are they?"

Frank nodded again. "Leo Benjamin has supplies freighted in from Virginia City at least twice a week, and he still can't keep stock on his shelves. A couple of other mercantiles have come in to take up some of the slack. The Silver Baron and the other saloons make money hand over fist. The blacksmith shop and Hillman's Livery are doing fine. The boardinghouse is full, and most of the abandoned houses and cabins have been claimed, at least until the rightful owners come along and reclaim them, if they ever do."

"Like that fella Munro did with the old hotel."

"Yeah. He probably doesn't need the money, but if he wanted to, he could turn the place into a hotel again. All the rooms would be rented in a week or less, I'd say."

"So you've got money flowing in, and pretty soon silver flowing out, I reckon. The mines are producing, aren't they?"

"The Lucky Lizard and the Crown Royal are," Frank said. He didn't know for sure how much ore Garrett Claiborne's crew was taking out of the Browning mine, but they were finding some color, Claiborne had reported. "I don't know about the Alhambra."

"Any new claims paying off?" Clint asked.

Jack said, "You're a mighty curious little fella, ain't you?"

Clint didn't appear to take offense at the blunt question or the description of him. He laughed and said, "I've already signed on as a deputy, but I still like to know what I'm getting myself into."

"You're getting into a town that's already busting at the seams," Frank said, "and it's only going to get worse before it gets better. Those new claims you asked about haven't produced any significant finds yet, at least not that I know about, but somebody could stumble onto a new vein at any time. If that happens, everything that's already going on in Buckskin will just go through the roof."

"In other words, there'll be plenty of trouble for three good lawmen to handle."

Frank nodded. "Yeah . . . but we can handle it."

He hoped the confidence he felt in himself and Jack— and in Clint Farnum—wasn't misplaced.

Chapter 16

Gunther Hammersmith wasn't expecting anything like the blonde who opened the door of the suite on the second floor of the old hotel. She said, "You must be Mr. Hammersmith," then smiled at him. The smile hit him in the gut harder than any punch he could remember ever taking.

He wanted this woman. He would *have* this woman.

But she had to belong to Munro, which meant she was off limits to Hammersmith, no matter how beautiful she was, no matter what that smile of hers did to his insides.

He recalled hearing something about how Munro had gotten himself a pretty wife back there in San Francisco. Hammersmith hadn't worked for Munro recently, and he hadn't been to San Francisco either. If he had ever seen this woman before, he would have remembered her, that was for damned sure.

He became aware that she was standing there in the doorway with an expectant look on her face. She was waiting for him to respond to what she had said, he realized. He took off the battered old derby he had crammed on his head before he rode into Buckskin and said, "Yes, ma'am.

I'm Hammersmith." His voice sounded thick and awkward to his ears.

She stepped back, still holding the door. "Come in. Hamish has been waiting for you."

That wasn't good. Munro didn't like to be kept waiting. Hammersmith worried that they would get off on the wrong foot.

That concern was justified. As Hammersmith walked in to the sitting room, Munro stalked out of the bedroom and glared at him. "I expected you earlier," the mining magnate snapped.

"We had a problem with one of the shoring timbers this morning," Hammersmith explained. "I thought I ought to stay until it was taken care of. A cave-in would have just set us back." With uncharacteristic humility, he added, "But I'm sorry I kept you waiting, Mr. Munro."

Hamish Munro was one of the few men in the world Hammersmith would have taken that tone with. Mostly, he despised other men for being weaker than he was, and he didn't bother trying to hide that disdain. Munro was different, though. Even though Hammersmith was almost twice as big as him and could have picked Munro up and broken him in two with his bare hands, he didn't want to cross the man. Everyone who had ever tried that had lived to regret it—but sometimes they hadn't lived much longer than that.

Munro waved a hand and said, "I suppose it was better that you stayed at the mine and made sure the problem was repaired properly." His voice took on a harsher tone as he continued. "But you're here now. What do you have to report? How soon will we be taking ore out of the Alhambra?"

"The shaft and the main drift have been cleaned out and the timbers that needed it have been repaired or replaced," Hammersmith said. He was on firmer footing here. No matter what else anyone said about him, no one could dispute that he was a good mining man. "We did some work on the rails for the ore carts. The stamp mill is in good working order, and we've installed all the new equipment for the amalgamation process. All we need now is the ore."

"And what about it?" Munro asked. "Have you located the vein?"

Hammersmith hesitated, then shook his head. "Not yet, but I haven't been able to spare as many men to look for it as I'd like. I'm going to hire some more miners, and I'm sure we'll find color any day now."

"You'd better." Munro scowled. "It's bad enough the Lucky Lizard has a jump on us. I don't want the Crown Royal getting too far ahead."

Hammersmith smiled. "They've had some trouble at the Crown Royal. Somebody tore up their rails. They'll have to fix all that damage before they can really get started bringing any ore out of the ground."

Munro took a cigar from his vest pocket, clipped the end of it with a fancy silver cutter, and put it in his mouth. He gave Hammersmith a cold, thin smile as he struck a match and lit the cheroot.

"That's good to know," he said.

Hammersmith hated talking around a subject. He liked things blunt and simple. It would have been fine with him to just say, *We sabotaged the Crown Royal like you told us to.* Munro liked to maintain the fiction that he was an honest, upright businessman, though, and that meant never admitting that he would stoop to sabotage to damage a competitor.

The mines were close enough together that the vein in the Crown Royal might well connect to the one in the Alhambra. In that case, the miners had the right to follow a vein as far as they could, as long as it didn't run into another mine's tunnels. That meant it was to Munro's advantage, at least potentially, to slow down the Crown Royal's operation. Hammersmith understood that and didn't mind doing something about it. Munro was paying his wages, after all, and they were good wages at that.

Hammersmith had been aware of the blonde moving around the room behind him. He could smell her perfume. He could damn near feel the warmth coming off her skin. He wanted to feel that warmth. She was enough of a distraction that he almost had trouble keeping his mind on what Munro was saying to him.

Now, she moved around where he could see her again. In the light, summery dress, she was prettier than any picture Hammersmith had ever seen. He recalled that he had once seen a picture in a magazine of a painting called "September Morn." The painting was of a pretty woman standing stark naked at the edge of a stream, her arms and hands covering the important parts, her head tipped up and back and a little surprised expression on her face, like she was looking at somebody who had just come along and caught her skinny-dipping. Hammersmith didn't know a damned thing about art, but he knew he liked that picture, and as he looked at the blonde now, he could imagine her just like that, all bare creamy skin glowing in the morning light . . .

"Can I offer you a drink, Mr. Hammersmith?" she asked, and the question forced that tantalizing image out of his mind.

"For God's sake, Jessica," Munro said. "It's not even noon yet."

"Almost," she said.

"Hammersmith's got to get back to work. He can't stand around here all day lollygagging." Munro jabbed a finger at his mine superintendent. "Hire as many men as you need, but *find that ore*. Let's keep the pressure on the

Crown Royal too. I don't care how hard it is or how many hours the men have to put in. If you can't handle the job, I'll find someone who can."

"I can handle the job, Mr. Munro," Hammersmith said. "Don't you worry about that. I'll drive those bastards from can to can't." He glanced at the woman. "Beggin' your pardon, ma'am."

"It's all right," she told him. The sound of the words made a shiver go through him. He imagined himself lying under a tree somewhere, in soft grass, with his head pillowed on her lap as she stroked cool fingers along his cheek and said, "It's all right. It's all right." He thought that if he could ever have an experience like that, he could die a happy man.

Assuming, of course, that he could throw her skirts over her head and get some sweet lovin' from her too.

He tried to banish that thought as he turned his derby over in his hands. Lusting after his employer's wife wasn't going to do him any good, especially when the boss was as rich, ruthless, and powerful as Hamish Munro. Hammersmith forced himself to say, "I'll be goin' now."

As he turned toward the door, Munro said to his back, "Remember, Hammersmith . . . my mine is going to come out on top. Whatever it takes."

"Yes, sir," Hammersmith said over his shoulder.

Why was it so important to Munro that the Alhambra outproduce all the other mines? If they found the vein again, the mine would make money, maybe a lot of it. And Munro already *had* more money than he could ever spend in the rest of his life.

It had to be the winning, Hammersmith thought. Munro didn't really care about anything except having more and being better than his rivals. He probably felt the same way about that wife of his.

Hammersmith understood both of those things. He liked nothing more than to crush his enemies too.

And now that he had seen Jessica Munro . . . well, he might just be willing to kill for her, if he ever got the chance.

Even though Frank had been halfway expecting it, the rate at which Buckskin grew in the next few weeks surprised him. Newcomers continued to pour into the settlement, and once all the buildings were occupied, men went up to the hillsides and began to fell trees. A sawmill opened inside a big tent, and the chugging of the donkey engine and the whine of the saw could be heard from early in the morning until dusk, seven days a week. Mixed with those sounds was the racket of hammering, as the rough boards from the sawmill were slapped together into new buildings. A whole new street grew up, running parallel with the main street that was already there. More saloons and stores opened, as did an assay office. A man showed up with a printing press in the back of a wagon and started a newspaper, the Buckskin *Bulletin*. A couple of lawyers hung out their shingles, as did a doctor. A red-and-white-striped barber pole appeared on the boardwalk in front of one of the new buildings. A Chinese laundry began taking in washing. Two new whorehouses opened up.

Back in the summer of '76, when he was still a young man, Frank had spent a little time in Deadwood, Dakota Territory. Buckskin wasn't quite the hell-with-the-hide-off town that Deadwood had been, but it was as wild and woolly a place as he had been in in quite some time. He and Jack and Clint had their hands full keeping the peace. Along with all the miners who descended on Buckskin came the cardsharps, the swindlers, the soiled doves, the cutthroats, thieves, and killers whose life work it was to empty the miners' pockets of what precious few riches they were lucky enough to obtain.

Deadwood had averaged a little more than a killing a day at its worst. Buckskin wasn't that bad. There were only a couple of murders a week.

Luckily, no more would-be gunfighters showed up to challenge Frank in an attempt to build a reputation. He supposed word might have gotten around about what had happened to the kid called Conwell and Harry Clevenger and Charlie Hampton.

But even if the men who fancied themselves fast guns were being wary right now, that wouldn't last, Frank knew. Sooner or later, one of them would get an itch to prove himself, and then he would ride into Buckskin and force a showdown with the notorious Drifter.

On the mining front, trouble still continued to plague the Crown Royal, and an angry Tip Woodford reported that somebody had stolen some blasting powder and other supplies from the Lucky Lizard. Frank had his suspicions about who was responsible for this mischief—the culprit was big and bald and answered to the name of Gunther Hammersmith—but he didn't have any proof that Munro's superintendent was to blame. Tip and Garrett Claiborne had both posted guards at their respective mines, and Frank tried to ride out and keep an eye on them when he could, but his duties in town took up most of his time.

He wondered if Hamish Munro had ordered the sabotage, or if Hammersmith was carrying it out on his own. Assuming, of course, that Hammersmith was responsible. Munro seldom budged from the old hotel that he had turned into his headquarters.

That wife of his came out from time to time, though, and she always drew plenty of attention when she did.

Many of the men in Buckskin hadn't seen a woman in quite a while, and it had been even longer since they had seen one as breathtakingly lovely as Jessica Munro.

That caused some trouble of its own one day. Frank was in Leo Benjamin's store, talking to the proprietor, when he heard angry voices in the street outside. With a frown on his face, Frank muttered, "What the hell's going on now?" and strode toward the front door.

There was a high porch in front of the store that served as a loading dock. Wagons could be backed up to it and supplies placed inside them without much trouble. A set of steps at each end of the porch led back down to the regular boardwalk that ran along both sides of the street.

From that porch, Frank had a good vantage point on the fracas taking place in the street. A miner was sprawled on his back, obviously having just been knocked down by Gunther Hammersmith, who loomed over him with clenched fists. Hammersmith reached down, grabbed the miner's shirt, and hauled him to his feet, only to draw back and wallop him again. Hammersmith's big fist landed on the man's jaw with a meaty thud, and the miner flew through the air to come crashing down on his back again.

"I'll teach you to be disrespectful to a lady, damn you!" Hammersmith bellowed.

Frank glanced to his right. Jessica Munro stood on the boardwalk just past the porch in front of Leo's store. She was dressed up in a fancy gown and carried a parasol to keep the sun off her face, which at the moment was set in an agitated expression.

"Please, Mr. Hammersmith!" she called. "This isn't necessary—"

"Beggin' your pardon, ma'am, but it is," Hammersmith insisted as he grabbed the hapless miner again, jerked him to his feet, and poised a malletlike fist to strike another devastating blow.

Frank palmed his Colt from its holster, eared back the hammer so that the metallic ratcheting of the action sounded loud in the street, and said, "Hold it right there, Hammersmith."

Chapter 17

Hammersmith froze with the punch undelivered. He looked over his shoulder and found himself staring down the muzzle of Frank's gun. Eyes narrowing in anger, he said, "This is none o' your damn business, Marshal."

Remembering what Garrett Claiborne had told him about some of the things Hammersmith had done in the past, Frank said, "It's my business if you're about to try to beat a man to death in my town, mister."

Hammersmith's lip curled. He gave the miner a hard shove that sent the man off his feet again. "If I was to beat this bastard to death, it wouldn't be any more than he had comin' to him."

"What did he do to deserve that?"

"He was tryin' to get a peek under Mrs. Munro's dress while she walked along that high porch!"

Frank glanced at Jessica Munro. Her face was flushed with embarrassment now as she looked down at the ground. "Is that true, ma'am?" he asked her.

"I . . . I don't really know. I was just out walking . . . I like to take a daily constitutional, you know . . . and that man . . . that man came up in the street alongside the porch. He was talking to me . . . paying his respects, he said—"

"Disrespects is more like it!" Hammersmith broke in. "I was coming the other way along the boardwalk and saw what he was doin'. Sneakin' peeks at the lady's calves!"

"Really, Mr. Hammersmith," Jessica said in a weak voice, and Frank wondered if she was more embarrassed by what the miner had done or by Hammersmith's bellowing about it like an angry old bull.

Frank had seen Hammersmith in town several times over the past few weeks, usually going in or out of the hotel that Hamish Munro had taken over. Whether by accident or design, though, their paths hadn't crossed. Frank had heard that the miners who worked for Munro had struck the vein again in the Alhambra, and the mine was producing a decent amount of high-grade ore. He knew from talk he had overheard in the saloons that Hammersmith had hired enough men to have a full crew at the mine, and he worked them hard too, keeping shifts down the shaft day and night, and the stamp mill working full-blast too. He was known to be a hard, even brutal taskmaster, just as Claiborne had said.

This incident today didn't have anything to do with the mine, though. The man Hammersmith had been abusing wasn't one of his workers. Frank recognized the miner as being one of Tip Woodford's employees. He also suspected that the man *had* been trying to get a peek under Jessica Munro's dress. That wasn't a very gentlemanly thing to do, but it probably didn't deserve a beating like the one that Hammersmith had been handing out to him.

"All right, this is over," Frank said. "Whatever that hombre did or didn't do, he's been walloped a few times for it, and that's punishment enough." He glanced at Jessica.

"Unless Mrs. Munro wants to press charges of disturbing the peace against him . . ."

She shook her head. "No, that's all right. Let the poor man go, Marshal."

The miner had managed to sit up, and was shaking his head back and forth groggily. Frank said, "He's a mite addled right now, ma'am, but when he gets his wits about him, I'll send him on his way."

"Thank you."

"As for you, Hammersmith," Frank went on, "I reckon I can't blame you for defending a lady's honor. Remember, though, we've got law in Buckskin. If you've got a problem with somebody, you can come take it up with me."

A harsh laugh came from Hammersmith. "I stomp my own snakes, Morgan. You'd best remember that. And this is the second time you've pointed a gun at me."

"Second time you're lucky I didn't shoot you," Frank countered.

Hammersmith glowered even more. "Next time, we're liable to finish this," he threatened.

Frank lowered the Colt's hammer and holstered the gun. "Reckon that'll be up to you," he said.

Hammersmith glared at him for a second longer, then turned to Jessica and said, "I'll escort you back to the hotel, ma'am."

"Really, Mr. Hammersmith, that's not necessary."

"I insist."

Jessica smiled, and Frank thought that despite her protests and her embarrassment over the incident, she was pleased that Hammersmith had been willing to give somebody a thrashing on her account. With that coy smile on her face, she allowed Hammersmith to slip his arm through hers and walk beside her as they headed along the street toward the hotel. They hadn't gone a block before she was laughing at something Hammersmith had said.

Leo Benjamin had come out of the store to stand on the porch and watch the confrontation. He said to Frank, "That woman is the sort who can cause trouble, Marshal. She likes to have men fighting over her."

Frank nodded. "I know. But there's not much the law can do about something like that. It's not a crime for a woman to be beautiful."

"No, but perhaps flirting and stirring up trouble should be."

Frank laughed and clapped a hand on the storekeeper's shoulder. "Tell you what. I'll deputize you and you can go out and arrest all the flirty females in the world. Let me know when you're done."

Leo just sighed, rolled his eyes, and went back in the store. Frank watched Hammersmith and Mrs. Munro go into the hotel, and his expression grew more serious.

He had been joking with Leo, but he knew that the storekeeper was right in a way. Going all the way back to Helen of Troy, some women just had a natural-born talent for getting all hell to bust loose.

Frank had a feeling that Jessica Munro was one of those women.

That evening, Frank left Catamount Jack and Clint Farnum in charge of things in town and rode out toward the Crown Royal. Clint had asked if Frank wanted him to come along, but Frank had said no. The deputies would have enough on their plate keeping things peaceful and quiet in the settlement. Frank's interest in the Crown Royal was less official and more personal. He went out to the mine several nights a week, just to keep an eye on the place and maybe catch any would-be saboteurs.

Once again, Frank was acting on his son's behalf. When Conrad had been building that spur rail line down in New Mexico Territory, bitter rivals had done their best to stop him. Frank had stepped in then too, taking a hand in the fight. This was no different. He had a stake in the Browning Mining Syndicate, just as he did in the Browning railroad interests.

It might have been nice, he reflected as he rode toward the Crown Royal on Stormy, if Conrad had taken the name Morgan. After all, Frank was his father.

But Vivian's second husband had raised the boy, and Conrad had thought of that man as his father until after he was grown. Couldn't expect him to just forget about all those years as if they hadn't meant anything, Frank thought. At least, he and Conrad weren't enemies anymore. They had grown to respect each other. That was something at least.

If he could have taken back all those lost years when he and Conrad hadn't even been aware of each other's existence, though, he would have. In a heartbeat.

Dog trotted along beside the Appaloosa. Frank intended to ride up to a hilltop overlooking the bench where the mine was located and spend a few hours there, just watching the place. He had a pair of field glasses in his saddlebags, and once the moon rose he would be able to see if anybody came skulking around the mine.

Before they reached the hill, though, Dog let out a sudden growl and took off like a shot, dashing away into the darkness. Frank started to call out after the big cur, then stopped himself. Chances are, Dog was after a rabbit or a gopher or something like that, but there was also a possibility he had caught the scent of a two-legged varmint who was up to no good. Frank reined in, swung down from the saddle, and ground-hitched Stormy. The Appaloosa was well trained and wouldn't go anywhere unless Frank whistled for him.

Frank pulled his Winchester from the saddle boot and then went ahead on foot, going the same direction Dog had. He knew that once Dog was on the scent of some prey, he would go in a straight line toward it, as much as possible, so Frank did the same. As silent as an Indian, he moved through some brush and came to the bank of a small creek that wound through the hills. Frank knew this creek ran beside the stamp mill at the Crown Royal and provided the water for the steam engine that powered the mill.

He dropped to a knee as the scent of tobacco smoke drifted to him. The smoke was a dead giveaway that somebody was out here, since no wild creature had ever mastered the art of rolling a quirly. Silent and still, Frank listened, and a moment later he heard the splashing of hooves as several riders moved along the rocky bed of the stream.

They moved into sight, heading away from the Crown Royal. Frank counted four men. They had to be riding in the shallow creek like that because they didn't want to leave a trail, and that told him beyond a shadow of a doubt that they were up to no good. It looked like his continued vigilance might finally pay off.

"The time ought to be up already, shouldn't it?" one of the men asked as they neared the place where Frank waited on the bank.

"Give it a few more minutes," one of the others replied. "We want to be well away from there before it blows, so I cut that fuse plenty long."

It was a warm night, but Frank's blood turned cold at

those words. The men had planted some dynamite or blasting powder or some sort of explosive and set it to go off soon. The only place around here they could have put a bomb like that was the Crown Royal.

Garrett Claiborne was there, along with all the other men he had hired to work the mine. Innocent men, each and every one of them, about to be blown to kingdom come.

And judging by what the riders had said, Frank had only minutes to stop the blast.

He came to his feet as his mind raced. The bomb could have been placed anywhere around the mine—in the stamp mill or the office or under the barracks or in one of the storage buildings. The Crown Royal had its own supply of blasting powder, and the bomb could be set to detonate that too. A blind search would take too much time. Frank had to force one of the men to tell him where the explosives were.

"Elevate!" he shouted as he levered a round into the Winchester's firing chamber and brought the rifle to his shoulder. "Hands up or I'll blow you out of the saddle!"

The men reacted instantly, as he had figured they would. They twisted toward him and clawed at the guns on their hips. In the thick shadows under the trees along the creek bank, Frank couldn't see them very well, but they couldn't see him either. As the first man to unlimber his Colt triggered a wild shot toward the sound of Frank's voice, Frank aimed just above the muzzle flash and fired.

The Winchester cracked and the gunman yelled in pain as he slewed backward and toppled off his horse, landing in the creek with a splash. Frank caught a glimpse of a large, furry shape flashing through the air as Dog leaped from the creek bank toward the riders. Then Frank threw himself to the side and rolled over as a fusillade of shots roared out and orange flame jumped from gun barrels, throwing a harsh, inconstant light over the scene.

Bullets whipped through the brush around Frank as he came to a stop on his belly. From that prone position, he fired the Winchester again, working the lever fast as he cranked off four rounds. Another man fell, and a third galloped off, hunched forward over his saddle.

The fourth man was already down, thrashing around in the water and screaming as he tried to fight off Dog. The big cur had knocked him out of the saddle with that leap.

Frank surged to his feet, pivoted, and tried to draw a bead on the man who was riding off. Before he could pull the trigger, though, the man swayed violently and then toppled off his horse, falling into the creek. Obviously, he had been hit by one of Frank's shots.

"Dog!" Frank called. "Hold!" He didn't want the hombre Dog had been attacking to get away, but neither did he want Dog to tear out the man's throat.

That fella might be the only one of the saboteurs left alive.

Frank ran out into the creek and checked the two men who had fallen close by. Both of them were dead, drilled cleanly through the body. The other man, who had fallen about fifty yards down the creek, had crossed the divide also. One of Frank's bullets had caught him low in the belly, the sort of wound that took a long time to kill a man, but in this case, the fellow had passed out, fallen out of the saddle, and broken his neck when he landed. His head was twisted at an ugly angle on his neck.

Frank ran back to the survivor, who had scooted up against the bank and sat there staring in terror at the huge dog standing right in front of him. The fur on Dog's back bristled, and his teeth were showing in a savage snarl. The animal quivered from the desire to launch himself at the man again.

"Listen to me, mister," Frank said. "Tell me what you did at the Crown Royal, and be damned quick about it or I'll turn him loose on you."

"K-keep that wolf away from me, mister!" the man said. "He's loco!"

"And he'll be tearing your throat out in about two seconds if you don't tell me what I want to know."

"All right! All right. We . . . we planted some dynamite up there at that mine. It ought to be goin' off any time now."

"Where is it?"

When the man hesitated, Dog growled and leaned closer.

"In the stamp mill! Oh, God, don't let him get me! The dynamite's in the stamp mill!"

"What about the guards?" Frank asked.

"A couple of the boys snuck up on 'em . . . cut their throats . . . but I swear I didn't have nothin' to do with that, mister! I swear it!"

Frank didn't know whether to believe the man or not, but it didn't really matter. The bastard had been part of the killings, even if he hadn't wielded a knife. And he had helped plant the explosives that might kill a lot more men. Frank was tempted to let Dog have him.

But instead he said, "Dog. Back."

The saboteur started to relax and heaved a sigh of relief.

Frank stepped forward and drove the butt of the rifle against his jaw. He felt the satisfying crunch of bone shattering under the impact. The man slumped back against the bank, out cold. He wouldn't be going anywhere for a while. Frank could come back and pick him up later.

"Come on, Dog!" he said as leaped onto the bank. A shrill whistle brought Stormy pounding toward him. As the

Appaloosa came up, Frank grabbed the saddle horn, stuck a foot in the stirrup, and swung up before Stormy even stopped moving. He took off toward the Crown Royal as fast as the big horse could run.

He hoped that the shots had roused the men at the mine. Maybe they had found the slain guards and discovered the dynamite as well, in time to put out the fuse. The explosion hadn't gone off yet, so that gave Frank hope.

On the other hand, rigging a fuse was an uncertain art unless a man was an expert. Maybe the fella who had set this one cut it so that it was burning quite a bit longer than he had expected it to.

At any rate, Frank wanted to draw anybody out who might be inside the stamp mill, so as he galloped toward the mine he slid the Winchester back in the saddle boot, pulled his Colt, and began firing into the air. He shouted, "Tell it, Dog!" and the big cur began to bark. Frank yelled too, raising such a ruckus that everybody at the mine would come outside, he hoped.

As he came within sight of the buildings, he saw that was the case. A couple of dozen men were milling around in the open area between the stamp mill and the barracks. Some of them held lanterns while others clutched rifles or shotguns. As Stormy pounded closer, Frank waved his arm and shouted, "Get away from the mill! Get away from the mill!"

Then, as a huge red and yellow ball of fire bloomed inside the big building, Frank knew that time was up.

The world shook, as hell came to call at the Crown Royal Mine.

Chapter 18

The blast was so strong that the ground jumped under Stormy's hooves, making the rangy Appaloosa stumble. At the same time, the concussion struck Frank and knocked his hat off. Stormy almost went down, but Frank hauled up hard on the reins and kept the horse from falling.

Dog wasn't as lucky. The big cur was thrown off his feet, and with a startled *"Yipe!"* he went rolling across the ground. He wasn't hurt, though, and leaped right back up.

Frank pressed on toward the mine as a thick cloud of black smoke billowed up from the stamp mill. Shattered boards and other bits of debris pelted down around Frank, Stormy, and Dog. The debris had been thrown high in the air by the explosion, but what had gone up was now coming down.

A large piece of machinery crashed to the ground no more than ten yards to Frank's left. He hoped none of the wreckage had his name on it, because he couldn't see the stuff falling in order to avoid it.

The fire inside the stamp mill lit up the night for a long way around. In its hellish glare, Frank saw that the miners were scattered around the clearing between the mill and the barracks like ninepins. Some of them were moving around, crawling and trying to struggle to their feet, while others just lay there motionless. But at least not all of them had been killed.

That was small consolation. For all Frank knew, some of the men were dead, and the stamp mill was destroyed. If only he'd been a little quicker getting here. . . .

He reined in and swung down from the saddle while Stormy was still coming to a halt. He ran over to the nearest man and helped the miner to his feet.

"Where's Claiborne?" Frank asked, raising his voice so he could be heard over the loud crackling of flames from the inferno inside the mill.

The miner looked stunned. Blood leaked from his nose. He shook his head and said, "Dunno. I ain't seen him."

The man was still shaky, but Frank left him there anyway and hurried over to the next fallen miner. He wasn't moving, and as Frank drew closer, he saw why. A jagged piece of wood had been blown all the way through the poor bastard by the blast. The ends of the deadly debris protruded from the front and back of his torso.

The next man was still alive, though. Frank helped him up, and saw that he didn't seem to be seriously hurt.

"Have you seen Garrett Claiborne?"

The miner waved toward the mill. "He was over that way, the last I saw of him." The man's eyes widened in realization. "Oh, hell! I think he ran inside the mill!"

If Claiborne had been in the mill when the dynamite went off, he was dead. No one could have survived such a terrible explosion. The grim possibility crossed Frank's mind that they might not even find enough left of Claiborne to give a proper burial.

"You two," he called to the men he had already assisted. "Check on the others. Help the ones you can."

While they were doing that, Frank headed for the blazing

mill. The heat from the fire was so bad he had to throw his arm up to shield his face. He lowered his head and kept going. He thought he had spotted something on the ground, not far from the mill. . . .

"Garrett!" he shouted as he recognized the shape as a body. With waves of heat washing out and battering him like physical blows, he fought his way forward until he reached the side of a man lying facedown on the ground. The man's clothes were smoldering in places. Frank slapped out those hot spots and then grasped the man's shoulders to roll him over. As he did so, the man let out a groan of pain. His left arm flopped loosely, and Frank saw the white of a broken bone sticking out through bloody flesh.

Claiborne was alive, though. Mighty scorched around the edges, and he had a broken arm at the very least, but he was still breathing. Frank guessed that Claiborne had been running away from the mill when the blast picked him up and threw him forward like a rag doll. He was lucky his insides weren't pulverized.

The engineer surprised Frank by opening his eyes and peering up in a bleary, confused fashion. "Where . . . what . . ." Claiborne rasped. "M-Morgan . . . ?"

"Take it easy," Frank told him, leaning close so that Claiborne could hear him over the roar of the flames. Both of them were baking. They had to get farther away from the fire.

Several of the miners ran up, wincing and grimacing from the heat. Frank knew it was going to hurt Claiborne even worse, but he had no choice except to order, "Pick him up! We'll carry him back to the barracks!"

A couple of men got Claiborne's legs. Frank and the other miner took his shoulders. Frank tried to be careful of the broken arm, but there was only so much he could do.

Claiborne moaned as the men lifted him and moaned again as they started to carry him off.

Frank was glad to see that some of the miners had gotten buckets and were using water from the creek to douse the roofs and walls of the other buildings. As green as everything was at this time of year, he wasn't too worried about the fire getting out of control, but he didn't want it spreading to the barracks and the storage buildings. He wasn't certain where the blasting powder was kept, but he sure didn't want any stray sparks getting close to it.

As they took Claiborne closer to the barracks, Frank spotted one of the supply wagons sitting there and said, "Hold on. Let's go ahead and put him in the wagon instead. He'll have to be taken to town to have that busted arm tended to, and we may have some other men who need medical attention."

"There are some who need buryin'," one of the grim-faced miners said.

Frank nodded. "I know, but Claude Langley can take care of that later." He called one of the other men over and told him to fetch some blankets from the barracks and spread them in the back of the wagon.

As they were placing Claiborne in the wagon, he came to again long enough to say, "Frank?"

"I'm right here," Frank told him.

"The . . . the mill . . . ?"

"Don't worry about that right now. We'll tend to it. Just take it easy, Garrett. You've got a broken arm, and you may have some other injuries. We'll be taking you to town in a few minutes."

"The men . . . ?"

"Anybody who needs help, we'll see to it," Frank assured him.

Claiborne's eyes closed and a long sigh came from him,

and for a second Frank thought the engineer had just died. But Claiborne's chest still rose and fell. He had just passed out again.

Frank grabbed the arm of one of the miners who wasn't hurt at all, just shaken up, and said, "You're in charge. Gather up all the men who are injured badly enough to need a doctor and put them in the wagon. Then you and a couple of other men take the wagon and head for Buckskin. Make sure you're armed, just in case you run into trouble along the way. Everybody else needs to stay here and keep that fire under control."

The miner nodded. "What are you gonna do, Marshal?"

Frank's eyes narrowed in anger. "I'm going to find out who's responsible for this."

As Frank, Stormy, and Dog hurried back toward the scene of the gunfight at the creek, Frank wished he had asked the man he'd knocked out who had hired him and the other three to plant that dynamite, before walloping the son of a bitch. But at the time, he had figured it was more important to find out where the bomb had been hidden so he could still try to stop it from going off.

That hadn't worked out, but Frank was willing to bet that he could still get the prisoner to talk. All he'd have to do was threaten to turn Dog loose on him.

As he approached the spot, letting his instincts guide him back to it, it occurred to him that the man might have regained consciousness and fled, in which case Frank probably would have to wait until morning to try tracking him.

The fella might be waiting to ambush him too, Frank thought, so he said in a low voice, "Dog. Find!"

Dog took off into the darkness. Frank knew that if the saboteur was hidden somewhere, waiting to bushwhack him, Dog would find him and spoil that plan. Frank reined in and waited for Dog to return.

He didn't have to wait long. Dog came loping out of the shadows a few minutes later. He let out a whine, then turned, ran off a few feet, and stopped, looking back over his shoulder at his trail partners.

"Want me to follow you, eh?" Frank nudged Stormy's flanks with his boot heels and sent the Appaloosa forward at a walk.

Frank followed Dog a couple of hundred yards to the creek. He hadn't followed the stream all the way from the mine because of the way it twisted and looped around. Faster to cut across country. As Frank reached the creek, he saw the dark shape still leaning against the bank.

"Must've hit the fella harder than I thought for him to still be out cold," he muttered to himself as he dismounted. Drawing his gun, he approached the saboteur with care.

Frank's nerves prickled, and the hairs on the back of his neck stood up. His gut told him that something was wrong. Keeping the gun trained on the man, he stepped out into the shallow stream and kicked his foot.

"Wake up, mister."

The man didn't budge. His head hung forward on his chest, motionless.

Frank reached into his pocket and found the little tin box where he kept matches. One-handed, he shook one loose from the box and put the wooden shaft between his teeth while he tucked the box away again. Then he took the match in his left hand again and used his thumbnail to snap it into life.

"Son of a *bitch*," Frank said as the glare from the match revealed a huge crimson stain on the front of the man's shirt. Blood appeared to have flooded down from his throat. That could mean only one thing.

Frank pouched his iron and reached forward with his right hand to grasp the man's hair. He jerked the man's head back. In the light from the match, Frank saw the gaping wound in the saboteur's throat. It looked like someone had taken a bowie knife or a similar weapon to him and nearly sliced his head clean off.

Remembering what the man had said about the guards at the Crown Royal having their throats cut, Frank thought this hombre's death was pretty appropriate. He still wished it hadn't happened, though.

The match burned down to Frank's fingers. He shook it out and dropped it in the creek, then lowered the dead man's head. The saboteur wouldn't be answering any questions, and Frank was sure that was exactly why he had been killed. Whoever had hired the men to blow up the stamp mill had come along to check on them and found all of them dead except for this one.

Frank straightened. There was no point in brooding over missed opportunities. He would come out here again in the morning and have a good look around, see if he could find anything that might lead him to the man who had hired the saboteurs.

Gunther Hammersmith. That was the name uppermost in Frank's mind. At the moment, though, he had nothing even faintly resembling proof that would tie Hammersmith to what had happened tonight.

In the meantime, now that he was a lawman, it went against the grain for Frank to leave a bunch of corpses littering the countryside. He mounted up and went looking for the dead men's horses, hoping that they hadn't wandered off too far.

He would take the bodies into Buckskin, he thought. Maybe someone there would recognize them.

Frank never did find one of the mounts he was looking for, so one of the other horses had to carry double in the grim procession back to the settlement. It was almost midnight by the time Frank rode into Buckskin, leading the three horses with the dead men lashed facedown over their backs.

The saloons were still lit up and doing some business. So were the doctor's office and Claude Langley's undertaking parlor. Frank wanted to check on Garrett Claiborne and the other injured men, but he figured it would be best to drop off the corpses with Langley first.

He rode around back, where a lantern was burning. Langley was hammering coffins together in the work area behind the building. He looked up as Frank came around the corner leading the three horses with their grisly burdens.

"More work, eh?" the little Virginian said.

"That's right. You're going to wind up the richest man in town, Claude."

"Who are these?"

"The men who blew up the stamp mill at the Crown Royal," Frank answered.

Langley nodded. "I heard about it, of course. That fellow Claiborne and several of the other men are over at the doctor's office. The men who brought them in stopped by and told me that they would be returning later with the bodies of the miners who were killed in the explosion."

Frank jerked a thumb at the dead saboteurs. "Need a hand with these?"

Langley reached for the reins and said, "No, I can

handle them. Roy's inside. I'll call him to help me get them off their horses."

Frank handed over the reins and turned Stormy around. He rode at an angle across the street toward the doctor's office. All the windows in the building glowed yellow with lamplight.

"Stay," Frank said to Dog as he dismounted and looped Stormy's reins around the hitch rail. He stepped to the door and didn't bother knocking, just opened it and went inside.

He had met Dr. William Garland briefly when the man came to Buckskin and hung out his shingle, but hadn't spent any great amount of time with the medico. Garland was young, probably no more than thirty, and slightly built with a shock of brown hair, a thin face, and intense brown eyes. When Frank came in, he was winding a bandage around the arm of a shirtless miner. The miner also had bandages around his torso.

Several other men sat around the doctor's front room, all of them sporting bandages and taped-on plasters in various places. Frank didn't see Garrett Claiborne among them.

"Hello, Doctor," he said.

Garland glanced up from his work. "Marshal Morgan," he said. "I understand you were there when these men were injured."

"That's right."

"The way they described that explosion, I'm surprised there weren't more serious injuries . . . and more fatalities."

"Where's Garrett Claiborne? How's he doing?"

Garland leaned his head toward the door into another room. "He's in bed in there. I've given him medication to ease his pain and help him rest."

"How bad is he hurt?"

"Well, if you saw him, you know his left arm is broken."

Frank nodded. "Yeah, that was pretty obvious."

"He has burns on the back of his neck from the explosion itself and in other places on his back because his clothes were set on fire. None of those are too bad, though. He has at least one cracked rib. I can't be certain yet if there are any other internal injuries. I'm hopeful that there's not."

"What about the others who were hurt bad?"

"I have four beds for patients," Garland said, "and they're all full. I'm pretty sure that one of the men has a fractured skull. I don't know if he'll pull through. He hasn't regained consciousness, and he may not. He's the worst of the lot, though. One of the other men has a broken leg, the other one a dislocated shoulder and a possible broken ankle. They'll be laid up for a while."

"I sure appreciate what you're doing for them."

Garland gave Frank a thin smile. "That's why I came to Buckskin, to help the sick and injured."

"Can I see Claiborne?"

"Yes, but I don't know if he'll be awake enough to talk to you."

Frank went into the other room and stood beside the bed where Garrett Claiborne lay. A single lamp burned in here, and it was turned low. But there was enough light for Frank to see how pale and drawn the engineer's face was.

"Claiborne," he said. "Garrett, can you hear me?"

After a second, Claiborne's eyes flickered open. He seemed to have trouble focusing on Frank, who remembered what Dr. Garland had said about giving him something for the pain. Laudanum, more than likely, which meant Claiborne's brain would be pretty foggy.

"F-Frank . . ." Claiborne whispered.

"You're at the doctor's in Buckskin," Frank said. "You'll be well taken care of. Don't worry about a thing."

"The . . . mine. The stamp mill . . ."

"It's gone," Frank said, "but we'll rebuild it, better than before."

"Mister . . . Browning . . . will be . . . upset . . . disappointed in . . . me . . ."

"Not hardly. This wasn't your fault, Garrett. If anybody's to blame, it's me for not taking the threat seriously enough."

But that wasn't really true either, Frank thought. The only people really to blame for such evil destruction were the ones who had carried it out—and the one who had paid to have it done.

Hammersmith. The name rang in Frank's head again.

"Mister . . . Browning . . ." Claiborne began.

"Let me worry about him," Frank said. "I'll ride to Virginia City and wire Conrad to let him know what happened."

Even in his drugged state, Claiborne frowned. "C-Conrad . . . ?" he said.

"Yeah. He's my son. You didn't know it, Garrett, but you've been working for me, too."

"Well . . . I'll be . . . damned."

Frank doubted that. The men who were responsible for what had happened tonight were the ones who would be damned. In fact, his bullets had already sent some of them to hell.

But he wasn't finished yet. Not by a long shot.

Chapter 19

"Hold it right there," the guard said in a low, menacing voice from the trees. His tone made it clear that he had the rider approaching the Alhambra Mine covered, probably with a rifle.

But that tone changed right away as he continued. "Oh, sorry, Boss, I didn't realize it was you. Didn't know you'd ridden out earlier."

"It's all right," Gunther Hammersmith said from the back of his horse. "Everything quiet around here?"

"Yeah," the sentry answered. "Well, I guess so. I heard some shots in the distance a while back, and then what sounded like the biggest clap of thunder I ever heard. Couldn't have been thunder, though. The sky's clear tonight. If I didn't know better, I'd say that somebody was doin' some nighttime blastin' at one of those other mines."

"Maybe that's what it was," Hammersmith said. He lifted the reins and heeled his horse into motion. "Stay alert."

"You can damn sure count on it," the sentry promised as Hammersmith rode past, heading for the stamp mill and the office.

When Hammersmith reached the office, he dismounted and tied his mount to a hitching post. He would unsaddle and tend to the horse later. Right now, he needed a drink.

He went into the office and lit the lamp on his desk. A bottle and a glass were inside one of the drawers. Hammersmith opened the drawer, looked into it for a moment, and then lifted out the bottle, leaving the glass where it was. Sometimes a man didn't want to bother with niceties, and this was one of those occasions.

He lifted the bottle to his mouth, tilted his head back, and swallowed a long, healthy slug of the whiskey. It burned all the way down his throat, a cleansing, purifying fieriness, and then kindled a warm glow in his belly. As he lowered the bottle and sank into the chair behind the desk, that warmth began to spread through his body, counteracting the chill of the blood that ran through his veins.

In his life, Gunther Hammersmith had killed four men with his fists, and he had done for another one with an ax handle, crushing the gent's skull with one blow. All of those deaths had occurred during fights. Maybe not *fair* fights, mind you, since Hammersmith knew he was bigger and stronger than most men he would ever encounter. But at least the men he'd been battling with had had a chance to strike a blow in return. Because of that, he had never lost a minute's sleep over what happened to those men.

Tonight was different. That sorry son of a bitch tonight was in too bad a shape to fight back. He'd been mauled by Morgan's wolf, or whatever it was, and the marshal had also clouted him over the head with a six-gun. Perry was hurt, and he thought that Hammersmith had come to help him.

It hadn't taken him long to figure out otherwise. Then he had begged and whimpered and pleaded for his life.

Hammersmith knocked back another drink of whiskey, then set the bottle on the desk and reached for a leather sheath on his belt, just behind his right hip. He pulled out the heavy, long-bladed knife and laid it on the desk next to the whiskey bottle. The blade was clean; Hammersmith had used Perry's shirt to wipe off all the blood. It glittered in the lamplight, cold and hard and deadly-looking.

Tonight was the first time Hammersmith had ever killed anyone with a knife, the first time he had killed somebody in cold blood, without the heat of combat to mitigate the violence. But Perry had to die. That bastard Morgan had stuck his nose in and knew that the four men had been hired to blow up the stamp mill at the Crown Royal. But Morgan didn't know *who* had hired them; Hammersmith had made certain of that before he cut Perry's throat.

It would have been a lot simpler if Morgan had gone ahead and killed all four of the saboteurs. The fact that he had left Perry alive told Hammersmith that Morgan intended to come back and ask the man more questions, after failing to prevent the explosion. Hammersmith couldn't allow that.

He had thought about bringing Perry back to the Alhambra with him. But if he had done that, some of the miners might have seen him, and as chewed up as Perry was, they would have remembered. Not only that, but Morgan had gotten a look at Perry and might go around describing him. Somebody could have recalled seeing Hammersmith helping an injured man who fit that description.

Hammersmith had been careful not to meet with Perry and the other three hired gunmen where anybody could see them. There was nothing to connect him to the four men. With Perry dead, there was nobody to testify, no evidence that Hammersmith had anything in the world to do with the blast at the Crown Royal. Once Hammersmith had figured that out, there was no real question about what he had to do.

Other than the fact that he had never before gotten his arm around a man's neck, jerked his head up, and pulled a knife across his throat, cutting deep so that the blood shot out like a black fountain in the shadows.

Hammersmith took another drink to steady his nerves. Munro wanted production slowed down at the other mines, by whatever means necessary. He didn't care about the details, just the results.

Well, tonight's action would bring production at the Crown Royal to a grinding halt. Without the stamp mill, they couldn't process the ore, and there was no telling how many men had been killed in the explosion. They could still ship out the raw ore, but that was a lot slower and less lucrative.

Now if something could happen to cause problems for the Lucky Lizard too, Munro would be happy. Or as happy as he ever got, Hammersmith amended. The man was driven, filled with a ruthless bitterness. Hammersmith wondered how much of that came from being married to a woman like Mrs. Munro, a beautiful woman so much younger than him, who probably wasn't satisfied by him and would therefore turn elsewhere for her pleasure. . . .

To a man like Gunther Hammersmith.

A smile spread across Hammersmith's rugged features. He took another long pull on the bottle, but the attack of nerves he had experienced earlier had been eased by thoughts of Jessica Munro. She would be enough to make a man forget anything he had done in the past. . . .

Even cold-blooded murder.

All Hammersmith had to do was bide his time.

As Frank had told Garrett Claiborne he would do, he rode to Virginia City the next day and sent a telegram to

Conrad to let him know what had happened. He wired his own lawyers in Denver and San Francisco too, to let them know that he was throwing his considerable financial resources behind the Crown Royal Mine near Buckskin, Nevada. Some minor sabotage was one thing; this attack on the mine was an act of war as far as Frank was concerned. Hammersmith and Munro had made this personal.

Frank stayed in Virginia City for several hours, burning up the telegraph wires. When he started back to Buckskin that afternoon, he brought with him his son's assurances that new equipment for the stamp mill would be on its way to the Crown Royal as soon as Conrad could arrange to have it freighted out there. He would send some professional armed guards to beef up the mine's security too.

In the meantime, Frank would see about having the mill rebuilt, so that it would be ready when the new equipment arrived. Conrad had considered having the men who were all right continue to mine the raw ore, but in the end he had decided it would be better for them to devote their efforts to repairing and rebuilding the mill.

Frank was torn between wanting to help out at the mine and taking care of his duties as the marshal of Buckskin. He had promised Tip Woodford and the other citizens that he would enforce the law, and he couldn't do that if he was out at the Crown Royal all the time. He couldn't dump all the responsibility for law and order in the settlement on Catamount Jack and Clint Farnum. He would talk to Claiborne and get his advice on which of the men might be able to handle the job of temporary superintendent.

It was dusk when he reached Buckskin. His empty belly reminded him that he hadn't eaten anything since the middle of the day, and he was tempted to stop at the café and let Lauren, Ginnie, and Becky feed him a good supper.

But he wanted to check on Claiborne and the other injured miners, so he headed for Dr. Garland's house instead.

Frank reined in and said, "Hell," as he recognized the wagon parked in front of the doctor's place. It belonged to Claude Langley. As he watched, Langley and Roy, the undertaker's assistant, emerged from the house carrying a blanket-wrapped figure. Frank had ridden Goldy to Virginia City, since Stormy had had the hard run the night before. Now he walked the horse over to the wagon and asked, "Who are you picking up, Claude?"

"Oh, howdy, Marshal," Langley greeted him. As they placed the body in the back of the wagon, the undertaker went on. "This is that poor fella who had the fractured skull. Lambert, his name was. Dr. Garland said he passed away a little while ago without ever regaining consciousness."

That was one more mark against the man or men responsible for last night's carnage, Frank thought. One more score to settle.

He dismounted and tied Goldy at the hitch rail while the wagon rattled off toward Langley's place. When Frank went inside, he found Dr. Garland at a desk in the front room, writing out some notes.

"I talked to Claude Langley outside," Frank said as the physician glanced up from his work.

Garland nodded. "Yes, I didn't hold out much hope that poor fellow would pull through, and unfortunately, I was right. He never woke up."

"How are the rest of your patients doing?"

"As well as can be expected." The doctor smiled. "In fact, they have some visitors at the moment, if you want to go in and see for yourself."

"Thanks," Frank said. "I'll do that."

He opened the door to the other room, and stepped in to find Diana Woodford sitting in a ladder-back chair beside

Garrett Claiborne's bed, spooning soup into his mouth from a bowl she held in her other hand. Ginnie Carlson was feeding one of the other patients, the miner with the broken leg, which by now Dr. Garland had enclosed in a plaster cast as he had done with Claiborne's busted arm. Frank took off his hat and nodded to the two women.

"Hello, Marshal," Claiborne said after he swallowed the mouthful of soup. "Were you able to get in touch with Mr. Browning?"

Frank was glad to see Diana taking care of Claiborne. That boded well. He nodded and said, "We exchanged several telegrams, and the upshot is, new equipment for the stamp mill will be on its way in a day or two."

"Excellent! By the time it gets here, we'll have the building rebuilt and waiting for it. I need to get back out to the mine tomorrow to see about starting work—"

"Dr. Garland said you weren't going anywhere for at least a week, Garrett," Diana put in. "Remember, he's not sure you don't have some internal injuries."

"I'm fine, confound it," Claiborne declared. "This arm of mine hurts, but it's nothing I can't put up with."

Frank pointed his Stetson at the mining engineer and said, "You'd better do what the doctor says. It won't do any good for you to go back out there and collapse. There's bound to be somebody on the crew you can trust to supervise the work on the new mill."

Claiborne frowned and looked like he wanted to argue the matter, but then he glanced at Diana and saw the stern expression on her face. He said, "I suppose Ernest Truman could handle the job. He's been an assistant superintendent at other mines before."

"There you go," Frank said. "I'll ride out there tomorrow and tell him what's going on, so he can get started."

Diana said, "All right, now that that's settled, no more

business talk until Garrett's finished this soup. It's getting cold."

Frank smiled and pulled up a chair to sit down. "Go right ahead," he told her.

Diana finished feeding the soup to Claiborne, and then he and Frank talked for several minutes about what would need to be done at the Crown Royal to get the mine operating again as soon as possible. Claiborne agreed with the idea that they should get the stamp mill rebuilt right away, but once that was done, if the new equipment hadn't arrived yet, the men could start stockpiling raw ore to be put through the pulverization and amalgamation process as soon as the mill was running.

Diana looked at Frank and said, "By the way, Marshal, I find it a little odd that you never mentioned you own a considerable interest in the Crown Royal."

Frank's eyes narrowed. He looked at Claiborne, who shrugged his right shoulder. The left one wouldn't move, strapped down the way it was.

"I'm sorry, Marshal. That fact slipped out earlier when Miss Woodford and I were talking."

She turned her gaze back to him. "I thought you said you were going to call me Diana."

"Of course . . . Diana. My apologies to you too."

Frank said, "Don't worry about it where I'm concerned. My connection with the mine isn't a big secret or anything like that. I just happen to have an interest in the Browning Mining Syndicate."

"That makes you and my father competitors."

"Not really. I reckon there's enough silver in these hills to go around."

"Not everyone feels that way," Claiborne said. "Otherwise, we wouldn't have had all that trouble at the mine. Someone's trying to put us out of business, Frank."

"That's what it looks like," Frank agreed with a nod, thinking about Hamish Munro and Gunther Hammersmith. "I've got an idea who it is, too."

"What are you going to do about it?"

"Conrad's sending a passel of men to serve as guards. Once they get here, whoever was responsible for that blast will have a hard time getting up to any more mischief."

"What about the things they've already done?" Claiborne asked. "What about the men who died?"

"There'll be a day of reckoning," Frank said. "You can count on that."

Chapter 20

Claude Langley had propped up the corpses of the four saboteurs in their coffins out in front of the undertaking parlor so that the citizens of Buckskin could come by and take a look at them. That was an accepted, if grisly, practice in frontier towns. Frank had never cared much for the custom, but in this case he put the word out that if anybody recognized the dead men, he wanted to know about it. He still hoped to find something that would tie the men to Hamish Munro, Gunther Hammersmith, or both.

But while a few people recalled seeing the men drinking in some of the saloons, nobody really knew them or had witnessed them talking to Hammersmith or Munro. No one who would admit it anyway.

Frank went up to the hotel to see Munro. He wasn't sure what he would say to the mining magnate, but he wanted Munro to know that he wouldn't rest until he got to the bottom of the explosion that had destroyed the stamp mill at the Crown Royal.

Munro's secretary, Nathan Evers, opened the door of the suite to Frank's knock. "Hello, Marshal," he said. "What can I do for you?"

"I want to talk to your boss," Frank replied. "Is he here?"

"As a matter of fact, he's not. He and Mrs. Munro have taken a drive out to the Alhambra. Mrs. Munro hadn't seen the mine yet, and she wanted to."

Frank nodded. "All right. Say, you haven't gone by Langley's undertaking parlor and had a look at the bodies of those four men who blew up the Crown Royal's stamp mill, have you?"

Evers blanched and said, "Good Lord, no. Why would I want to do a thing like that?"

"I've been asking people around town to see if they recognized any of those men."

"Well, I can tell you the answer to that without looking at them. I never saw them before. I wouldn't associate with ruffians like that. Why would I have any reason to?"

"I don't know," Frank said. "You tell me."

Understanding dawned on Evers. "You think Mr. Munro had something to do with that explosion!"

"He's competing with the folks who own the Crown Royal," Frank said without mentioning that he was one of those folks.

"So is Mr. Woodford," Evers replied. Rather than pale, his face was now flushed with anger. "I don't hear you accusing *him* of engaging in criminal acts."

"That's because I know Tip Woodford," Frank pointed out. "I don't know Munro all that well yet. But he has a reputation as a ruthless man."

Evers gripped the edge of the door, his fingers tightening on it. "I think this conversation is over, Marshal, unless you have some other official business with me."

Frank shook his head. "Nope, no official business. I was just talking, that's all."

"Yes, of course," Evers said in a cold tone that showed he didn't believe Frank at all. He swung the door closed, shutting it with a little more force than was really necessary.

Frank smiled to himself. He didn't know if Evers would report the details of this conversation to Munro, but it seemed likely that he would. That would be just fine with Frank. He wanted Munro to know he was suspicious. If Munro was behind what had happened and viewed Frank as a threat, he might get rattled enough to do something foolish—like coming after Frank next time.

Frank knew that by goading Munro, he was sort of painting a target on his back, but it wouldn't be the first time he had done such a thing. Sometimes, a man had to place himself in a little bit of danger in order to smoke out some varmints.

In fact, he decided he didn't want to count on Evers to do the job for him. After going by the marshal's office to let Catamount Jack know that he would be gone for a while, he went to the livery stable, saddled up Stormy, and headed for the Alhambra Mine with Dog trotting along beside him.

Gunther Hammersmith was surprised to hear the clatter of wheels outside his office at the mine. He stood up and went to the door, which stood open to let in some breeze along with the sound of the donkey engine that pulled the ore carts up the shaft and out of the mine. The miners were bringing out more ore all the time, and it looked like re-opening the Alhambra was going to turn out to be a lucrative proposition.

One of the last things Hammersmith expected to see rolling up to the office was that damned blue stagecoach of Munro's. But that's what rocked to a halt in front of the building, with the usual driver and bodyguard on the box.

The men climbed down, and the guard opened the door. Hamish Munro climbed out, followed by his wife.

Hammersmith's breath caught in his throat a little at the sight of Jessica Munro. She had that effect on him every time he saw her.

Hammersmith was aware that he was wearing rough work clothes, with the sleeves of his shirt rolled up over brawny forearms. He rolled them down as Munro took his wife's arm and brought her to the foot of the steps that led up to the office.

"Good morning, Gunther," he said with an unusually pleasant expression on his face. Munro usually looked like he had just bitten into something that had gone bad.

"Uh, morning, sir." Hammersmith nodded to Jessica. "Ma'am."

"My wife wanted to see the mine," Munro explained, "and I'd like to look over the assay reports. I assume they're in the office?"

"Yes, sir, of course. And they're up to date too."

Munro nodded. "Fine. I'll take a look at them while you show Mrs. Munro around. All right?"

It was unusual for Munro to ask if something was all right. Mostly, he just barked orders and expected everybody to go along with them without any hesitation.

Hammersmith looked at Jessica, saw the smile she gave him, and said, "Yes, sir, that'd be just fine. The reports are on my desk."

"I'll find them," Munro said as he started up the steps. Hammersmith reached back inside the door to snag an old slouch hat from a nail driven into the wall. He put it on as he waited for Munro to go into the office. Then he went down the steps to join Mrs. Munro.

He didn't offer to take her arm. That would have been too forward, he thought, especially out here in the open like that, with the stagecoach driver and the guard loung-ing near the coach as they rolled quirlies. Instead, he pointed toward the mouth of the shaft and asked, "Do you mind walking, ma'am?"

"Not at all," Jessica replied. "It's a beautiful day."

Not half as beautiful as you.

He kept that thought to himself as he led her over to the shaft, pointing out the stamp mill, the barracks for the miners, and the storage buildings as he did so.

"It looks like you have everything you need here," she commented.

"Well, we have to bring supplies out from town, of course. But other than that, we're pretty self-sufficient."

She wore a green traveling outfit and hat today, and Hammersmith wondered just how many different outfits she had brought with her to Buckskin. He didn't think he had seen her in the same one twice.

When they reached the mine shaft, she hesitated, look-ing a little nervous as she said, "Are you sure it's safe to go in there?"

"There are a couple of dozen men down there right now, working," he told her. "They wouldn't be there if they didn't think it was safe."

Actually, that was stretching the truth a mite. The men were down there because they wanted the wages they were being paid—and because they feared the big, iron-hard fists of Gunther Hammersmith. They knew he wouldn't take it kindly if any of them tried to quit without a good reason. And as far as Hammersmith was concerned, there *weren't* any reasons good enough.

Following the rails that the ore carts used, Hammer-smith and Jessica walked down the steps that had been cut into the steeply inclined plane of the entrance shaft. That gave Hammersmith an excuse to take her arm. He had to steady her so she wouldn't fall. It was just coincidence that his elbow nudged the warm softness of her breast as he linked his arm with hers.

Their way was lit by oil lanterns hung on the walls of the shaft at regular intervals. Many of the sturdy shoring timbers on the sides and ceiling of the shaft were new. Hammersmith pointed them out to Jessica and said, "See? Nothing to worry about."

"Not for you, perhaps, Mr. Hammersmith, but I've never been underground before."

Hammersmith couldn't contain his surprise. "What, you're married to Mr. Munro and you've never seen one of his mines before?"

"I was just never interested in them . . . until now." She looked up at him and smiled as she said it.

Hammersmith felt his heart speed up. "Well, I won't let anything happen to you, you can count on that. I'd sacrifice my own life to keep you safe, ma'am."

"Why, Mr. Hammersmith, how gallant of you."

And she squeezed his arm, which meant that his elbow pressed against her breast again.

They descended several hundred feet to the main drift, the tunnel that followed the vein of silver through the mountain. Hammersmith knew that it stretched for more than a mile under the earth. Several crosscut tunnels intersected it; the crosscuts provided ventilation and access to smaller drifts that paralleled the main tunnel. There were also some vertical shafts leading to lower levels.

"You mean the mine goes even lower?" Jessica asked when he pointed out the vertical shafts to her.

"That's right. Some mines where I've worked go down several thousand feet."

She looked up at the ceiling, no doubt thinking of the tons of rock and dirt perched there over her head, and

Hammersmith felt a shiver go through her. "I can't imagine such a thing," she murmured. "We're already so deep that it's frightening."

"Nothing to be scared of," he assured her. "As long as you take the right precautions, mines like this are perfectly safe."

"But things sometimes go wrong, don't they? There are cave-ins and things like that?"

Hammersmith shrugged. "Most problems are caused by carelessness. I don't allow my men to get careless. They know they'll be in for trouble if they do."

"From a cave-in, you mean?"

Hammersmith laughed. "From me. I reckon most of them would rather have to deal with a cave-in than face me when I'm mad at them."

"You *are* a rugged man, Mr. Hammersmith."

"You can call me Gunther if you want," he ventured.

"All right . . . Gunther."

She didn't invite him to call her Jessica, and while he noticed that, he didn't really care. As long as he got to walk along beside her and touch her now and then, it didn't matter to him what he called her.

There was quite a bit of noise underground. Picks rang against the walls; steam-powered drills known as widow-makers chattered as they gouged holes in the rock so that dynamite could be planted in them; men shouted back and forth to each other. In some mines, the rock was balanced so precariously that a loud noise could set off a cave-in, meaning that the hard, dangerous work of shoring up had to be completed before the real job of taking the ore out could begin. In the Alhambra, that had already been done. An earthquake or a badly placed blast might bring the place down, but short of those things, it was safe down here, as Hammersmith had explained to Mrs. Munro.

He didn't try to take Jessica all through the place. That would have taken too long and exhausted her. He settled for showing her the general layout and letting her watch some of the men at work for a few minutes. At this level, they still wore their grimy, dust-covered shirts. Lower down in the earth, where the temperature rose, the miners often stripped their shirts off and worked bare-chested. Hammersmith recalled doing that himself, when he was a young man and too stupid to do anything except swing a pick all day long. He had learned a great deal since then.

Even here, it was warmer than on the surface, and Jessica's face shone in the lantern light as a fine layer of perspiration appeared on her skin. "My goodness," she said as she fanned herself with a hand, "if you dig down far enough, do you reach Hades itself?"

Hammersmith laughed and said, "I wouldn't be surprised. That's probably how folks got the idea that Hell's somewhere under the earth. Once you get past the upper level, where it's cooler, the deeper you go, the hotter it gets. Smells a little like brimstone too."

"I think I'm ready to go back out and get some fresh air."

"Sure. You've seen all there really is to see anyway."

They started back up, the light from the mouth of the shaft growing brighter as they climbed. Before they reached it and stepped back out into the sunshine, Jessica stopped and said, "Gunther, thank you for showing me around."

"Oh, it was my pleasure," he said without hesitation, meaning every word of it.

"You're just being polite. I'm sure you couldn't have enjoyed getting stuck with your boss's wife like this."

He shook his head. "You've got that all wrong, ma'am. I didn't mind a bit, truly. Fact is, I, uh, really enjoyed spending the time with you."

"Really?" She smiled up at him. "Why, that's such a nice thing to say, Mr. Hammersmith . . . I mean, Gunther."

He had never liked his name all that much. It sounded coarse and harsh to him. But when she spoke it, in that honeyed voice of hers . . . well, that was different. He looked down at her, realizing just how close she was standing to him. Nobody was around; all the men were down at the bottom of the shaft. And she had this look on her lovely face, like she expected him to do something. . . .

What the hell.

He pulled her into his arms and brought his mouth down on hers in a hard, urgent kiss.

Chapter 21

The same sort of racket came from the Alhambra that had come from the Crown Royal until the explosion a couple of nights earlier. The donkey engines, the compressor that powered the steam drills down in the mine, the shuddering thumps of the stamp mill in action . . .

A mine was a noisy place, and one that stunk a mite too, Frank thought as he rode up. The frontier had been a lot more peaceful before all this newfangled machinery came along, starting with the railroad. Frank was old enough to remember what it had been like before. He could only imagine the changes that some of the real old-timers, like Catamount Jack, had seen in their lifetimes.

Frank brought Stormy to a halt and dismounted in front of the building where the office was located. The place had been cleaned up and repaired a lot since that day he and Garrett Claiborne had stopped by here and almost gotten themselves gunned down for their trouble. At least, Hammersmith wasn't taking potshots anymore at anybody who happened to come riding along.

Hamish Munro's private stagecoach was parked in front of the building. His guard and driver sat on the edge of the porch, smoking. The guard had his rifle across his lap, and his eyes followed Frank closely.

"What do you want, Marshal?" he asked.

"I'm looking for your boss," Frank replied. "Is he inside?"

Before the guard could answer, the door of the office opened and Hamish Munro stepped out. "What do you want, Marshal?" the mining magnate demanded.

"Hammersmith around?"

"I thought I heard you say you were looking for me."

Frank nodded. "Oh, I was. I just thought I'd talk to both of you together, save a little time that way."

"Hammersmith is tending to some chores I assigned to him," Munro said. "Anything you have to say, you can say it to me. If I deem it worthwhile of his time, I'll pass it along to him."

"All right then, if that's the way you want it." Frank hooked his thumbs in his belt and asked, "Have you had any trouble out here at the mine?"

"What sort of trouble?"

"I reckon you heard about what happened at the Crown Royal a couple of nights ago."

Munro pursed his lips. "Yes, of course. A terrible accident. Sorry for the loss of life. But nothing like that has happened here."

Frank didn't think Munro sounded the least bit sorry. He said, "I want you to know, I'm going to find out who was responsible for that blast and bring them to justice."

"I thought you killed the four men who set that dynamite," Munro said with a frown.

"I shot three of them when they threw down on me. I reckon the fourth one was killed by whoever hired them, so that he couldn't answer any questions about who was really to blame for what happened."

Munro shook his head and scowled. "I wouldn't know anything about that."

"Didn't say you would," Frank pointed out. "All I'm saying is that I'm going to continue to investigate until I get to the bottom of that business, and when I do, whoever came up with the idea of blowing up the Crown Royal's stamp mill is going to be mighty sorry."

In a harsh, angry voice, Munro asked, "Why are you telling me this?"

Frank shrugged. "So you'll know that if anything suspicious happens around your mine, I'll look into it the same way. If you have any trouble, just let me know and I'll see what I can do."

Munro's bushy, reddish-gray eyebrows lowered even more, as Frank's reply appeared to confuse him. "All right," he said. "Is that all?"

"You're sure nothing's happened out here that you want to report?"

"I'm certain," Munro snapped.

Frank reached for Stormy's reins. "I reckon I'll be getting back to town then." He swung up into the saddle. "Come on, Dog."

He turned the Appaloosa and rode away. Without looking over his shoulder, he felt Munro's eyes on him anyway, gazing after him with what had to be a mixture of hatred, anger, and puzzlement. Munro had been ready to take offense when he thought that Frank was about to accuse him of being involved with the explosion at the Crown Royal, but Frank's sudden change of tactic had confused him.

That was the idea. It was always better to keep an enemy off balance—and Frank was still convinced that Munro was the enemy. He had put the man on notice that he was going to continue investigating that dynamite blast until he found the true culprits. Maybe that would spook Munro into doing something rash, like trying to have him killed.

Frank hoped that Munro *would* send a bushwhacker after him. He would take his chances, willing to run the risk because he was confident that if he could get his hands on a prisoner, he could get a confession implicating Munro or Hammersmith—or both of them.

Then, as he had promised Munro, he would see to it that they got what was coming to them.

Hammersmith fully expected Jessica to pull away from him, to slap him across the face, to run screaming for her husband. He figured it would be worth losing his job to taste the sweetness of her mouth and feel the warmth of her body in his arms.

She did none of those things.

Instead, she returned the kiss with the same passionate intensity that Hammersmith put into it.

When she finally took her lips away from his after a long, delicious moment, she said in a half whisper, "My goodness, Gunther, I was beginning to think you were *never* going to get around to that."

He couldn't believe what he was hearing. "You . . . you wanted me to kiss you?"

"Of course. What girl *wouldn't* want to be kissed by a big, strong, handsome man like you?"

A tiny voice in the back of his head warned him that she had to be flattering him like that for a reason. Big and strong he was, sure enough, but handsome? No one had ever accused him of that.

Logic was one thing, though, and the incredible feeling he had inside him at this moment was something else entirely. Maybe she had some unknown motive for playing up to him. He didn't care. All he knew was that she hadn't objected when he kissed her, so he clutched her to him and did it again.

This kiss was just as potent as the first one, but when it ended she put both hands against his broad, muscular chest and said, "That's enough now. You don't want to muss me up too much, or Mr. Munro is liable to notice. I don't want him to know that I've been up to any mischief."

"Neither do I," Hammersmith agreed. "I don't want to cause any trouble for you."

"Then we'll just pretend this little incident never happened. . . ."

His heart sank.

"Until we get a chance to do it again," she went on as she reached up to rest a gloved hand against his cheek. "And maybe more."

Hammersmith's excitement rose again. "You mean it?"

"Gunther, honey, I never say anything I don't mean."

With that statement to give him hope, Hammersmith said, "I guess we'd better get back to the office."

"Lead the way," Jessica said with her sweet smile.

Hammersmith took her the rest of the way out of the shaft, letting go of her arm as they emerged into the sunlight. As they started toward the office, he spotted a man riding away. He couldn't be sure, but he thought the man on horseback was Frank Morgan.

"What the hell?" he muttered.

"Is there a problem?" Jessica asked.

"Nothing I can't handle," he answered. He didn't want her to see how much the idea of Morgan poking around the Alhambra bothered him. He had been able to put aside in his mind that killing from a couple of nights earlier, but he didn't want Morgan stirring things up again.

When they reached the office, Hamish Munro was waiting

on the porch. He looked distracted by something, but he put a smile on his face and asked Jessica, "Did you enjoy your look around the mine, my dear?"

"Very much," she replied. "Mr. Hammersmith was quite informative about what was going on down there, and he watched out for my safety every step of the way."

Munro grunted. "That's good." He turned his attention to the superintendent. "Hammersmith, I have to talk to you—"

"I'm really a little tired, Hamish," Jessica broke in. "I'd like to go inside the office to sit down and rest for a while before we start back to town, if that's all right."

"Of course," Munro said. He came down the steps to take her arm and help her up. "You go right on inside. The chair behind the desk isn't all that comfortable—"

"I'm sure it'll be fine, dear."

Munro pointed a finger at Hammersmith and ordered, "Wait right there."

Hammersmith did so, and then after a moment, when Munro came back out of the office, the owner of the Alhambra said, "Let's walk over toward the shaft."

The guard asked, "You want me and Billy to come with you, Mr. Munro?"

"No, you can stay here. I'm in no danger here at the mine."

Munro stalked off toward the shaft. Hammersmith went with him, and as soon as they were out of earshot of the men at the office, he asked in a low voice, "Was that Morgan I saw riding off?"

"It certainly was."

"What did that bastard want?"

"He believes that you and I are responsible for that explosion at the Crown Royal two nights ago."

"Damn it!" Hammersmith burst out. "How could he know about—"

Munro lifted a hand and made a curt gesture to stop him. "*I* don't know anything about how that explosion happened, Hammersmith, and I want to keep it that way. You'd do well to remember that."

"Yes, sir," Hammersmith said. Munro was touchy about things like that and always had been. He would hint around about what he wanted accomplished, but he never wanted to know any of the details of how the dirty work got done. Hammersmith supposed that was Munro's way of protecting his own ass. Munro wanted to be able to swear in court, if it ever came down to it, that he had no guilty knowledge of anything.

That seemed a little cowardly to Hammersmith, but Munro was the one with the money and power. He was the one who made the rules.

"If Morgan's not careful, something's liable to happen to him," Hammersmith said. "Some folks don't like it when a lawman starts poking around in their affairs."

He phrased the comments with care, thinking that this was a damned waste of time. It would be a lot easier if he could just come right out and ask Munro if he wanted the marshal killed.

Munro would balk at that, though, so Hammersmith talked around the idea instead.

After frowning in thought for a moment, Munro said, "I think that's exactly what Morgan hopes will happen. He'd like to stir up a hornet's nest so that someone will come after him. The wise thing to do would be to not give the marshal what he wants."

"It would?" Hammersmith asked, getting a little confused now himself. He wanted to make sure he was clear on what Munro wanted.

"That's right. Morgan can investigate all he wants to. He's not going to find out anything. The men who planted that dynamite at the Crown Royal are all dead, aren't they?"

"Yeah," Hammersmith said, his voice heavy. "They're all dead."

"So if anyone else *was* involved, Morgan won't be able to discover it. He's wasting his time. Doesn't it seem that way to you?"

Hammersmith knew what Munro was asking. He wanted to know if there was anything to tie the four dead men to either of them. Hammersmith had taken great care to insure that there wasn't.

"Yeah, he's wasting his time."

Munro nodded. "Good. We can move on to other things. That terrible accident at the Crown Royal has given us a definite advantage for a while. Our only real competition now is Woodford's Lucky Lizard Mine."

"Something might happen there too," Hammersmith said, knowing that Munro would take his meaning correctly.

"Not an explosion, though. That would be an incredible coincidence. Some people might not believe that it *was* a coincidence."

"What do you reckon might cause the most problems for them?"

Munro smiled. "It would be very unfortunate for Woodford if he was hit with the bane of all mining men: labor troubles. A miners' strike would shut down the Lucky Lizard for no telling how long."

Hammersmith rubbed his heavy jaw in thought. "I don't think Woodford has to worry too much about that," he said after a few seconds. "From what I hear, he treats the fellas who work for him pretty good."

"Well, you never know. All it takes is one or two hotheads to stir things up. Miners are like sheep, Hammersmith.

They're easily led, and once they get some idea in their head, it's almost impossible to get it out."

"Yeah, maybe. Let me think about it, Boss."

"Don't think too long," Munro snapped. "Every mine I've ever been involved with has been the largest and most successful in its area. Things aren't going to be any different here."

"We're well on our way. I got a feeling the Lucky Lizard's in for a run of bad luck, one way or another." Hammersmith paused, then added, "Did you want to talk about the assay reports?"

"I looked them over," Munro said. "The preliminary tests indicate that with the new methods, the ore will assay out at a satisfactory amount of silver per ton. I think you should go ahead and increase production as much as possible right away."

Hammersmith nodded. "I'll take care of it."

"I've no doubt of that."

It should have made Hammersmith feel better for Munro to express his confidence that way, but for some reason, it didn't. For one thing, only half an hour earlier, Hammersmith had been kissing Munro's wife and running his eager hands over her body. For another, Hammersmith couldn't forget that Munro had things set up so that if anybody ever got in trouble with the law over the things they had been doing, it would be him, Gunther Hammersmith. Munro wasn't that worried about Morgan because the marshal couldn't prove anything against him. It might be a different story where Hammersmith was concerned.

Despite what Munro had said earlier, maybe it was time to start thinking about how some "accident" might befall Frank Morgan. . . .

When they got back to the office, they found Jessica rested and ready for the ride back to Buckskin. She took

Hammersmith's hand in hers and squeezed it as she said, "Thank you again, Mr. Hammersmith. You were an excellent host."

"Always glad to oblige, ma'am," he told her. "Come back and visit the Alhambra any time you want."

"I think one visit will be enough for Jessica," Munro said. "Come along, my dear."

He helped her into the coach and followed her inside. The driver and the guard climbed onto the box, and a moment later the stagecoach was rolling over the dusty trail back to the settlement, a couple of miles away. Hammersmith watched it go, thinking about what Munro had said. He'd been forced to hide his disappointment when Munro decreed that Jessica wouldn't be coming out to the mine anymore. He figured that she would be able to change his mind about that if she wanted to. He hoped she wanted to.

If not, he would just have to find a way to see her in town. Hammersmith's mind was full at the moment, thoughts about various subjects whirling around inside his head. He had to worry about Frank Morgan and come up with a way to foment a miners' strike at the Lucky Lizard.

But uppermost in his thoughts were Jessica Munro and his need to see her again. To hold her in his arms once more and feast on those sweet lips of hers. To experience all the wonders that her sleek, supple body promised.

All the other problems sort of paled beside that, and he was very glad that she had accompanied her husband today.

"You look tired, my dear," Hamish Munro said as they rocked along in the coach.

"I am," Jessica said. "This visit to the mine was interesting, but I'm exhausted now."

"Really?" Munro frowned. "I was hoping that when we got back to the hotel. . . ."

"I'm sorry, Hamish. I'm afraid all I want to do when I get back is soak in a hot tub to get this rock dust off of me, then have a nice long nap."

The look of disappointment on his face was priceless, she thought. He was so easily manipulated. She could dictate his moods according to her whims, jerking him around like a puppet on a string. To the world, he was Hamish Munro, as rich and powerful as a king. But to Jessica he was just another man, powerless in the face of his need for her. He actually thought that she loved him, and as long as he believed that, he would do anything she wanted him to.

She had looked over the assay reports in the office while her husband was off talking to Gunther Hammersmith. They were probably plotting something together, as men liked to do. Jessica didn't care. Let them play their games. She had found out what she wanted to know. She knew how the ore assayed out, and her brain could calculate the income per ton even faster than Munro's could. It was easy to speculate on how much the mine would be worth in the long run.

It had been a productive day in other ways too. Hammersmith had bitten hard on the hook, and now she had him on the line if she needed him. Pulling him in would be no challenge at all. When the time came, with Hammersmith's help, she could make herself a very rich woman indeed. All she had to do was wait for the right moment. . . .

Jessica became aware that Munro was looking at her from the stagecoach's other seat. There was no suspicion in his eyes, only longing.

She smiled at him. She could throw him that bone anyway.

It was all he was going to get.

Chapter 22

Since keeping the corpses of the dead men on display in front of the undertaking parlor didn't seem to be doing any good, Frank told Claude Langley to go ahead and bury them. Frank and Dog had gone over the scene of the gun battle with the men and hadn't found anything to indicate who they had been working for. Riding in the stream the way they had prevented Dog from backtracking them. The man who had slit the throat of the surviving outlaw must have also ridden in the stream, because Frank couldn't find his track either.

Frank's frustration grew over the next few days as it seemed that his visit with Munro wasn't paying any dividends either. That attempt on his life he had halfway expected didn't happen. In fact, things in Buckskin were pretty peaceful again. The rush of newcomers into town finally seemed to be slowing down. The settlement was still crowded, and there were drunken brawls in the saloons, fights over poker games and women, and the occasional robbery. But nothing happened that Frank couldn't take care of easily with help from Catamount Jack and Clint Farnum.

The new deputy seemed to be settling right in. He had

made some friends, including Becky Humphries, who seemed to have given up her interest in Garrett Claiborne now that Diana was spending so much time with the mining engineer. Frank went by Dr. Garland's place every day, and knew that Claiborne was getting more and more restless. He was anxious to get back out to the Crown Royal and go to work, even though the new equipment for the stamp mill hadn't arrived yet. There was still rebuilding work to do, and Claiborne wanted to supervise it. The doctor's orders were firm, though. Claiborne still had some more recuperating to do.

Frank was coming out of Leo Benjamin's store one morning, carrying a box of .45 cartridges he had just picked up, when he saw Tip Woodford hurrying toward him. The mayor's urgent manner, plus the worried look on his face, told Frank that Buckskin's peaceful respite was probably over.

"What's wrong, Tip?" Frank asked.

"Got some trouble out at the Lucky Lizard," Tip replied. "The fellas are sayin' that I ain't treatin' 'em right."

Frank frowned in surprise. "You're talking about the men who work in the mine?"

Tip nodded. "Yeah."

"That's crazy. You pay them fair wages, you do everything you can to make sure the working conditions are safe, you don't expect more than an honest day's work for an honest day's wage."

"Yeah, but that ain't stopped a couple o' the boys from tryin' to get all the rest stirred up and mad at me." Tip pushed his hat back and scratched his head. "To tell you the truth, Frank, I ain't sure I ought to be talkin' to you about this, seein' as you and me are rivals, so to speak."

Frank shook his head. "Diana told you what Claiborne said about me."

"Yeah. You wouldn't expect her to keep somethin' like that a secret, would you?"

"No, I reckon not. But listen to me, Tip. My late wife and my son were the ones who built up that business empire. I had nothing to do with it. For years I was just a drifter, like that nickname somebody hung on me. It was only after my wife died that I inherited a stake in all those holdings, including the Browning Mining Syndicate. I don't have anything to do with the running of it, and I let my lawyers in Denver and San Francisco handle all the money. As far as I'm concerned, my only real job is being the marshal of Buckskin."

"Well, it ain't that I doubt you . . ."

"Good, because I'm not in the habit of lying," Frank said.

Tip nodded, wearing the look of a man who had just made a decision. "All right. In that case, I reckon I done the right thing by comin' to you for help. Can you come out to the mine and have a talk with those fellas?"

"Problem is, I'm not sure how much I can do," Frank said. "The mine's not in my jurisdiction—"

"That didn't stop you from goin' after the sons o' bitches who blew up the Crown Royal," Tip pointed out. "And remember, there's that old offshoot tunnel that runs all the way down here under the office. Since that's in town, I reckon you could say that by extension, the rest o' the mine is too."

Frank chuckled. "That's a little bit of a stretch," he said, "but I can't argue with that reasoning. Anyway, my job is to keep the peace here in town, and if there's unrest at your mine, it could spill over down here any time."

Tip nodded and said, "Yep, that's what I was thinkin' too."

"I'll go out there and see if I can find out what the problem is. You want to come with me?"

Tip rubbed his jaw. "Might be better if you went by yourself. Those boys might come closer to shootin' straight with you if I ain't around."

"Who's the ringleader?"

"There's two of 'em, a couple o' brothers I hired not long ago. Their names are Fowler. Mike and Gib Fowler."

Frank nodded. "I'll see what I can do."

"I'm obliged, Frank. Things have been goin' pretty well. I don't need some new trouble."

"None of us do," Frank said.

He left Tip and headed for Hillman's livery stable. Having two horses had worked out fairly well, since one of them was always fresh and well-rested. Stormy hadn't gotten over his resentment of the fact that sometimes Frank saddled up Goldy and rode out on the other horse, as he did today, but Frank supposed the Appaloosa would get used to it sooner or later.

The Lucky Lizard was the closest of the mines to the settlement, close enough so that the noise from the mill could be heard in Buckskin most of the time. It didn't take long for Frank to ride out there. Tip Woodford served as his own superintendent, but he had several foremen who supervised most of the day-to-day operations. When Frank rode in, he spotted one of the men walking from the stamp mill toward one of the storage buildings and hailed him.

"I'm looking for the Fowler brothers," Frank told the foreman. "Got any idea where I can find them?"

"Mr. Woodford talked to you about the trouble out here, right?" the foreman asked.

Frank nodded.

"Well, Gib Fowler is down in the mine right now, but Mike is over in the barracks, I think. He came off shift just a little while ago."

"You put them on different shifts?"

"Thought it would best," the foreman replied. "The way those two run their mouths, if they were both in the same crew no work would ever get done."

"If they're causing trouble, why doesn't Tip just fire them?"

"I've asked him the same question, Marshal. He says that he can't fire somebody for having an opinion, that it just wouldn't be right. But if you ask me, he ought to boot both of 'em out of here."

The foreman had just brought up a point that bothered Frank. As long as the Fowler brothers were just talking, he didn't see what he could do about them. This was America, where folks had a right to express their opinions, no matter how annoying or upsetting or downright stupid they were.

Frank nodded his thanks and reined Goldy over toward the barracks. The door of the building was open, and as Frank dismounted he heard a loud, angry voice coming from inside.

"If you don't stand up to Woodford, he's just gonna keep takin' advantage of you," the man said. "He ain't ever gonna treat you fair unless you make him do it!"

Frank stepped into the doorway. He saw a wiry man with a bristling red brush of a beard standing in the center of the aisle between the bunks, waving his hands in the air as he talked.

"Just because Woodford's the boss don't mean he's got the right to treat us like animals!"

Half-a-dozen miners were either stretched out or sitting on their bunks, listening to the man. Some of them noticed Frank's entrance and looked past the speaker at him. The man with the red beard noticed that and fell silent, turning toward the door with a suspicious glare on his face.

"Are you Mike Fowler?" Frank asked, even though he was pretty sure he already knew the answer to that question.

"I'm Red Mike," the man replied, and his beard made it obvious how he had gotten the nickname. He squinted at the badge pinned to Frank's shirt and went on. "I can see who *you* are, mister. Woodford's called in the law to try to shut me up and keep me from tellin' the truth!"

"The only reason I'm here is because I've heard reports that somebody was trying to stir up trouble out here at the Lucky Lizard," Frank said.

"Trouble!" Fowler practically yelped. "The only one stirrin' up trouble around here is Woodford, because he don't pay fair wages nor treat his workers right!"

Frank looked at the other miners scattered around the barracks and asked, "How do you boys feel about that? Do you think Woodford's not treating you right?"

None of the men responded for a moment, but then one of them said, "I always figured he was a pretty good boss, but then I found out that Mr. Munro over at the Alhambra is payin' ten cents an hour more."

Another man spoke up. "Yeah, and he's got his men workin' in ten-hour shifts, instead of twelve hours at a time."

"Mike says the shaft is shored up better over there too," a third man added.

"Is that a fact?" Frank asked, casting a speculative look at Red Mike. "Were you the one who told them about the pay and the hours too?"

"Somebody's got to tell the truth," Fowler replied with a defiant glare on his bearded face.

"How is it that you know so much about the wages and the hours and the working conditions at the Alhambra?"

Fowler shook his head. "You ain't gonna twist things around and make these men distrust me, Marshal. I been honest with them from the first. They know that my brother and me used to work over there for Munro."

"If it's so much better at the Alhambra, why aren't you still working there?"

"Because Munro fired us, me and Gib both." Fowler shrugged. "We got a mite likkered up one night and got in a fight with one of the foremen. Hammersmith actually fired us, the bald-headed bastard, but Munro backed him up on it. So you see, we ain't got no love for Hammersmith or Munro either one, and we damn sure got no reason to be tellin' folks that their mine is better than this one, except for one . . . it's the truth."

Frank pondered that. He had thought in the back of his mind that Munro might have something to do with the problem developing here at the Lucky Lizard, but it appeared that wasn't the case.

He nodded toward the other miners and asked Fowler, "Are you saying these fellas should go to work for the Alhambra?"

Fowler made a face. "Wouldn't do 'em any good if they tried. Hammersmith's got a full crew over there. What I think they should do is get Woodford to pay them right and treat them better."

"Has anybody talked to him about that?"

A disgusted snort came from Fowler. "We tried. He won't listen to reason. Just says that he can't afford to pay us any more than he already is, and he claims the mine is safe. All he'd do is promise to think about cutting back on the number of hours in a shift, but thinkin' about it ain't gonna get it done."

Tip hadn't told Frank all those details, and hearing them just made the situation more troublesome. The wages that Tip was paying seemed fair enough to Frank, but he wasn't the one working for them. A twelve-hour shift was pretty common, but gouging ore out of the earth *was* pretty hard work. As for the mine's safety, Frank couldn't say about that, because he hadn't taken a good look at the inside of the Lucky Lizard. Maybe there were some improvements that should be made.

"If you don't get what you want, what do you plan to do?"

Red Mike crossed his arms over his chest and glared at Frank. "We'll do the only thing we *can* do to make Woodford listen to us. We'll call a strike." He looked around at the others. "Ain't that right, boys?"

Frank noticed that some of the miners looked pretty dubious about that idea, but the rest gave enthusiastic nods and one man said, "Damn right we will!"

Strike. It was a word Frank didn't want to hear. There had been miners' strikes before, as well as strikes in other businesses, like the railroads. They nearly always led to violence. Back East, there had been riots and bombings connected with strikes. The business owners usually brought in armed men to break the backs of such work stoppages. The Pinkertons had come to specialize in such work. Because of that, these things were seldom if ever resolved in a peaceful manner.

Folks usually had to die first before anything got done.

Frank didn't want to see that happen here. He liked Tip Woodford too much for that, and besides, it was his job to keep things as peaceful as possible.

"I think you ought to try to talk to Woodford again," he began, not knowing if it would do any good or not. "If you want, I'll say something to him—"

A sudden rumble from somewhere nearby interrupted Frank's words. He felt a faint vibration in the floor under his feet and knew it couldn't have come from anything good. Thunder sometimes sounded like that and shook the earth. . . .

But this wasn't thunder.

Fowler's eyes widened with shock as the other miners bolted up from the bunks. The bearded man's exclamation put into words what whey were all thinking.

"Oh, my God! *Cave-in!*"

Chapter 23

Frank whirled around and headed for the doorway at a run. Fowler and the other miners were right behind him. They burst out of the barracks building and turned toward the mine entrance, where a cloud of dust boiled out of the dark mouth of the shaft.

They weren't the only ones who had heard the rumble and felt the earth shake. Anyone who had worked around mines for very long had experienced those sensations, and once experienced, they were never forgotten. Men came running out of the stamp mill and the office to stare toward the shaft with stricken looks on their faces. Someone began to ring an alarm bell.

Frank ran toward the mine entrance. So did most of the other men.

"Gib!" Fowler shouted. "My brother's in there!"

So were probably a dozen other men, maybe more. Although Frank was no expert on such things, it seemed to him that the cave-in must have occurred fairly close to the entrance for the dust to be coming out like that so soon after the collapse. Of course, there was no telling what might have happened deeper in the mine, but Frank's hope was that even if the shaft was blocked, the tunnels were all right. In that case, they would have at least a chance to get any trapped men out of there before they ran out of air.

The choking dust kept men from reaching the entrance right away. They tried to penetrate it but staggered back, coughing and hacking. Frank pulled a bandanna from his pocket and tied it over his mouth and nose like a bandit, then started forward into the dust. He took off his wide-brimmed hat and waved it back and forth in front of his face, trying to clear the air a little as he pressed ahead. He heard some of the other men following him, but didn't look back.

Blinded, eyes stinging from the dust, Frank knew he had reached the cave-in only when he ran into it. He barked his shins against something hard and stopped. Clapping his hat on, he reached out with his hands and felt a jumbled barrier of rock, dirt, and broken timbers. "Hello!" he shouted. "Anybody hear me?"

No response came from the other side of the cave-in. Men crowded around Frank on this side. Fowler said, "We've got to get these rocks out of here and see how bad it is!"

That made sense. Frank grasped a chunk of rock so big and heavy that he needed both hands to carry it. Turning, he stumbled under the weight and headed back toward the mouth of the shaft. The dust was beginning to thin a little, and now he could see that the cave-in was about thirty yards inside the shaft.

As he emerged and dropped the rock to one side of the tunnel mouth, more men rushed past him carrying picks and shovels. A couple of men trundled wheelbarrows into the mine. The foreman Frank had spoken to earlier rushed up carrying a lantern.

"What's it look like in there?" he asked.

Frank shook his head. "Couldn't tell. The dust was still too thick. Looks like it's clearing out now, though."

The foreman nodded. "That's a good sign. You can tell there's some air blowing out of the mine. That means the shaft isn't sealed off completely. There have to be some little openings somewhere, and the ventilation holes deeper in the mine are supplying air."

"You're saying the men trapped down there will be able to breathe?"

The foreman nodded. "Yeah. Anybody who wasn't caught in the collapsed area and killed by falling rock ought to be all right. We'll have them dug out before they can die of starvation."

"What about water?"

"There are water barrels down in the tunnels. They can make it for a day or two, if it takes that long."

Frank felt a sense of relief wash through him. Although they wouldn't know for sure until they cleared away the cave-in, it appeared that this accident could have been a lot worse than it was turning out to be.

But that didn't mean there was no danger. Men could have been crushed when the roof of the shaft collapsed. Others could have been hurt badly enough to need medical attention as soon as possible. It was still imperative that they reach the trapped miners just as quickly as they could.

He followed the foreman with the lantern into the shaft. All the lamps along the walls had been blown out by the gust of air caused by the collapse of the ceiling. Dust motes danced thickly in the yellow glow as the foreman approached the site of the cave-in.

Frank could see the barrier now that he had only felt earlier. It was a tumbled mess formed mostly of rock. With the practiced swings of men who had been using picks for years, several of the miners chipped away at the barricade, loosening chunks of rock so that other men could pick them up and carry them out or pile them in the wheelbarrows to be hauled out later. The foreman didn't have to issue orders. The miners were already doing what needed to be done.

The men worked in silence for the most part, the only noise being grunts of effort and the chinking impact of picks against stone. But after a while, Red Mike Fowler began to curse bitterly and said, "This never would've happened if Woodford had listened to us. We told him this mine wasn't safe! Now my brother's trapped in there, or maybe dead already!"

Some of the other men muttered agreement with Fowler's complaints. The foreman spoke up, saying, "Damn it, that's not true! There was no reason for this shaft to collapse. The timbers were in fine shape, and the rock was stable!"

Fowler swung his pick with savage strength and drove it into a crack between two pieces of rock. "Yeah," he said, "we can all see for ourselves just how safe it is!"

Time didn't mean much underground like this. Frank had no idea how long they had been working at clearing the blocked area. He knew he wouldn't be much good with a pick, so he took over the job of using one of the wheelbarrows, rolling it toward the mouth of the shaft when it was full. His muscles strained against the weight of the rocks, and after several trips he was drenched with sweat.

At last, an excited shout went up, filling the tunnel, and Frank knew that meant the rescuers had broken through the barrier. Everyone crowded forward to see as the air moving through the shaft from inside the mine picked up. The irregular opening that had been created was a small one, no more than a foot square, but that was enough for

Mike Fowler to put his face up to it and shout, "Gib! Gib, can you hear me?"

A voice answered faintly from the other side. "Mike! Is that you?"

A triumphant cheer went up from the miners as they heard the proof that someone was still alive on the other side of the cave-in.

"Yeah, it's me!" Fowler called back. "Is everybody all right over there?"

"Most of us," Gib Fowler replied. "A couple of men were caught when the ceiling came down, but the rest of us weren't hurt!" His voice cracked a little from the strain as he went on. "Are you gonna get us out of here?"

"Hang on!" his brother told him. "We'll have you out of there in no time!"

Actually it took another hour of hard, backbreaking labor before the hole was enlarged enough for Gib Fowler and the nine other miners with him to crawl through to safety. They were taken out into the sunlight and open air, which they greeted with gratitude.

As Frank came out of the mine, he saw that Tip Woodford had arrived at the Lucky Lizard, summoned from the settlement along with his daughter Diana. They wore expressions of great concern that eased a bit when they saw the men who had been rescued. Woodford's frown returned, though, as he counted the miners and said, "We're two men short, aren't we?"

Mike Fowler turned toward him and said, "Damn right we are, Woodford! There are still two men in that mine, buried under tons of rock because of you!"

Tip looked shocked at the accusation. Diana was surprised, too, but also angry. "What are you talking about?" she demanded. "My father didn't have anything to do with that cave-in!"

"He had everything to do with it, little missy," Fowler snapped. "All of those timbers that shored up the ceiling should have been replaced when the mine was opened up again, not just some of them."

"I inspected every one of those timbers myself. Most of 'em were fine," Tip insisted. "We replaced all the ones that needed replacin'."

"That's what you say now," Fowler responded with a sneer. "You didn't care if the shaft fell in on the poor miners you pay slave wages to! A couple of men get killed, you'll just replace 'em with some other unlucky devils!"

The miners' mood was starting to turn ugly. From the edge of the crowd, Frank heard a lot of angry muttering. Tip looked confused and hurt and unsure of himself, and he moved closer to Diana and gripped her arm.

"Go on in the office," he told her. "You don't need to be out here."

"No," she said. "I'm not leaving. Somebody's got to talk some sense into these men."

It wouldn't be her, Frank thought. Tip was right—Diana needed to get inside one of the buildings where she would be safe in case trouble broke out. Three of Tip's foremen were on hand, and Frank figured they would back their boss, but there were a couple of dozen angry, resentful miners crowding around them.

It was time for him to step in.

Raising his voice so he could be heard over the hubbub, Frank called in a powerful, commanding tone, "Everybody just settle down!"

That brought a moment of surprised silence, but the respite didn't last long. Mike Fowler said, "This is none of your business, Marshal. We ain't in town! You've got no right to interfere."

"I'm making it my right," Frank snapped. His right hand

rested on the butt of his Colt. Men eyed him warily and began to move back. Everybody here knew that before pinning on the badge as marshal of Buckskin, Frank had been the famous gunfighter known as The Drifter.

"This don't have anything to do with you," Red Mike insisted.

"Tip Woodford's my friend, and so is Miss Diana. If you think I'm going to stand by while they're threatened, mister, you're dead wrong."

"What are you gonna do, Morgan? Shoot all of us?"

"No," Frank said, "but I can damn sure shoot *you* if I need to."

Fowler's face tensed and turned pale at the cold menace in Frank's voice.

"Tip," Frank went on, "you and Diana both get out of here. Go on back to town."

"The Lucky Lizard is mine, blast it," Tip said. "I'm as upset about what happened as anybody, but I still don't think it was my fault."

"You just don't give a damn about the people who work for you," Fowler accused. "Well, we won't work for you anymore, will we, boys? We're on strike!"

"Strike! Strike!" the other miners began chanting.

Tip looked sick. "You can't strike," he said. "That'll shut the mine down!"

"That's right," Fowler said with an ugly grin. "We're shuttin' you down, Woodford. We won't work for you again until you agree to meet all our demands!"

"I . . . I'll hire more men!" Tip shot back. Frank wished that he hadn't. Under the circumstances, that was one of the worst things he could have said.

"You try it and you'll be sorry," Fowler threatened. "So will anybody who tries to work for you."

One of the supervisors said, "We need to finish getting that shaft cleaned out. . . ."

"Clean it out yourself!" Fowler said. "Come on, boys. Back to the barracks!"

With angry scowls and muttered, defiant curses, the miners tramped off toward the barracks building. "God," Tip Woodford said. "What am I gonna do now?"

Frank nodded toward the mine entrance. "I'm no expert, but I'd say you need to finish getting that shaft cleaned out, like this fella said, so you can see how bad the damage is." Frank's voice grew more solemn as he added, "And there are a couple of bodies in there that need to be gotten out too."

Tip sighed and nodded, then said, "You're right. With only a handful of us, it ain't gonna be an easy job. I won't blame you fellas if you don't want to stick."

The foremen looked at each other, then one of them said, "We signed on to do a job. We'll do it."

"Let's get to work then," Tip said. "Frank, if you'd take Diana back to town—"

"Town, hell," she said. "I can handle a wheelbarrow."

"Now, blast it—"

"Haven't you learned by now, Pa, that you're wasting your time arguing with me?"

For the first time in quite a while, Frank felt like smiling. Diana Woodford was one stubborn young woman, living proof of the old saying about the apple not falling far from the tree.

"All right," Tip growled after a moment. "But when I tell you to get out of the tunnel, you get out, hear?"

Frank knew what he was getting at. As they cleared away the debris from the cave-in, they were bound to come across the bodies of the two men who had been trapped in the collapse. Tip didn't want his daughter to see that gruesome sight, and Frank couldn't blame him for feeling that way.

Diana must have understood what her father meant too, because she nodded and sounded uncommonly agreeable as she said, "Of course."

They all set to work. Mike and Gib Fowler watched them from the door of the barracks, but they didn't try to interfere. Progress was slow with only a half-dozen people working now, but gradually Frank began to see that only about ten feet of the ceiling had collapsed. The two men who had been caught in the cave-in had just been unlucky. A few yards either way in the tunnel, and they would have been able to avoid being crushed.

Tip Woodford had been swinging a pick, loosening the fallen rock, but he suddenly straightened from that task and said, "Go on out of here, girl." His tone made it clear that he wouldn't put up with any argument.

Diana didn't try to give him one. She just said, "All right," and left the tunnel.

"Here's the first one of those fellas," Tip said when she was gone. The men gathered around to remove the rocks from the body.

Frank had seen plenty of gory sights in his life, but the body of an hombre crushed by tons of falling rock was right up there with the worst of them. One of the men went to a storage building and came back with some sheets of canvas. The mangled remains were taken from the rocks as carefully as possible and wrapped in the canvas. A few minutes later, they found the second body and accorded it the same respectful handling.

"We'll put them in one of the wagons and take them to town," Tip said. "Reckon the coffins Langley makes will have to be closed at this funeral."

Frank nodded. Tip looked very upset, and Frank couldn't blame him. Despite his insistence that the mine was safe,

Tip had to be wondering if maybe, in some way, these two deaths *were* his fault.

As the bodies were being carried out, something in the rubble caught Frank's attention. He bent and pried it loose from the rocks that were piled around the object. It was part of one of the shoring timbers that had been holding up the ceiling before it collapsed. The jagged edge showed where it had snapped. Frank inspected it intently, holding it up and bringing his face close to it as he studied it in the light from the lantern.

"Well, how about that?" he said in a soft voice, more to himself than to any of the others. They weren't paying attention to him anyway. The men were all too upset and grieving over the deaths of the two miners.

They would be even more upset if they knew what the broken piece of timber had told Frank.

But he was going to keep that knowledge to himself for now, until he figured out what to do with it.

Chapter 24

It was well after nightfall before Frank got back to Buckskin. He rode straight to the office and tied Goldy at the hitch rail outside. When he came in, he found Clint Farnum behind the desk, leaning back in the chair with his booted feet propped on top of the desk.

Clint sat up and said, "Sorry, Frank. Didn't mean for you to catch me loafing."

Frank waved a hand and said, "Don't worry about it. Everything all right here in town?"

"Yeah. I did the rounds a while ago, then came back here and sent Jack to get himself some supper. We heard about what happened out at the Lucky Lizard. One of the townspeople came by and said two bodies had been brought in, claimed they were men who'd been killed in a cave-in."

Frank nodded. "That's right."

Clint stood up and came out from behind the desk so that Frank could sit down. "Better take it easy for a while," Clint advised. "You look like you've been rode hard and put away wet. I reckon digging out a collapsed mine tunnel must be pretty hard work."

Thinking about what they had found in that tunnel, Frank nodded and said, "Yeah. Really hard work."

"Why don't I go over to the café and get the girls to fix up something for you to eat? I'll bring it back here."

With every muscle and bone in his body screaming their weariness, Frank settled down in the chair. He figured Clint's offer had something to do with the deputy wanting to see Becky Humphries, but either way Frank appreciated it.

"That would be fine," he told Clint. "You might take my horse down to Amos's place too while you're at it."

Clint nodded. "Be glad to." He hurried out of the office, leaving Frank there to lean back in the chair and close his eyes for a moment.

As tired as he was, his brain was racing. In his saddle-bags was a piece of the broken timber he had slipped out of the mine shaft. The wood wasn't just broken, however. It showed signs of some other sort of damage, as if something had eaten away at it, and when Frank had brought it close to his face to inspect it, he had caught a whiff of a vaguely familiar odor. It had taken him a few seconds to identify the reeking smell.

Sulfuric acid.

The impact of that realization had hit Frank almost like a physical blow. He didn't know much about mining, but it seemed to him that the only logical way sulfuric acid could have gotten on that timber was if somebody *put* it there. The stuff was highly corrosive. A concentrated application of it could have weakened that support beam.

If the acid had been applied to several of the beams, that might have weakened the whole structure enough to bring part of the ceiling crashing down—which was exactly what had happened. If the theory forming in Frank's mind was correct, then the death of those two miners hadn't been a tragic accident after all.

It was murder.

He would check with Garrett Claiborne to be sure, but it seemed likely to him that sulfuric acid could be found pretty easily around a mine. The Lucky Lizard had a small assayer's laboratory adjacent to the stamp mill, and such places were full of chemicals that the assayers used in their tests on the ore. For all Frank knew, the acid might be used in some other process too.

The details weren't all that important. What mattered was that the cave-in had been caused deliberately, and when Frank asked himself who would benefit from such sabotage, his mind went right back to Hamish Munro and Gunther Hammersmith. With the Crown Royal pretty much shut down because its stamp mill had been destroyed, and now with work stopped at the Lucky Lizard because of the miners' strike, that left the Alhambra as the only producing mine in the area of any significance.

Would Munro go that far to gain an advantage on his competitors? A normal businessman wouldn't.

But who was to say that Munro was normal?

By the time Clint Farnum came back in carrying a tray full of food from the café, Frank had poured himself a cup of coffee and was standing in the doorway of the office drinking it. Clint said, "I thought you were going to take it easy."

"Compared to what I was doing earlier today," Frank said, "this *is* taking it easy."

He stepped aside so that Clint could carry the tray into the office and set it on the desk. The food was covered with a clean cloth.

"Miss Stillman asked after you," Clint said as he stepped back.

"Did she now?"

"That lady might be a little interested in you, Frank," Clint said with a grin.

That was an intriguing possibility, except for Frank's less-than-stellar history with women. Too many of them wound up dead because he was a famous gunfighter, and he wouldn't wish that fate on Lauren Stillman. Anyway, he had plenty of his plate already, what with all the trouble that had cropped up since Hamish Munro came to Buckskin.

"Lauren's a fine woman," Frank said, keeping his voice expressionless.

"Used to be a madam, from what I hear. Of course, I never hold it against a woman what she had to do to get along in the world."

"Neither do I. But I'm too tired tonight to think about things like that. I think I'll eat this supper and then get some shut-eye. You can go home, Clint. I'll stay here on the cot tonight."

"You sure?"

Frank nodded. "I'm sure."

Clint thumbed his hat back. "All right. Maybe I'll mosey on back over to the café. They were getting ready to close down for the night, and Miss Becky might need somebody to walk her home."

"You do that," Frank said with a smile.

Clint left the office, and Frank sat down behind the desk with his cup of coffee. He took the cloth off the tray, found a platter full of steak, potatoes, gravy, and biscuits. Simple fare, but mighty good.

At least, it would have been if he'd been able to pay any attention to what he was eating. Instead, he took the chunk of wood from his pocket and placed it on the desk where he could see it. The acid wasn't the only thing that had been put on it.

To Frank's eyes, it was also stained with the blood of two innocent, murdered men.

The next morning, Frank told Catamount Jack he was going to be gone for a while, then fetched Stormy from the stable and rode out to the Alhambra.

Earlier in the morning, he had stopped by Dr. Garland's house to talk to Garrett Claiborne, and the engineer had confirmed Frank's suspicion that quantities of sulfuric acid could be found around most mines. He also agreed that it was corrosive enough to eat deeply into a wooden beam such as the shoring timbers, especially if it was applied in a highly concentrated form.

"I heard about what happened at the Lucky Lizard," Claiborne had said. "Diana was here last night and told me all about it. She's very upset, and she says that her father is too."

"I'm not surprised," Frank had replied. "Tip Woodford's a good man, and despite what those no-good Fowler brothers are claiming, he cares about the men who work for him. Mining is dangerous work and everybody knows it, but I don't think Tip would take reckless chances with anybody's life."

"You think that cave-in was caused deliberately?"

"That makes the most sense to me," Frank had said. "Not only did it cause physical damage to the mine that will have to be repaired, but it made Tip look bad and bolstered all the troublemaking talk that the Fowlers had been doing. After the cave-in, all Red Mike had to do was point at Tip and yell that it was all his fault, and the rest of the men went along with that strike."

"Which stopped work completely at the mine."

Frank had shrugged. "Tip's foremen are still doing what

they can, I reckon, but they won't be able to accomplish much without some help. And that's going to be hard to come by as long as the rest of the crew is on strike and claiming the Lucky Lizard is such a dangerous place to work."

"A diabolical scheme, if ever I heard of one," Claiborne had said. "You lay it at the feet of Munro and Hammersmith?"

"They benefit more than anybody else. And Red Mike and his brother used to work at the Alhambra."

"They claim that they were fired and implied that they have a grudge against Hammersmith and Munro."

Frank had smiled at that, but there wasn't any genuine humor in the expression. "They could be lying to throw me off the trail. Could be they're still working for Munro, and have been all along."

"If history is any indication, you'll have a devil of a time proving it."

"I know," Frank had said with a nod. "But that's not going to stop me from poking my nose into it anyway."

Now, as he approached the Alhambra, he didn't forget his visit to the mine a couple of days earlier, when he had attempted to prod Munro and Hammersmith into doing something rash, like trying to bushwhack him. He kept his eyes open, figuring that they weren't likely to have him ambushed this close to the Alhambra but unwilling to bet his life on it. Experience had taught him that it always paid to be careful.

He came within sight of the mine. No stagecoach was here today, so he supposed Munro was back in Buckskin. That was all right. Hammersmith was big and brutal, but he wasn't as smart as Munro. It would be easier to get him off balance and maybe get him to say something that he shouldn't.

A man stood on the porch of the office building with a rifle cradled in his left arm. Frank pegged the man as a sentry, and sure enough, the hombre went inside the office a second later, no doubt to let Hammersmith know that a rider was coming.

By the time Frank drew rein in front of the building, Hammersmith was stepping out onto the porch, an unfriendly frown of recognition on his face. "You're getting to be a regular visitor out here, Morgan," he said, "but not a welcome one. What the hell do you want today?"

Frank leaned forward in the saddle. "I reckon you heard about what happened yesterday over at the Lucky Lizard?"

Hammersmith gave a harsh laugh. "Yeah. It seems like you're always bringing bad news for somebody else when you come out here."

"You have to ask yourself why I think of you every time something bad happens at one of the other mines," Frank said.

Hammersmith glared at him. "It's because you've got it in for us," he said. "You've got to blame somebody, so you try to make it look like me and Mr. Munro are responsible for everybody else's problems."

"The Crown Royal and the Lucky Lizard are both shut down right now," Frank pointed out. "The Alhambra is the only big mine that's producing any ore."

Hammersmith sneered and waved that off. "Coincidence. It's not our fault the Lucky Lizard ain't so lucky after all, and we didn't have anything to do with hiring those men to blow up the Crown Royal."

"One of these days I'll prove otherwise."

His face flushing with anger, Hammersmith demanded, "Is that a threat?"

"No, just a promise," Frank replied. "Somewhere out there is the proof I need to tie you and Munro to what's been going on around here, and I'm going to find it, Hammersmith. And when I do, both of you will wind up behind bars where you belong . . . or dancing at the end of a hang rope, since men were killed at both of those other mines. That makes it murder as far as I'm concerned, and I'll bet a jury would go along with that verdict."

Hammersmith's big hands clenched into fists. "Get the hell off this property," he said. "You got no legal authority out here, Morgan. You know it and I know it." He turned to the guard and snatched the rifle out of his hands. "Gimme that gun!"

Frank tensed. If Hammersmith made to shoot him, he would have no choice but to draw. He didn't want that. He didn't want to be forced to kill Hammersmith now, not until he had uncovered the evidence he needed to bring Hamish Munro to justice too.

Hammersmith swung back around toward Frank, but he didn't raise the rifle. Obviously struggling to control his anger, he said, "Are you leavin'?"

"I'm going," Frank said, "but that won't save you and your boss from what's coming to you. It's only a matter of time, Hammersmith."

Frank turned Stormy, well aware that by showing his back to Hammersmith, he was providing a target. Hammersmith cursed in a low, furious voice, but he kept the rifle pointed toward the ground, Frank saw when he glanced back over his shoulder.

He didn't think Hammersmith could take too much more prodding. The man's temper was too hair trigger for that. And now Frank had put Hammersmith on notice, as he had done with Munro, that he wasn't going to stop investigating until he had the evidence he needed against them.

Now it was just a matter of time.

Chapter 25

Hammersmith was so furious at Morgan—and so worried that the marshal would make good on his promise to get the evidence he needed—that he didn't even think much about Jessica Munro during his ride into town later that day. He was looking forward to possibly seeing her again, but today her loveliness didn't fill his thoughts the way it often did.

No, the image in his brain now was that of Frank Morgan, dead and shot full of holes.

Unfortunately, that was never going to happen in a stand-up gunfight, and Hammersmith knew it. He was deadly with his fists and a fair shot with a rifle or a shotgun, but he couldn't handle a revolver worth spit. He knew as well that he couldn't hope to match Morgan's blinding speed. If he had tried to bring that rifle up during the confrontation this morning, Morgan would have killed him without blinking an eye. Hammersmith was well aware of that, and so he had struggled mightily to control his temper.

He didn't want to come *that* close to dying again any time soon.

Still, he was convinced that Morgan had to be dealt with. The marshal had to go. Otherwise, Hammersmith and Munro ran the risk of Morgan finding someone who would testify against them. That was unlikely but not impossible, and the threat of prison or a hanging was great enough to convince Hammersmith that action was necessary.

Now he just had to see to it that Munro felt the same way. He brought his horse to a stop in front of the old hotel Munro had taken over for his headquarters, dismounted, and went inside.

At Hammersmith's knock, Nathan Evers opened the door of Munro's suite. The two men had been acquainted for several years, but that didn't mean they liked each other. In fact, Hammersmith didn't have much use for the prissy secretary.

He shouldered past Evers and said, "I need to see Mr. Munro."

"He's not here," Evers said.

"Well, where is he?"

Evers shook his head. "I'm not sure. He said he was going to talk to several of the businessmen here in town. I think he plans to make offers to them for their establishments."

"He wants to buy a bunch of stores?" Hammersmith asked with a frown.

"Mr. Munro believes in maintaining diversified financial holdings."

Hammersmith grunted. "You mean he wants to own everything, not just the mine. He wants to turn Buckskin into a company town, so when the poor bastards who work for him have to buy anything, they'll be giving their wages right back to him."

"Mr. Munro is nothing if not a canny businessman," Evers said with a shrug.

Hammersmith rubbed his jaw and frowned in thought. He wanted to talk to Munro about the problem of Frank Morgan, but he couldn't wait around all day for the mining magnate. On the other hand, he *had* ridden all the way into town. He ought to get something out of the visit. . . .

"Is Mrs. Munro here?" he asked.

"I believe so."

"I'll talk to her then," Hammersmith declared.

It was the secretary's turn to frown. "What business do you have with Mrs. Munro?"

"That's between her and me," Hammersmith snapped.

The two men glared at each other for a moment before Evers gave in—as Hammersmith had known he would. "Just a moment," he said.

He went to the door of the suite's other room and knocked on it. When Jessica Munro answered, Evers said, "Mr. Hammersmith would like to speak with you, ma'am."

The door opened. Jessica wore a green silk dressing gown that looked good on her. She smiled and said, "What can I do for you, Mr. Hammersmith?"

She was so lovely she took his breath away, as usual. He managed to say, "I, uh, have an important message about the mine that you can pass along to your husband if you'd be so kind, ma'am."

"If it has to do with business, you could have told me," Evers said.

Hammersmith bared his teeth and said, "I'd rather speak to the lady."

"It's all right, Mr. Evers," Jessica said. "I'm glad to help Hamish with his business. He never lets me do anything really important." Her full red lips pursed in a little pout that made Hammersmith's heart thud even harder. "Why don't you go downstairs to the kitchen and get some coffee for us?"

Evers looked reluctant to leave them alone. "Are you sure you want me to do that, ma'am?"

"I'm certain."

He sighed and nodded. "All right then." He looked at Hammersmith and added, "I'll be right back."

When he was gone, Hammersmith grinned and said, "I don't think that fella likes me very much."

Jessica ignored that comment and asked, "Do you really want to talk to me about the mine, Gunther . . . or did you come for this?"

Just like that, she was in his arms, and her mouth met his with an eager urgency as he bent his head to hers. Her body molded against his, and he could feel every curve of it through the dressing gown.

When she pulled back from him after a long, intense moment, she said, "That will have to be enough to satisfy us both for now. I don't think Nathan will be gone for very long."

Hammersmith's voice was rough with need as he said, "Are you sure?"

"Yes," she said, her voice firm. It softened a little as she added, "But there'll be another time, Gunther."

He dragged in a deep breath in an attempt to get control of himself. He said, "I really did want to talk to Mr. Munro about some things. Can you tell him that Morgan was out at the mine again this morning?"

"You mean Marshal Morgan?" Jessica asked with a frown.

"Yeah. He was talking about that cave-in and the strike over at the Lucky Lizard."

Jessica shook her head. "That doesn't have anything to do with the Alhambra, does it?"

Hammersmith thought for a second about how to approach this, then said, "No, but Morgan's got a burr under his saddle about it anyway. Everything bad that happens around here, he blames on me and your husband. I think Mr. Munro needs to know that Morgan's still causing trouble."

"But what can be done about that?"

Hammersmith's massive shoulders rose and fell. "I wouldn't know about that," he said. "Mr. Munro handles all the problems like that. Just tell him about Morgan coming out there, and if he wants me to do anything about it, he can let me know."

"All right." She gave a little laugh. "I'm glad I don't have to worry about all these things. I just don't have any head for business at all."

"Well, that doesn't matter," he assured her. "You've got me and your husband looking out for you."

"That's right." She rubbed her hand up and down his arm. "And I know I can count on you, can't I, Gunther?"

He swallowed hard. "Yes, ma'am. You sure can, Mrs. Munro."

"Oh, I think when we're alone, you can call me Jessica. Would you like that?"

He bobbed his head and said, "Yes, ma'am. I mean, Jessica."

She pointed to a chair on the other side of the room. "Now, I think you should go over there and sit down, because I think I hear Evers coming back."

Sure enough, by the time Hammersmith was seated in the chair Jessica had indicated, Evers was right outside the door. He came in carrying a silver tray with two cups of coffee on it. Jessica was all the way across the room, standing by the window. Judging by appearances, nothing improper had happened here while Evers was gone.

He looked suspicious anyway, and Hammersmith wondered if he would tell Munro about him being here alone with

Jessica. Well, Munro either trusted Jessica or he didn't—and any man with a young, beautiful wife like that *shouldn't* trust her too much, in Hammersmith's opinion. He had acted on impulse and couldn't do anything about it now.

And remembering the sweet warmth of Jessica's lips and the pliant heat of her body, he wouldn't change anything even if he could.

Except for maybe killing Frank Morgan before now. *That* he wished he had done.

When Hammersmith was gone, Nathan Evers asked, "What did he tell you, Mrs. Munro?"

"I believe that's between Mr. Hammersmith and myself," Jessica replied. She didn't fully trust Evers, mostly because he had never acted the least bit interested in her as a woman. Any man like that had to have something wrong with him, as far as she was concerned.

It was a shame too, because he was rather handsome in a bespectacled way.

"If it has to do with the mine, I should be privy to the information as well," Evers insisted. "I *am* Mr. Munro's confidential secretary, after all."

"If Hamish wants you to know something, he'll tell you," Jessica snapped.

She went back into the bedroom, leaving Evers fuming in the sitting room. As she sat down at the dressing table and began to brush her hair, like she usually did whenever she was worried or upset about something, she thought about what Hammersmith had told her.

This lawman Morgan was becoming a problem. Even though Hamish would never take her into his confidence, Jessica was convinced that her husband and Hammersmith were responsible for the explosion at the Crown Royal and the cave-in at the Lucky Lizard. Those were the sorts of things that Hamish would do, although Hammersmith would take care of all the details so that Hamish could keep his own hands clean.

Still, somewhere there might be some bit of evidence tying him to the sabotage, and if that connection ever came out, Hamish Munro would be ruined. He would wind up in prison or worse. Jessica had never planned to wait years before making her move, but she wasn't sure if she was ready for Munro's downfall just yet.

On the other hand, it would simplify things if the law did some of her work for her. If anything happened to Hamish, she would inherit his business empire. His first wife had died years ago, without ever having any children. Jessica was the only heir left. Of course, she was sure that Hamish would leave his lawyers in charge of everything . . . but they would just see how long *that* lasted. Men always underestimated her. She would wrest control away from those stuffy old attorneys in their suits before they knew what was happening.

"You're getting ahead of yourself, Jessica," she told her reflection in the mirror. "Nothing has happened to Hamish yet."

Perhaps it was time to tilt the odds a little more in her favor.

From inside the marshal's office, Frank had seen Hammersmith ride up to the hotel, dismount, and go inside. The burly mine superintendent had stayed in there for a while and then left. Frank could make a pretty good guess why Hammersmith had ridden into town. Hammersmith had come to warn Munro that Frank was pushing his nose in where it wasn't wanted. Probably, he would have tried to talk Munro into sanctioning an ambush attempt, too, if Munro had been there.

Unfortunately for Hammersmith, Munro wasn't at the hotel. Frank had seen him leave earlier, and he hadn't come back yet.

A few minutes after Hammersmith rode off, Jessica Munro emerged from the hotel, wearing a long, dark blue skirt and a pale blue blouse. Frank saw her through the open door of the marshal's office. She angled across the street, seemingly unaware of the avid stares directed toward her by most of the men she passed.

Frank realized to his surprise that she seemed to be heading for his office. He got to his feet.

Jessica stepped onto the boardwalk and came straight to the door. "Marshal," she said as she paused there, "I'd like to talk to you."

Frank came out from behind the desk and held out a hand. "Come on in and sit down, Mrs. Munro," he said. "The furnishings aren't fancy, but that chair's not too uncomfortable."

Jessica came in and sat down. Frank perched a hip on a corner of the desk and asked her, "What can I do for you, ma'am?"

"I'd like to talk to you about Mr. Hammersmith, the superintendent of my husband's mine."

Frank nodded. "Yes, ma'am, I know who he is. What about him?"

"I think . . ." She drew in a deep breath, making her breasts lift. Frank tried not to notice that, but he wouldn't have been human if he hadn't. "I think he's been doing some things behind my husband's back that aren't in Hamish's best interest."

"How do you mean?"

"I believe he may have had something to do with the trouble at the other mines in the area. You know, that explosion at the Crown Royal and the cave-in and strike at the Lucky Lizard."

Frank's interest quickened. "You think Hammersmith was responsible for those things?"

"I . . . I don't know. I think, from a few things he said, that he might have some connection with them."

"But your husband wouldn't know anything about any of that?"

Jessica stared at him, all wide-eyed innocence. "No, of course not. Hamish is an honest businessman, Marshal. He would never resort to unscrupulous tactics like that."

Frank scratched at his jaw with a thumbnail. "Why are you telling me this, ma'am?"

"Because I don't want Hamish getting into any trouble for something that's not his fault! If Mr. Hammersmith is responsible for what's been happening at those other mines, I'm sure he's doing it to help the Alhambra, but at the same time he's been acting without my husband's permission or knowledge. I don't want Hamish being blamed for those things."

"Does your husband know that you're here?"

She shook her head. "No, certainly not, and I don't want him to know. He doesn't like for me to involve myself in his business affairs." She laughed. "He says I shouldn't worry my pretty little head about such things." A look of concern appeared on her face. "You won't tell him, will you? You can look into Mr. Hammersmith's actions without Hamish having to know that I talked to you?"

"I reckon I can try to keep your name out of it," Frank promised.

She sighed in relief. "Thank you, Marshal. I'm just trying to help Hamish, not get him angry."

"I can understand that, what with you being his wife and all." Frank stood up. "Is there anything else I can do for you?"

"No, I don't believe so. You *will* try to find out what Mr. Hammersmith has been up to?"

"Yes, I will." Frank didn't tell her that he had already suspected Hammersmith before she ever came over here. He didn't share her conviction that her husband was blameless in the matter, though. But she didn't have to know that.

Jessica stood up and offered him her hand. "Thank you, Marshal. You don't know what a load this is off my mind."

"Might be a good idea not to say anything to Mr. Munro about Hammersmith," Frank said as he took her hand. It was warm and supple. "Just let me look into it."

"All right." She smiled, making her face light up. "Good-bye, Marshal."

Frank said good-bye and watched her walk out of the office. As he settled back down in his chair, he thought about what she had told him. The more he thought about it, the less sure he was that he believed *anything* she had said. Was she really so trusting that she thought Hammersmith would be carrying out that sabotage without her husband's knowledge?

Just because she acted like a pretty, brainless fool didn't mean she actually was one. Maybe she was *trying* to increase Frank's suspicions not only of Hammersmith but of Munro as well. But why would she do such a thing?

Frank couldn't answer that question just yet, but he was going to keep it in mind. It looked like Jessica Munro was playing some sort of game of her own. She might turn out to be just as dangerous as her husband and Hammersmith.

And the female of the species, Frank reminded himself, was often deadlier than the male. . . .

Chapter 26

Frank went about his business in a normal fashion for the next couple of days, waiting to see how—or if—Hammersmith and Munro would react to the prodding he had given them. If anyone tried to kill him, he planned to capture the bushwhacker and force him to reveal who had hired him. Most hired gunmen would spill their guts when faced with the prospect of hanging—or having Dog turned loose on them.

On the evening of the second day, Frank was making his rounds when Colt flame suddenly spurted from the darkness of an alley mouth he was passing. He had heard a faint noise just before the gun went off, nothing solid enough to identify, but alarm bells had gone off inside his head anyway, sending him plunging forward. The bushwhacker's bullet went just behind his head, close enough so that he felt the wind-rip of its deadly passage.

By the time Frank landed on one knee, his Peacemaker was already in his hand and he was twisting toward the spot where the muzzle flash had lit up the shadows. Aiming low, he triggered twice, in hopes that he could knock the would-be killer's legs out from under him.

The gunman must have been moving as soon as he fired his first shot, though, because two more blasts came from the far side of the alley. Either that or there were two bushwhackers, Frank thought as slugs chewed splinters from the planks of the boardwalk—in which case his attempts to draw an ambush might have worked a little *too* well.

He dived off the boardwalk into the street as more bullets whistled around his head. As he landed on the dirt, he rolled fast to his left, a move that brought him behind a water trough. He came to rest on his belly with the Colt still clutched in his hand. Slugs thudded into the thick wood of the trough, but didn't penetrate it.

Running footsteps pounded on the boardwalk from both left and right. Frank lifted his head and shouted, "They're in the alley! Go around back!"

The men who had been running toward him darted into other alleys, heading for the narrow lane that ran behind the buildings. When Frank started on his rounds tonight, Clint Farnum had been about a hundred yards ahead of him, while Catamount Jack trailed him by an equal distance. Both deputies stayed hidden in the shadows as much as possible, so that anyone laying a trap for Frank would be less likely to notice them. Unknown to the bushwhackers, Frank had been setting his own trap, and the gunmen in the alley had sprung it.

As the shots fell silent, Frank heard a muttered curse and then a man said in an alarmed voice, "They're gonna get behind us!" That confirmed there were at least two bushwhackers.

"Blast our way out the front!" a second man urged. "We gotta get to the horses!"

A couple of saddle mounts were tied to a hitch rail in front of the next building along the street. Frank figured the horses belonged to the two gunmen. The men must have reloaded, because they burst out of the alley firing their six-guns like they had an endless supply of bullets. Frank had to stay low, behind the water trough, or else the deadly storm of lead would have ventilated him.

The killers dashed for their horses. The one in front made a leap for his saddle. Frank rose up and snapped a shot at him. The other man returned the fire, and Frank felt a bullet tug at the side of his shirt. It missed the flesh underneath, though.

Frank must have missed the first man to try to mount up, because the hombre reached the saddle and jerked his reins loose as he twisted around and threw more lead. Bullets kicked up dust around Frank and forced him to roll behind the water trough again. That gave the second man time to leap onto the back of his horse. Now they were both mounted and ready to gallop out of Buckskin.

Frank wanted to take at least one of them alive. He came up on his knees and drew a bead on one of the killers, aiming at the man's shoulder. The light was uncertain and a haze of dust hung in the air, but Frank trusted his aim. He pulled the trigger.

At that instant, the other man's horse, evidently spooked by all the gunfire, danced to one side. That unexpected movement brought his rider directly in line with Frank's shot. Frank heard the grunt of pain as his bullet thudded into the man's chest. The bushwhacker was rocked backward and slid out of the saddle.

That left the other man, who by now was leaning forward and raking his spurs against his horse's flanks as he raced down Buckskin's main street.

A figure dashed out to try to stop him. "Hold it!" Frank heard this man shout, and he recognized Catamount Jack's voice. The old-timer must have realized that the bushwhackers were no longer in the alley and doubled back.

The rider didn't slow down. He fired from the back of his horse, and Frank saw Jack stumble and go to a knee. Fearing that his deputy was hit, Frank leaped to his feet.

The shotgun in Jack's hands boomed, twin flowers of flame blooming from its barrels. Horse and rider both went down.

Frank ran along the street. He heard someone huffing and puffing behind him, and glanced back to see Clint Farnum trying to catch up. "Check on that one!" Frank called as he waved his gun at the man he had inadvertently shot. Then he dashed on past.

Catamount Jack was getting to his feet by the time Frank reached him. The old-timer leaned on the empty shotgun, using it as a makeshift crutch.

"Jack, are you all right?" Frank asked.

"Yeah. The sumbitch nicked my leg with that shot, but it ain't nothin' to worry about. I had a grizzly just about gnaw that leg clean off one time. This ain't near that bad."

Frank was willing to take Jack's word for that, for the time being. He turned toward the man and horse lying in the street. The horse was struggling to get up, and as Frank reached the animal, it made it to its feet. Frank saw several dark streaks on the horse's hide that he knew were places where buckshot had raked it, but the animal didn't seem to be hurt too badly.

The same couldn't be said of its former rider. Most of the double load of buckshot had ripped into the gunman's body, shredding flesh and shattering bone. Frank felt for a pulse in the man's neck, but knew he wasn't going to find one. Jack had blasted the hell out of the hombre.

Sure enough, the man was dead. Although Frank was disappointed, he couldn't blame Jack for what had happened. In the heat of a gun battle, already wounded, Jack had just obeyed his instincts and blown his enemy out of the saddle. Anybody else would have done the same thing.

Clint Farnum trotted up. Frank turned to him and asked, "What about the other one?"

"He's dead," Clint replied. "This one too?"

"Yeah," Frank said.

Clint shook his head. "That's a tough break. I know you wanted to take at least one of them alive."

"Bullets don't always follow the plan."

"Yeah," Clint agreed. "They sort of have minds of their own sometimes, don't they?"

People came along the street, drawn by the sounds of the gunfight. Frank sent someone to fetch Claude Langley, then told Catamount Jack, "Let's get you down to Dr. Garland's and let him patch up that bullet hole."

"I ain't sure it's worth the bother," Jack protested.

"Come on," Frank insisted. "You can act like a stubborn old pelican some other time."

Jack grumbled about it, but he did as Frank said.

The wound was minor, as Jack had said. Dr. Garland cleaned and bandaged it, then said, "Just out of curiosity, is there anywhere on your body that *doesn't* have a bullet or a knife scar on it?"

Jack grinned and said, "Only the parts that been chewed on or clawed by grizzly bears, wolves, and mountain lions. You think this is bad, you ought to see an old mountain man I used to know called Preacher. That hombre was nothin' but a walkin' scar. Probably still is, if he's still alive. Wouldn't doubt it for a second. He'd only be in his nineties by now, and he was always tough as whang leather."

"Well, if you ever run into him again, bring him to see me," Garland said. "A specimen like that should be written up in the medical journals."

Since the doctor was finished, the three lawmen told him good night and headed for the marshal's office. "What now, Frank?" Clint asked as they walked along the street. "You think maybe anybody can testify that there was a connection between Hammersmith and Munro and those two dead bushwhackers?"

Frank shook his head. "Munro is too smart and careful for that, and Hammersmith probably is too. I'd say I'm back where I started."

"Not quite," Jack said. "Them two hired guns are dead. They won't be comin' after you again."

"No, they won't," Frank said, "but I'm afraid there are plenty more where those two came from."

If Munro was disappointed that the marshal of Buckskin was still alive, he gave no sign of it when Frank went to see the mining magnate the next morning. He found Munro and his wife in the dining room of the hotel, having breakfast. Munro didn't invite Frank to join them.

"What can I do for you, Marshal?"

Frank had decided it was time to change tacks for the moment. "You know that strike is still going on out at the Lucky Lizard."

Munro patted his lips with a napkin and his wife looked disinterested. "I'm afraid I haven't been keeping up with that, since it's not really any of my business," Munro said.

Tip Woodford had been by the office earlier that morning to talk to Frank about the strike, and he seemed very discouraged about it. The miners were standing firm in their demands for higher wages, shorter hours, and more safety precautions in the mine. As Tip had put it, "I can go along with shorter shifts, and I already want the mine to be as safe as I can get it, but I just can't afford to pay the wages they're askin' for."

Now Frank said to Munro, "I'm a mite curious about the way you're paying your workers more than Tip Woodford was paying the fellas who were working for him."

Munro shrugged and said, "I don't know what concern it is of yours what I pay my men, Marshal. It's not really a matter for the law, now is it?"

"It might be, if you were paying those wages in a deliberate attempt to cause a strike at the Lucky Lizard and put Woodford out of business."

"It's called competition," Munro snapped.

"Yeah, but if you sent those Fowler brothers over there to stir up trouble—"

"Hammersmith fired the Fowler brothers," Munro cut in.

"So he claims. What I'm wondering is if they're still working for the Alhambra."

Munro glared up at Frank. "Those are very serious accusations," he said.

"I'm not finished." Frank reached into his shirt pocket and drew out a bit of wood. He placed it on the table. "This came from one of the timbers inside the Lucky Lizard where that cave-in happened. Somebody used acid to weaken it and some of the other timbers, so they would give way and let the ceiling collapse."

Munro shot to his feet and asked in a cold, angry voice, "What are you saying, Marshal?"

"I'm saying that I think you're behind that cave-in and the strike at the Lucky Lizard, and I think you had something to do with the explosion at the Crown Royal's stamp mill too."

Munro trembled with rage. His face was flushed a dark red by now. "By God, you go too far, Marshal! To come in here and . . . and accuse a man of cold-blooded murder in front of his wife like this! The gall of it!" He leaned forward and rested his knuckles on the table. "Well, you'll be sorry, Morgan. You'll rue the day you decided to take on Hamish Munro!"

Frank ignored the apoplectic mining magnate for the moment and looked over at Jessica Munro instead. He nodded to her and tugged on the brim of his hat. "I'm sorry if I've upset you, ma'am," he said, although as far as he could see, Jessica wasn't upset at all. She was keeping her face carefully expressionless, as if she didn't really understand what was going on, but Frank saw the intelligence and awareness in her eyes. Again, he wondered if in the long run she might be more dangerous than her husband.

"Get out!" Munro said, flinging up an arm and pointed at the door. "This is private property, and I want you out of here, Morgan!"

"I'm the law in Buckskin," Frank pointed out. "That gives me the right to go pretty much where I need to."

"No crime has been committed here. Get out of here, and I warn you, if you continue to spread vicious lies about me, I'll take legal action against you!"

"I reckon you already took action against me," Frank said in a calm voice, "although it sure wasn't the legal kind."

Munro stared at him. "What are you talking about now?"

"Maybe you heard . . . a couple of hombres tried to kill me last night."

Munro sneered and said, "From what I've seen, people are *always* trying to kill you. It must have something to do with the fact that you're a notorious gunfighter."

"This was different. This was an ambush, by the same sort of hired guns who blew up the Crown Royal for you."

"Not for me," Munro insisted with a shake of his head.

"And I didn't have anything to do with any attempt on your life last night either."

"So you say," Frank said. "So you say."

"Are you going to leave us alone?" Munro asked in a voice that shook with rage.

"I reckon I've said what I came to say. All the cards are on the table now, Munro. We both know what you've been doing around here, you and Hammersmith. And one way or another, it's going to end."

"Are you threatening me?"

Frank shook his head. "Just letting you know that there comes a time when all the sneaking around and trying to manipulate things behind the scenes is over. When you have to make a stand for good or bad and settle things like men."

"I'm not going to fight you," Munro said. "Good Lord, I'm not a gunslinger!"

"No," Frank said. "You just pay them to do your killing for you."

With that, he turned and walked out of the hotel. He had accomplished what he had come here to do. He had put Munro on notice that all hell was about to break loose. He was sick and tired of trying to play out this hand with all the legal niceties and pussyfooting around. If he had to take off his badge to settle things, that was just what he would do.

The sound of hurrying footsteps on the boardwalk made him pause and look around. Jessica Munro was coming after him. He stopped to wait for her.

"I told you my husband isn't involved in what Hammersmith has been doing, Marshal," she said as she came up to him. "You promised you'd keep Hamish out of it."

"I'm sorry, ma'am," Frank said, "but you know as well as I do that Hammersmith isn't the sort of man to go behind your husband's back. Mr. Munro knows everything that Hammersmith has been doing." Frank gave a little shrug. "Except maybe for that ambush last night. That might've been Hammersmith's doing." He looked past her at the front doors of the hotel. "I'm surprised your husband would let you come after me like this."

"Hamish doesn't know. He went upstairs in a rage to talk to Nathan Evers about going to Carson City and complaining to the governor about your actions. He doesn't know that I've ever even spoken to you, certainly not alone."

Frank gave her a faint smile. "Well, then, it seems more like *you're* the one used to going behind his back, not Hammersmith."

She gave him a long, cool look for a moment, then said, "Are you implying that I'm your enemy as well, Marshal?"

"I'm just saying that the trouble's gone on long enough. I'm going to end it . . . whatever that takes."

"I'm *not* your enemy," Jessica insisted. She started to back away. "I have to go."

Frank nodded. Jessica turned and hurried away, going back into the hotel.

Frank's intention had been to stir things up. He figured he had done that. He didn't know what would happen now, but at least everything was out in the open. Things would start to move faster now.

But he didn't expect what happened late that afternoon, when one of the men from the Alhambra rode into town and announced to a crowd of drinkers in the Silver Baron that the miners who worked for Hamish Munro had just gone on strike.

Chapter 27

Gunther Hammersmith was in the office at the mine when one of the guards ran in and reported in a breathless voice, "Trouble in the shaft, Boss."

Hammersmith came to his feet. "What sort of trouble?"

"The men are talkin' about goin' on strike."

Hammersmith grunted as if he had been punched hard in the belly. He had orchestrated the strike at the Lucky Lizard by sending the Fowler brothers in to stir up unrest. The cave-in was their work too. Hammersmith hadn't ordered them to cause the deaths of any of Woodford's miners, but the luck that had dropped those rocks on the two men had been good for Hammersmith, if unfortunate for the miners who had died. The deaths had made it that much easier to get the strike started.

In the meantime, Munro had raised the wages of the men working at the Alhambra, and Hammersmith had taken it easier on them than usual. What the hell were they thinking, talking about a strike under these conditions?

Balling his hands into fists, Hammersmith strode out of the office. "I'll put a stop to this," he told the guard.

"Want me to come along with you just in case there's trouble?" the man asked, hefting his rifle.

Hammersmith started to tell him no, that this was nothing he couldn't handle with his fists, but then he thought better of it. He was a match for any two or three or even more of the miners, but a whole mob of them might be too much. They were tough men too—just not as tough as him.

"Yeah, come on," he snapped as he stalked off toward the mine entrance. The rifle-toting guard followed him.

A tight knot of men had gathered just in front of the shaft's mouth. Hammersmith heard their angry voices, one in particular. As he drew closer, he recognized the burly, beard-stubbled figure. Dave Rogan had been working for the Alhambra for a couple of weeks, ever since he'd been fired from the Lucky Lizard after causing some sort of ruckus in town. He was a good worker, tireless with a pick and shovel, but surly all the time and prone to getting into fights with the other miners. Hammersmith wasn't surprised to see that he was the troublemaker.

"—ain't just the Lucky Lizard," Rogan was saying. "Sure, Munro's payin' us more than Woodford pays his men, but it's only a few cents an hour! That ain't enough more to make a real difference. We ought to be gettin' two bits more an hour at least! And you know damn well Hammersmith's gonna start workin' us like dogs again. You saw how he was up until a few days ago. Easin' up on us is just a damned trick! Hammersmith and Munro don't want us lookin' at what's goin' on at the Lucky Lizard and gettin' any ideas!"

One of the other men spotted Hammersmith coming and nudged Rogan to shut him up. Rogan didn't take the hint, though. He turned and saw Hammersmith approaching, and a snarl twisted his mouth.

"Here he comes now," Rogan said. "Gonna try to shut me up and scare you boys into not thinkin' for yourselves."

With an effort, Hammersmith reined in his temper. What he wanted to do was to sledge a couple of blows into Rogan's face and knock that smirk off the man's lips. Instead, he demanded in a harsh voice, "What the hell's goin' on here?"

"We're tired of bein' taken advantage of, Hammersmith," Rogan replied. "Ain't that right, boys?"

A cheer went up from the miners. Like any mob, they were brave, but it was a collective courage, not an individual one. Split them up and they'd be as craven as they normally were, Hammersmith knew.

And the first step in splitting them up was dealing with Rogan. The man was almost as tall as Hammersmith and only about twenty pounds lighter. The muscles of his arms and shoulders were corded and ropy from swinging a pick for endless hours. Despite that, Hammersmith had no doubt that he could defeat Rogan in a fight.

He might get the chance to find out, because Rogan had a crazed light in his eyes that said he wasn't going to be cowed. A man like that lived for conflict, and the more violent the better.

Hammersmith decided to try talking first for a change. He hadn't been around Munro so much without learning something. Munro used words—backed up by the threat of violence, of course—to get what he wanted.

"Listen, you men," Hammersmith began. "You know you just got a raise, and you're working ten-hour shifts now, not twelve."

"You can't buy us," Rogan shot back. "Not with a measly ten cents more than what caused the miners over at the Lucky Lizard to go on strike."

"You know it wasn't just the pay that made those men

decide to strike," Hammersmith argued. "They had a cave-in too. They don't trust Woodford to keep 'em safe anymore. You don't have to worry about that here."

"No?" Rogan asked. "Woodford claimed his mine was safe too, until the ceiling came down in the shaft!"

"You can see for yourself, damn it!" Hammersmith paused and forced himself to draw a deep breath. In a calmer tone, he went on. "Just look at the timbers and everything else in the Alhambra. You'll see that it's a safe place to work."

"Any mine can have a cave-in," one of the other miners pointed out. "It's a dangerous job, no matter how careful you are."

"Yeah!" another man called. "That's why you ought to pay us better, Hammersmith. We're riskin' our lives down there!"

"Blast it, that's true of any mine anywhere in the world!" Hammersmith said.

Rogan folded his arms across his brawny chest and glared at Hammersmith. "We're goin' on strike," he declared. "We want two bits more an hour, *eight*-hour shifts, and an independent inspection of the mine to prove that it's safe. And until we get what we want, we ain't goin' back down there." He turned to look at the other miners. "Are you with me, boys?"

Again, they cheered. Some snatched their hats off and waved them over their heads. Others pumped their fists in the air. Hammersmith couldn't believe what he was hearing and seeing. How had things gone so wrong so quickly and unexpectedly? It had never occurred to him that the strike at the Lucky Lizard might spread over here to the Alhambra!

Munro was going to be mad. Damned mad.

That was why Hammersmith had to put a stop to this *now* before it got more out of hand than it already was.

He stepped closer to Rogan and said between clenched teeth, "Get into that mine and get back to work, mister. Right now, or you're fired!"

Rogan gave a stubborn shake of his head. "You can't fire me," he said. "I'm on strike!"

And with that, he spit in Hammersmith's face.

That was more than Hammersmith could stand. With a howl of rage, he slammed a punch into Rogan's jaw. The blow landed with a solid thud and knocked Rogan back a couple of steps, but the miner didn't go down. He stayed on his feet, caught his balance, and roared in defiance as he charged Hammersmith.

The battle was on. A clash of titans, a poet might have called it. Actually, it was just two big men beating the hell out of each other. They slugged, they wrestled, they threw each other down and rolled on the ground. Hammersmith tried to knee Rogan in the groin, but Rogan twisted aside and took the blow on his thigh. Rogan tried to dig his thumbs into Hammersmith's eyes, but Hammersmith caught one of them in his mouth and bit down hard, tasting blood as his teeth went all the way to the bone. Rogan screamed, pulled free, and flailed at Hammersmith. Blood from the injured thumb spattered on Hammersmith's face as some of the punches got through and battered him.

All the while, the assembled miners cheered and shouted. Some of them grabbed the guard and took his rifle away from him, as well as the pistol on his hip. The man tore out of their grip and sprinted away, fearing for his life if he tried to stay and help Hammersmith.

The mine superintendent roared like a maddened bull, grabbed Rogan by the shoulders, and pitched him off to the side. Rolling to his feet, Hammersmith charged after

Rogan and kicked him hard in the side, hard enough to maybe break a rib. Rogan grunted in pain and tried to get up, but Hammersmith's foot thudded into his chest and knocked him onto his back. Hammersmith lifted his foot again, ready to drive the heel of his work boot down into Rogan's face. Caught up in the grip of rage like he was, he didn't care if he stomped the life out of the bastard.

Before Hammersmith could bring his foot down, the mob surged forward. Strong hands gripped him and pulled him back. He yelled in alarm as he felt himself lifted off his feet. He struck out, throwing wild punches as fast and hard as he could, in every direction. He knew that if he allowed himself to be overwhelmed by the miners, he might be the one who wound up being stomped to death.

"Hold it!" The shouted command cut through the noisy confusion. "Let him go, damn it! If you kill him, you'll be playin' right into Munro's hands!"

The orders came from Dave Rogan. He continued to shout as Hammersmith was shoved roughly back and forth. Gradually, the miners let go of him and moved back a little to give him some breathing room, although he was still surrounded. They looked like a pack of wild-eyed wolves, Hammersmith thought as he stood there with his chest heaving. His muscles already ached from the battering he had received, and his left eye was trying to swell shut.

"If you kill him, Munro will have the law on us," Rogan said as he shouldered his way through the crowd to confront Hammersmith again. "It's legal for us to strike, as long as we don't murder anybody." He sneered at Hammersmith. "No matter how much they might deserve killin'."

"Why the hell do you hate me?" Hammersmith burst out, genuinely puzzled. "I never did anything to you!"

"You work for Munro. That's enough. But I've heard

plenty about you, Hammersmith. You've beaten men to death before for not obeying your orders. And you've worked them to death in the mines, damn you."

Hammersmith wiped the back of his hand across his mouth. It came away bloody. "I never laid into anybody except lazy sons o' bitches who had it comin'," he insisted. "Either that, or they jumped me first."

"Well, it don't matter now. You won't run roughshod over us anymore." Rogan thumped his chest with a clenched fist. "We're on strike. Go tell Munro that he'd better meet our demands, or else he won't ever take any more ore outta this mine!"

Hammersmith didn't want to tell Hamish Munro any such thing. Munro would explode with fury when he heard about this. As if they didn't have enough trouble with that damned nosy marshal!

Rogan waved an arm at the other miners. "Come on, boys, let's get out of here. Somebody go down and make sure everybody's out of the mine."

"You won't get away with this," Hammersmith warned. "You'll all just lose your jobs and get nothin' for it. We'll bring in more workers."

"They'll have to get through us first," Rogan warned with an ominous glare.

"If that's what it takes, then so be it," Hammersmith snapped. Munro could afford to bring in an army of armed guards if he needed to. Rogan and the others would soon see that they had bitten off a hell of a lot more than they could chew.

But in the meantime, Hammersmith thought as he watched the miners stalk off, throwing angry glances over their shoulders at him as they did so, the Alhambra Mine was shut down.

Like it or not, Munro had to be told about this, and

Hammersmith knew he was the one who would have to bring that bad news to Buckskin.

It was the guard who fled for his life, though, who reached the settlement first. He was breathless from the hard ride into town as he came into the Silver Baron Saloon, went to the bar, and asked for a drink. After he tossed back the whiskey, he began telling anybody who would listen how the miners at the Alhambra had gone on strike and were rioting.

"They've probably killed poor Mr. Hammersmith by now," he said.

Frank was seated at one of the tables in the rear of the room with Tip Woodford. They had cups of coffee in front of them, and had been talking about Frank's confrontation with Hamish Munro that morning.

Now Frank stood up and strode over to the bar, where he faced the newcomer and said, "You should've mentioned that somebody was in danger first."

"Sorry, Marshal," the man said. "I know how you and Mr. Hammersmith feel about each other, though. I didn't figure you'd care what happened to him."

"I wouldn't stand by and let any man be torn to pieces by a mob," Frank said, not bothering to keep the scorn out of his voice.

The guard from the mine flushed. "There was nothin' I could do. They would've killed me too."

Frank just turned away. He said to Tip, who had followed him to the bar, "I'd better ride out there and see what's going on."

"Want some company?" Tip asked.

Frank shook his head. "No, but I'd appreciate it if

you'd find Jack or Clint Farnum and let them know where I've gone."

"Sure, I can do that," Tip said with a nod. "Be careful, Frank. You sure as blazes don't want to get yourself killed over the likes o' Gunther Hammersmith."

Frank knew what the mayor meant. Still, he had chosen to expand his jurisdiction to the mines in the area, whether he really had any legal right to do so or not, so to Frank's way of thinking, he had a job to do and wasn't going to shy away from it.

He left the saloon and went to Hillman's livery stable. Both horses were well rested, so he saddled Stormy and rode out, taking Dog with him. He headed straight for the Alhambra.

However, he had ridden only half a mile or so when he saw a man on horseback coming toward him and recognized Hammersmith's bulky figure. The man didn't sit a saddle all that well, and Frank knew he wasn't really comfortable on horseback. Hammersmith was moving along the trail at a good clip, though.

Frank reined in to wait for him. He held up a hand in a signal for Hammersmith to stop. Hammersmith pulled his mount to a halt, but looked like he didn't care for being delayed.

"What the hell do you want?" he asked in a guttural voice. His face was bruised and swollen and had several patches of dried blood on it.

"I'm a mite surprised to see you alive, Hammersmith," Frank drawled. "Fella who works for you out at the mine came galloping into town, said the men were on strike and were about to tear you limb from limb."

"Yeah, well, you can see for yourself that didn't happen."

"What about the part about being on strike?"

"What business is that of yours?"

"Anything that affects the community is my business," Frank said, "because it might have an effect on law and order too. Just answer the question, Hammersmith."

"Yeah, they went on strike," Hammersmith replied in a grudging tone. "That bastard Rogan started it."

"Dave Rogan?" Frank asked in surprise. "I didn't know he worked for the Alhambra."

"Yeah, he hired on after Woodford fired him."

Frank hadn't forgotten the ruckus at Ed Kelley's Top-Notch Saloon. That fight had gotten Rogan discharged from the Lucky Lizard, but evidently the miner hadn't had much trouble finding another job.

A part of Frank was tempted to tell Hammersmith that he had gotten just what he deserved. Frank was as convinced as ever that Hammersmith and Munro were behind the strike at the Lucky Lizard. Now their tactics had backfired against them, as their own workers, inspired by the strike at the other mine, had walked out on their jobs.

"You want anything else, Morgan?" Hammersmith snapped. "I got to tell Mr. Munro about what happened."

Frank would have enjoyed being a fly on the wall during that conversation. That wasn't going to happen, though, so he waved a hand in the direction of Buckskin and said, "Go ahead. I'm warning you, though, Hammersmith. . . . Your labor troubles had better stay confined to the mine. If they start reaching into town, I'll put a stop to all this myself if I have to."

Hammersmith's lip curled. "What can you do? There ain't no law against striking. More's the pity."

Again, Frank was struck by the irony of it. Hammersmith and Munro had struck at the Lucky Lizard, using the strike there as a weapon, but Hammersmith didn't like it so much when the tables were turned and there was nothing he could do about it.

Frank moved aside to let Hammersmith pass. The man rode off toward the settlement. Frank started again toward the mine, chuckling as he said to Dog, "Wonder what they'll do now."

He didn't figure he would have to wait very long to find out.

And he wasn't expecting to be pleased when he found out, either.

Chapter 28

Frank rode on out to the Alhambra and talked to Dave Rogan, warning him that any violence connected with the strike wouldn't be tolerated. Rogan remembered Frank from the ruckus in Kelley's, and for a few moments things had been pretty tense as Rogan debated whether to indulge his old grudge and try to cause more trouble for the lawman.

But in the end, Rogan had just said, "Talk to Hamish Munro, Marshal. If anybody causes any bloodshed, it'll be him."

Frank wasn't going to be surprised if Rogan turned out to be right. One thing seemed certain: Munro wouldn't take this setback lying down. He would fight and would try to hurt the striking miners just as much as they were hurting him.

For a couple of days, an uneasy pause seemed to hang over Buckskin. The strike at the Lucky Lizard continued, in addition to the one at the Alhambra. The new equipment for the stamp mill at the Crown Royal arrived, as well as a dozen hard-bitten, well-armed men who had been hired by Conrad Browning to keep any more sabotage from occurring at the mine. Their leader, a tall, rusty-bearded man named Burke, came to see Frank.

"We have our orders," Burke explained. "We're to protect the Crown Royal, and that's it. Mr. Browning doesn't want us getting mixed up in any other local troubles."

Frank nodded. "That's fine with me. I'd just as soon give things a chance to settle down on their own. We don't need a war here in Buckskin."

That looked like what the town might get, though, because a day later the army rode in.

Frank was in the office when Catamount Jack stuck his head in the door and said in an excited voice, "You'd better come take a gander at this, Marshal. Looks like Buckskin's bein' invaded."

Frank didn't know whether to be alarmed or puzzled by Jack's comment. He stood up and moved to the door, not wasting any time.

Sure enough, a military force was entering the settlement, riding into town from the northern end. The natty blue uniforms made Frank take them for United States cavalrymen at first, but he realized a second later that the markings and insignia were different. These uniforms were a little gaudier, a little fancier, than regular cavalry uniforms. All the riders, about two dozen of them, wore sabers in brass scabbards and had Winchesters in saddle boots instead of the usual army carbines.

The soldiers rode with their eyes fixed straight ahead, not paying any attention to the commotion their arrival was causing in the settlement. They came on down the street to the marshal's office, where the officer leading them reined in and raised a hand. The man right behind him, evidently a sergeant of some sort, turned in his saddle and bellowed, "Company . . . *halt!*"

The officer dismounted, handed his horse's reins to the

sergeant, and stepped up onto the boardwalk. He tugged a gauntlet off his right hand and offered that hand to Frank. "Marshal Morgan?" he said. "I'm Colonel Jefferson Starkwell, Nevada State Militia."

Frank had already started to wonder if these newcomers were members of the state militia. That was the only explanation that made any sense. What they were doing here in Buckskin was still an open question, though.

Frank shook hands with Starkwell and said, "Colonel. What brings you to Buckskin?"

Starkwell was a tall, stiff-backed man with iron-gray hair and a neat mustache and goatee. He said, "The governor has ordered us here to maintain law and order in the face of mounting civil unrest."

A frown creased Frank's forehead. He had been afraid that Colonel Starkwell would say something like that. Waving a hand toward the street, which was thronged at the moment with curious bystanders, he said, "What civil unrest? You can see for yourself that the place is plumb peaceful right now."

"At the moment, perhaps," Starkwell replied, unfazed by Frank's question. "But the governor has been informed that violent strikes have broken out at two of the area mines and may spread to other mines in the vicinity. Riots have been reported." A cold, thin smile curved Starkwell's lips. "Dealing with such problems is beyond the scope of local law enforcement; therefore the governor dispatched us to see to it that things don't get even more out of hand. The citizens must be protected."

"And the mine owners have to be protected too, is that it?" Frank didn't bother trying to hide his irritation now. "Since Jack and me and my other deputy are that local law enforcement you were talking about, don't you think we ought to have a say in whether or not we need help from a troop of militia men?"

"The governor received a full report on the situation here, Marshal, and he acted in what he believes to be everyone's best interests."

Frank looked at Jack and said, "Munro. He's the one behind this."

The old-timer nodded. "Sure as shootin'."

As far as Frank had known, Hamish Munro had been holed up in the hotel for the past few days, consulting with Hammersmith and Nathan Evers about the strike going on at the Alhambra. Now Frank realized that Munro had already taken action without him knowing about it. Munro must have sent a rider into Virginia City to wire the governor in Carson City and ask for help putting down the strike. The governor, like all politicians mindful of anyone with wealth and influence who might help him get elected again, had been only too glad to help. He had sent in the militia, ostensibly to keep order, but Frank knew how these things worked. He had seen similar situations in other places. Starkwell and his company of soldiers would actually be working for Munro, and their real goal would be to crush the strike crippling production at the Alhambra.

To accomplish that goal, they would crush the strikers if they had to.

Even though Frank knew it probably wouldn't do any good, he said, "Colonel, I'd appreciate it if you and your men would turn around and ride right back to Carson City. Tell the governor we appreciate his concern, but we don't need any help keeping a lid on things here."

"I'm sorry, Marshal," Starkwell said, not sounding the least bit apologetic, "but our orders are clear. We won't be leaving until the miners' strike is over, the men have returned to work, and the danger is ended."

"But that ain't right," Catamount Jack protested. "You can't force them fellas to work for Munro, nor for Tip Woodford neither."

"The governor disagrees, sir. He views continued silver production as vital to the state's interest. I'll be riding out to the Alhambra Mine to issue a warning to the striking workers. I'm sure they'll be reasonable."

"Damn it, if you go out there, those men are liable to think you've come to arrest them."

"If they don't cooperate, they'll be right about that," Starkwell snapped.

Frank thought about how hotheaded Dave Rogan was and said, "They're liable to open fire on you."

"If they do, they'll wish they hadn't. Our orders empower us to use all necessary force to maintain order."

Anger welled up inside Frank as he realized what Starkwell intended to do. Under the guise of "maintaining order," the colonel planned to massacre the striking miners, or at least some of them, in hopes that the others would surrender and go back to work. If not, Starkwell would wipe out all of them so that Munro could start over. This "militia" was really nothing more than a gang of hired killers.

"I'm going out there with you," Frank snapped. "Let me talk to those men first."

"You've had plenty of chances to talk to them before now, Marshal. I can't stop you from riding out there, but I warn you. . . . Stay out of our way."

Frank suppressed the impulse to knock the arrogant smirk off Starkwell's face. Instead, he turned to Jack and said, "Find Clint and tell him what's going on. The two of you stay here in town and be ready for trouble."

Jack nodded. "You be careful, Frank."

"It may be too late for that," Frank said. He headed for

the livery stable. As he hurried along the street, he glanced up at the hotel.

Hamish Munro stood in one of the windows of his suite, the curtain pulled back so that he could gaze out at the street. The mining magnate wore a self-satisfied smile, and the nod that he gave Frank was even more infuriating. Munro thought that everything was going his way again. He believed that his money and influence could always get him whatever he wanted.

And so far, Frank reflected with a grim, silent curse, nobody had proven that idea wrong.

Starkwell mounted up and the militia moved out, riding past Amos Hillman's place. Frank heard them go by as he was throwing his saddle on Goldy. The uniformed riders were still in sight as he emerged from the livery barn a couple of minutes later. They were following the main trail toward the Alhambra. Frank figured he could circle around and beat them to the mine, since he knew the area better than the militia men did.

Hearing his name called, he turned in the saddle to see Catamount Jack hurrying toward him. "I can't find Clint," the old-timer said.

"He's bound to be around somewhere. Keep looking, and warn the townspeople that there's liable to be more trouble."

Jack nodded. "All hell's about to bust loose, ain't it, Frank?"

"Not if I can help it," Frank said.

Problem was, he didn't know if he could.

A breeze set the leaves of the aspens to rattling together as Clint Farnum rode up the slope. It was a beautiful day, the sort of day he would have enjoyed getting out of the settlement and just riding around the hills, taking in the magnificent scenery. The years had taught him to appreciate such things. All the long, solitary, dangerous years of riding the owlhoot trail, never knowing when a day might be his last one on this earth. . . .

He hadn't ridden out here into the hills west of the settlement to look at the scenery, though. He had a job to do, and he intended to carry it out. He might not like it much anymore, but there was no turning back now.

The smell of tobacco smoke drifted to his nose. He grimaced. That was careless. Didn't really matter, though. Not now.

Clint topped the hill and saw the riders waiting on the other side. Between thirty and forty, he estimated. Roughly dressed and heavily armed, with a brutal eagerness stamped on their beard-stubbled faces.

The big, blond-bearded man spurred out to meet Clint and said, "I got the word you sent and brought the boys right on. What's goin' on down there?"

"A company of state militia rode in just as I was about to leave to meet you, Jory," Clint replied.

That brought mutters of concern from the outlaws. Jory Pool turned in his saddle and silenced them with a look. He swung back around to face Clint and asked, "What are they doin' there?"

"I don't know for sure, but I imagine they came to bust that strike out at the Alhambra Mine. The gent who owns it, Hamish Munro, is friends with the governor."

One of the other men said, "I guess that means we'll have to call the raid off, Jory. We can't attack the town if the militia is there."

"The hell we can't," Pool said. "This is a stroke of good luck for us."

Clint frowned. "I don't follow you, Jory."

A grin spread across Pool's face. "The soldier boys and them miners will be too busy fightin' with each other to worry about us. And the people in town will be so caught up in that they won't expect trouble to come at them from any other direction."

"I don't know," Clint said.

"What's the best time to jump somebody?" Pool asked. "When he's watchin' two other hombres fight. That's when you hit him with a sucker punch." He gave an emphatic nod. "That's what we're gonna do to Buckskin."

Clint knew it wouldn't do any good to argue. Once Jory Pool's mind was made up, especially when it came to the tactics of a raid, nothing would change it.

Like it or not, even more hell was to come to call on Buckskin.

"What about Morgan?" Pool asked.

"I was watching from one of the hills," Clint said. "I saw him ride out toward the Alhambra. My guess is that he was trying to get there before the militia did, so he could warn those miners."

"So the only law left in town is one old pelican."

Clint thought about Catamount Jack and nodded. "Yeah." His throat was tight for some reason, and the word didn't much want to come out.

Pool nodded and said, "You've done a mighty fine job spyin' out this job for us, Clint. You've already earned your share of the loot. I reckon you can be right proud of yourself." Pool leaned forward in the saddle and waved his men forward. "Let's go."

As the gang moved out, bound for Buckskin, Clint Farnum thought about what Pool had just said to him. Proud of himself? Clint thought about how Frank had given him a chance to wear a deputy's star, about how Catamount Jack had befriended him, about how folks in the settlement had started smiling at him and looking at him with something like respect in their eyes. He thought too about how Frank had saved his life during that shoot-out with the drunken miner who'd had the fight with Professor Burton.

Funny . . . he didn't feel proud of himself at all. He felt almost . . . ashamed, in fact.

But it wasn't the first time in his life he'd been ashamed of something he was doing, not by a long shot. And as he sighed and hitched his horse into motion, Clint thought that he was too old to change now.

Besides, money spent just as good whether you were ashamed of how you got it or not.

He spurred ahead to catch up to Jory Pool.

Chapter 29

Goldy responded magnificently as Frank left the trail and started cutting across country to try to get ahead of Colonel Starkwell and the militia company. The horse took to the steep slopes almost like a mountain goat, bounding from rock to rock going up, and then deftly keeping his hooves under him as he skidded down the far sides. Goldy leaped gullies and weaved through trees, and even though Frank felt a little guilty for thinking it, he didn't believe that Stormy could have done any better.

Dog raced alongside. The big cur seemed as happy to get out and stretch his legs, as eager for action, as Goldy did.

Frank came in sight of the bench where the Alhambra was located, with its overhanging cliffs and the rock formations that looked like battlements. He didn't see the militia on the trail approaching the mine and knew he had beaten them here. He couldn't be very far ahead of them, though, so he knew he didn't have much time. He galloped down the hill and brought Goldy to a halt in front of the bunk house.

"Rogan!" Frank shouted. "Rogan, it's Marshal Morgan from Buckskin! Trouble's on the way!"

There was no response from the building. Frank dismounted and hurried to the door. When he looked inside, he saw that the bunkhouse was empty. Where could the striking miners be?

He walked over to the office and stamp mill, keeping one eye on the trail as he did so. The other buildings were empty too, as if the mine had been abandoned.

That wasn't the case, though, as the warning shot that came from the mouth of the shaft proved a moment later as Frank walked back out into the open. The bullet whistled past, well above his head, and as instinct made him crouch and reach for his Peacemaker, a man shouted from the mine entrance, "Hold it, Morgan!"

Frank recognized Dave Rogan's voice. He turned in that direction and saw Rogan standing at the tunnel mouth, along with several more of the striking miners. He realized that they must have barricaded themselves inside the shaft to keep Munro from bringing in any other workers.

Frank straightened and walked toward the mine. He kept his hands in plain sight so that Rogan and the others could see them.

Rogan fired again. This time the bullet kicked up dirt and rocks from the ground about ten yards in front of Frank. Frank didn't break stride or slow down.

"Get out of here, Marshal!" Rogan shouted. "The next one might not miss!"

"Listen to me, Rogan," Frank said in an urgent voice that was loud enough so that the rest of the men inside the shaft could hear him too. "Munro's gotten the governor to send in the state militia to break this strike. A company of armed soldiers is on its way out here right now."

"Let 'em come!" Rogan replied. "We'll show 'em that we won't be budged!"

Some of the other men in the mine shouted in agreement with him.

"You'll all get yourselves killed, that's what you'll do," Frank said as he came to a stop in front of the mine entrance. "You boys are tough, but those militia men are professionals at this. They'll do whatever they have to in order to break this strike. They're liable to heave a bomb in there to blast you out."

Rogan sneered. "That would damage the mine," he pointed out.

"You think Munro wouldn't be willing to have the damage repaired if it meant that none of his workers would ever dare to defy him again?"

Rogan wasn't so quick to respond to that, and for the first time Frank saw doubt appear on the miner's rugged face. Rogan was a troublemaker, but he wasn't stupid. He knew that Munro would do whatever it took to suppress this challenge to his authority.

"We got a right to strike," Rogan said, but the doubt was in his voice now too.

"It's not about rights anymore," Frank said. "It's about Munro wanting to crush you and teach a lesson to anybody else who ever works for him."

"Yeah, well, what business is it of yours?"

"I don't want to see all of you massacred," Frank said. "Munro thinks that he's above the law. I don't like that."

"That's mighty funny, comin' from a gunfighter like you. I didn't reckon you ever worried all that much about the law."

"Maybe I didn't in the past." Frank tapped the badge pinned to his shirt. "That's before I put this tin star on."

Rogan lowered his rifle and frowned. "What do you think we ought to do?"

"Get out of here," Frank said without hesitation. "Clear out and let Munro have his mine back."

"But that's giving up!"

Frank shook his head. "Go over to the Lucky Lizard and get the miners there who are on strike. All of you come to Buckskin. There's a tunnel from the mine that runs under Tip's office in town, so you can get there without the militia seeing you. We'll all sit down and have a meeting with Tip Woodford and Munro. Tip's a reasonable man. His workers will be able to work out something with him."

"What about Munro? He ain't reasonable."

"No, but out in the open like that, where everybody in town can see what's going on, he'll have to make a show of listening anyway. And once he sees that Woodford is going to settle the strike at the Lucky Lizard, public opinion may force him to go along and reach a compromise too."

Rogan scratched at his jaw and frowned in thought. "Maybe," he allowed. "Might be worth a try."

This argument was taking too long. "You can decide what to do later," Frank said. "Right now, you've got to get out of here while you still have the chance. That militia company will be showing up any minute now."

Rogan turned to the other men clustered just inside the mouth of the shaft. "What do you say, boys?" he asked.

"I think we ought to do what the marshal says," one of the miners replied. "If we join forces with Woodford's men, then Woodford and Munro will have to listen to us."

"What about the Crown Royal?" Rogan asked Frank. "Once it starts up again, will the men who work there be treated fairly too?"

Frank nodded. "I can just about guarantee that. You see, I'm well acquainted with the fella who owns it."

"All right," Rogan said, reaching a decision. He waved to the men behind him. "Let's go."

As they began to file out of the mine, Frank said, "I'll go back down the trail and stall the militia. Head for the Lucky Lizard and then come on into town this evening. I'll have Woodford and Munro waiting for you."

Rogan jerked his head in a nod.

Frank hurried back to Goldy, grabbed the reins he had left trailing on the ground, and swung up into the saddle. "Come on, Dog," he said as he heeled Goldy into a run.

Following the main trail this time, Frank rode hard. He spotted a haze of dust in the air up ahead and knew the militia was only a few hundred yards away. He sighted them as he came around a bend where the trail looped around a cluster of large boulders.

Frank said, "Dog, stay," then reined in and sat there in the middle of the trail, blocking it as the riders approached. Of course, he was outnumbered by more than twenty to one, and if they really wanted to get past him, he wouldn't be able to stop them. He could take a few of them with him if they rode him down, but he wasn't sure he wanted to draw and fire on them. Even though they were being used for a purpose he considered corrupt, the militia men weren't outlaws or anything like that. He didn't want to have to kill any of them.

Colonel Starkwell rode in front of the troop. He raised a hand in a signal to halt, and the sergeant who rode behind him bawled out the order. Starkwell walked his horse forward to confront Frank.

"What are you doing here, Marshal?" Starkwell demanded. "I thought that when we left you back in Buckskin I made it clear this was none of your affair."

"I'm making it my affair," Frank said. "I took a shortcut and rode out to the Alhambra. You might as well turn around and go back. The mine's deserted. All the strikers are gone."

Starkwell's mouth thinned in anger under the mustache. "You mean you warned them and they fled," he snapped. "By God, I ought to put you under arrest! You should be clapped in irons and thrown in your own jail!"

"You can try it if you want," Frank said in a quiet, dangerous voice.

Starkwell glared at him for a couple of heartbeats, then said, "Move aside. I'm not going to take your word for it that the strikers have abandoned the mine. We're going out there anyway."

Frank hoped that Rogan and the others had had plenty of time to get into the thickly wooded hills above the mine by now. He pulled Goldy to the side of the trail and said to Starkwell, "Fine. Go right on ahead, Colonel."

Starkwell's eyes slitted in suspicion, as if he thought that Frank was playing some sort of trick on him, but he gigged his horse into motion and waved the rest of the soldiers ahead. Frank sat there beside the trail as the militia troop rode past him.

He followed them back to the Alhambra, but reined in a couple of hundred yards away to watch as the men searched the bunkhouse, the stamp mill and office, and the mine shaft itself. He could tell from the way Starkwell was stomping around that the colonel was getting madder and madder.

Frank turned Goldy and started back toward the settlement. He didn't want another confrontation with Starkwell right now. Starkwell might be angry enough at the fact that his quarry had eluded him to try making good on that threat to arrest Frank.

Pushing Goldy into a run, Frank reached Buckskin well ahead of the militia. He went straight to the office of the Lucky Lizard Mining Company, hoping he would find Tip Woodford there.

Tip was there, all right, and so was Diana. They greeted Frank warmly, but both of them could tell from the expression on his face that something was wrong. "What is it, Frank?" Diana asked.

"You know the militia was here earlier?"

Tip nodded. "Yeah, we saw the soldier boys. Heard that Munro got the governor to send 'em in. I wish he hadn't done that. It's liable to just make things worse. We would've worked things out sooner or later, if everybody would just leave us alone."

Frank nodded. "I know. That's why I rode out to the Alhambra to warn Rogan and the other men that the militia was coming to break the strike. I sent them to the Lucky Lizard."

Tip's eyebrows rose in surprise. "The Lucky Lizard? Why'd you want to do that?"

"Because all the men from both mines who are on strike are coming in to town tonight for a meeting with you and Munro. We're going to settle this without a war breaking out."

"I'd be glad to settle things with the fellas who work for me," Tip said, "if they'll just listen to reason."

"I think they will, once they realize they've been duped. The Fowler brothers are still working for Munro and Hammersmith. They caused that cave-in to stir up trouble and get the strike started, so the Lucky Lizard would be shut down. The only problem was that Munro didn't count on it spreading to his mine too."

Diana asked, "Do you have any proof of that, Frank?"

"Nothing that would stand up in a court of law more than likely," Frank replied with a shrug. "But I can prove somebody sabotaged the timbers in the mine and caused the cave-in. I'm betting that if Mike and Gib Fowler think they're facing a hang rope because of what they did, they'll be more than happy to testify that they were following orders from either Hammersmith or Munro."

Tip nodded his bulldoglike head. "Maybe. Munro bein' behind it all would explain why he raised his wages and cut back the hours his men are workin' too. Those things were just temporary to make the Lucky Lizard look worse."

"That's my theory," Frank agreed. "As soon as he put you out of business, things at the Alhambra would go back to being the way they were, if not worse."

"That fella was playin' a mighty deep game."

"Yes, but he's going to lose the final hand," Frank said. He gestured toward the back room. "Dave Rogan's the leader of the strike at the Alhambra. I told him about the tunnel that runs down here from the Lucky Lizard. All the men from both mines will be here after dark, coming through the tunnel so the militia won't be able to stop them."

"That fella Rogan's an ornery varmint. Are you sure we can trust him?"

"He's a hothead and a troublemaker, all right . . . but I think at the core he's an honest man."

Tip sighed. "Let's hope you're right."

"And let's hope everything can be settled without bloodshed," Diana added.

"That's the idea," Frank said.

"But you don't hold out much hope that it'll happen, do you?" she asked.

"It never hurts to hope for the best," Frank said.

And prepare for all hell to break loose, he added silently to himself.

Chapter 30

The militia arrived back in town a short time later. Colonel Starkwell dismounted and stalked into the hotel, no doubt to report to Hamish Munro about their lack of success at the Alhambra. From the boardwalk in front of the marshal's office, Frank watched Starkwell go into the building, and thought that it was pretty clear who was really in charge of the militia. The governor must have made it plain to Starkwell that Munro was really calling the shots in Buckskin.

At least, Munro *thought* he was. If Frank's plan worked, Munro might find himself with a problem a lot worse than some striking miners.

Catamount Jack walked up and said with a worried frown, "I still ain't found Clint. Where do you reckon he got off to?"

Frank shook his head. "I don't know. I'd feel a little better if he was in town, though, in case trouble breaks out between the militia and those miners." A short time earlier, before Jack left to take another turn around town in search of Clint Farnum, Frank had told the old-timer about the meeting he had set up for that evening.

Now Jack asked, "You gonna take a side in that fight if it happens?"

Frank shook his head. "No, but I'm going to do my best to keep the townspeople safe. I'm hoping that Starkwell won't start a full-scale battle right here in the middle of town. That would look mighty bad for the governor, no matter what caused it, and the colonel's bound to know that."

Frank had a shoulder leaned against one of the posts holding up the awning over the boardwalk. He straightened from that casual pose as he looked along the street and noticed a rider coming.

"There's Clint now," he said.

Jack looked in the same direction and said, "Sure enough is. Wonder where he's been."

Clint Farnum rode up and dismounted in front of the marshal's office. The little gunfighter looped his horse's reins around the hitch rail and said, "Sorry for disappearing like that, Frank. The wanderlust got me. Had to get out of town and ride around the hills for a while."

"You need to tell Jack or me where you're going before you do something like that again," Frank said. "For all we knew, you'd ridden off and weren't coming back."

"No, I'd never desert you boys like that. Wasn't any trouble while I was gone, was there?"

Jack snorted. "Just the damn militia ridin' in to bust the hell outta them strikes at the mines."

Clint's eyes widened in surprise. "You don't say! What happened?"

Frank filled him in on the day's events. Clint shook his head in seeming disbelief.

"So all those miners are coming into town tonight for a showdown with Woodford and Munro?" Clint asked when Frank was finished.

"I wouldn't call it a showdown. They need to stop fighting and get down to some serious talking."

"I can see the mayor going along with that," Clint said, "but not Munro, or that fella Hammersmith who works for him."

"They'll have more trouble of their own once I show everybody what I found inside the shaft at the Lucky Lizard." Frank took the acid-damaged piece of timber from his pocket so that the two deputies could look at it. "Somebody's bound to have seen one or both of the Fowler brothers hanging around those support beams that gave out. Once they realize they've been found out, they won't take the blame for those deaths by themselves."

Clint nodded and said, "Sounds like you've got it all figured out, all right."

"We'll have to wait and see," Frank said. "All three of us are going to be on hand for that meeting, to keep things as peaceful as we can."

"I'll go put my horse up." Clint looked back as he started to lead the animal toward the livery stable. "Again, I'm sorry for disappearing on you like that, Frank."

"You're here now," Frank said. "That's all that matters."

He couldn't have said for sure, but he thought he saw something flicker through Clint's eyes just then, an unreadable expression that was still somehow troubling, as if Clint were wrestling with some sort of inner demon.

But then the little gunman's face was as bland and smiling as ever, and Frank wasn't sure he had even seen anything unusual. He told himself not to worry about it.

With the meeting looming between the striking miners and the mine owners—a meeting that might well turn into a violent showdown despite his best efforts—Frank figured he had bigger problems on his plate right now than whatever was bothering Clint Farnum.

* * *

Hap Mitchell walked up to the top of the ridge where Pool was studying Buckskin through a pair of field glasses. "Any sign of the signal?" he asked.

Pool lowered the glasses and glared at Mitchell. "If there was, don't you think I'd've said somethin' before now?"

"I didn't mean any offense, Jory," Mitchell said. "I just figured from the way you were talking earlier that we'd ride right into the settlement and start lootin' the place."

"It never hurts to be sure everything's lined up just right. That's why we're gonna wait for Farnum's signal before we move in."

Mitchell nodded. "Sure, that makes sense. You know best, Jory."

"Damn right I do," Pool said in a harsh tone of voice that was almost a growl.

But despite what he had just said, Hap Mitchell wasn't so sure about that anymore. There came a time when bad luck caught up to every gang, no matter how careful they were. It had happened to Frank and Jesse James and their cousins the Youngers up in Northfield, Minnesota, and just a couple of years earlier the Dalton boys had run into the same thing in Coffeyville, Kansas.

Mitchell had to ask himself if Buckskin, Nevada, might turn out to be the Pool gang's Northfield or Coffeyville. If that was the case, he didn't want to be there for it. He ought to get Lonnie Beeman and slip away from here while there was still time. Hap and Lonnie had been riding together for a lot of years. Maybe they should git while the gittin' was good.

But if they did that and then the raid went off perfectly, just as planned, then not only would they miss out on their shares of the loot, but they would have earned the enmity of Jory Pool for deserting him. Jory wouldn't take kindly to that. In fact, he might just track them down and kill them for their disloyalty.

No, Mitchell thought with a sigh, it looked like he and Lonnie were stuck. They would have to join in the raid with the rest of the gang.

As soon as Clint Farnum gave the signal.

Frank was waiting in the back room of the building that housed the Lucky Lizard's office when dusk settled down over Buckskin. He had already lifted the trapdoor and exposed the ladder that led down to the tunnel from the mine. That tunnel ran for a mile or more into the nearby hills. Frank didn't know when the miners would be arriving, or even if they would come. Dave Rogan could have changed his mind and backed out of the deal. There was no guarantee either that the men from the Lucky Lizard would come along, even if Rogan and the other miners from the Alhambra did as Frank had suggested.

This room was where Frank's long vengeance quest against Charles Dutton had ended. Dutton had betrayed Vivian Browning and been responsible for her death, he had put Conrad Browning in mortal danger, and he had sent hired gunmen after Frank to kill him. Those gunmen had failed, and instead Frank had tracked Dutton to what had then been an isolated ghost town in the foothills of the Wassuck Mountains. Frank had caught up to Dutton here, and so had justice. . . .

A faint noise caught Frank's attention and pulled him out of his reverie. He leaned closer to the open trapdoor and listened. The echoing sounds of footsteps and voices came to his ears. Men were moving along the tunnel toward him.

A tight smile appeared on Frank's lips. The miners were on their way.

He stepped into the front room, where Tip Woodford, Diana, Catamount Jack, and Garrett Claiborne waited. Even though Claiborne, as the superintendent of the Crown Royal, had no direct stake in what happened tonight, he was here because of his belief that Munro had been behind the explosion that had almost cost him his life, and because he and Diana had grown closer as well. Claiborne's broken arm was still in a sling, but he was getting around well enough these days that he had been supervising the rebuilding of the mine's stamp mill.

"They're on their way," Frank reported. "I can hear them coming down the tunnel."

"I sure hope we can settle this mess," Tip said. "It'll get everything out in the open, anyway."

Frank nodded. "Jack, stay here and keep Rogan and the others here for the time being. There's no place in town big enough to hold everybody on both sides, so the meeting will take place in the street. I'll go tell Munro what's about to happen."

"What if he refuses to negotiate?" Claiborne asked.

Tip said, "Then I'll settle things with the fellas who work for me, and Munro's problems will be his own lookout." He glanced at Frank. "You know Munro's liable to tell that militia colonel to arrest Rogan and the rest of the bunch from the Alhambra."

"He can't do that, because they're already going to be in my custody. And as the duly appointed marshal of Buckskin, here in town I have the authority to make that stick."

"You and a couple o' deputies against a whole troop of militia?"

"I've been going around the town this afternoon talking to folks," Frank explained. "Amos Hillman said he'd back my play, and so did Professor Burton. Leo Benjamin and Johnny Collyer and Claude Langley want in on it too. Ed Kelley said he would come to the meeting and would spread the word, and so did the others. The citizens of Buckskin are ready to say that enough is enough and put a stop to all this squabbling."

"I hope you're right, Frank," Tip said with a sigh. "But I sure wish Hamish Munro had never come to town."

Frank jerked his head in a curt nod as he started out of the office. "You and me both, Tip," he said. "You and me both."

He crossed the street at an angle, heading for the old hotel. Munro had guards posted on the porch as usual, and they moved to block Frank's path as he started toward the door.

"You're not welcome here, Marshal," one of the men said. "Mr. Munro's orders."

"I'm here on official business," Frank said, "so step aside."

The men hesitated, but Frank's steely-eyed stare reminded them that while he might be the marshal of Buckskin now, he was also still the notorious gunfighter known as The Drifter. Finally, the guard who had spoken before said, "Well, I reckon if it's official business . . ."

The two of them moved away from the doors.

Frank went inside, into the lobby, and the sound of voices drew him to an arched entrance that led into the dining room. He found Hamish and Jessica Munro there, along with Gunther Hammersmith, Nathan Evers, and Colonel Starkwell. The men were gathered around a table talking while Jessica sat alone at another table.

Munro, Hammersmith, and Starkwell all glared at Frank. Evers was as blandly inscrutable as ever. Munro demanded, "What are you doing here, Morgan? I gave orders that I didn't want to be bothered by you."

"You'd better be bothered, Munro," Frank snapped. "Those men of yours who are on strike have come to town to negotiate a settlement."

Starkwell surged to his feet. "What! Those fugitives are here?"

"They're not fugitives. They haven't been charged with any crime. But I've placed them in protective custody, just as a precaution."

"You can't do that." Starkwell snatched up his hat from the table where he had been sitting with the others and jammed it on his head. "I'm going to get my troops and place those men under arrest—"

"I don't think so." Frank played his trump card. He had made the long, hard ride to Virginia City and back during the afternoon, pushing Stormy as hard as he dared, and the big Appaloosa hadn't let him down. Frank took a telegram from his pocket and handed it to Starkwell, who hesitated before taking it as if Frank were trying to give him a rattlesnake.

Starkwell's eyes went to the words printed on the Western Union form, and his face reddened with fury as he read them.

"As you can see, the governor has rescinded his previous orders to you," Frank said. "You're to assist me in maintaining order in Buckskin, *at my request*. I haven't asked for your help, Colonel."

"How . . . how . . ." Starkwell sputtered, too angry to go on.

Munro pushed himself to his feet and demanded, "What sort of trick is this, Morgan?" He jabbed a finger at the telegram in Starkwell's hand. "How do we know that wire isn't a fake? How do we know it's really from the governor?"

"I guess you'll have to go to Virginia City and wire him yourself," Frank said.

Starkwell crumpled the telegram. "It's real, all right," he said as his mouth twisted in a snarl. "I know how the governor sounds when he gives orders like this. How did you do it, Morgan? How the hell did you manage to go over my head like that?"

"I've got a friend or two in high places too," Frank drawled.

Like Conrad Browning, who counted senators and congressmen and various federal officials among *his* friends, as well as the presidents of numerous banks and railroads. A series of wires to Conrad and to Frank's own lawyers in Denver and San Francisco had produced the desired results. Political pressure had been brought to bear on the governor of Nevada, and wisely, the man had bowed to it.

"From the sound of this, my men and I are under *your* command," Starkwell fumed.

"This is outrageous," Munro said. "Outrageous!"

Frank shrugged. "Call it whatever you want. What it comes down to is that the striking miners from the Lucky Lizard and the Alhambra have come to Buckskin. Tip Woodford has agreed to meet with them, Munro. Whether you do or not is up to you. But I have a feeling that the strike at the Lucky Lizard is going to be settled tonight. Unless you want the Alhambra to fall behind, it might be a good idea for you to reach a settlement too."

"Go to hell!" Munro screamed. "No one tells me what to do!"

"Your choice," Frank said. He turned away, and as he did so he took the acid-damaged piece of wood from his pocket, tossing it up and down on his palm so that Munro could see it and recognize it. He walked out, leaving Munro sputtering and seething behind him.

Starkwell hurried after him. "My men are camped just outside of town," he said. "I'm going to bring them in. I don't trust those miners. If there's any trouble, I intend to suppress it with all due force, no matter what you say, Morgan."

"Fetch your men if you want, Colonel, but there won't be any riot. I'll see to that."

Diana and Claiborne stood on the boardwalk in front of the Lucky Lizard office. Frank made a motion toward them, and Diana turned to say something through the open door of the office. They moved aside, and a moment later Catamount Jack strode out, followed by Dave Rogan. The striking miners filed out of the building and began to form ranks in the street.

Catamount Jack hurried to one end of the street and set fire to a pile of branches and brush that had been stacked there earlier. Along with another bonfire at the far end of the street, the blaze would provide light for the meeting. After a moment, Frank realized that Clint Farnum wasn't lighting the other bonfire as he was supposed to, though.

"Where's Clint?" Frank called to Jack.

"Don't know. Has the little varmint up and disappeared again?"

That appeared to be the case. Jack trotted down to the far end of the street and lit that pile too. As the glow from the fires brightened, men carrying rifles and shotguns stepped out onto the boardwalk in various places, and Frank felt a surge of pride as he realized that his unofficial deputies were prepared to do their part if necessary. He nodded his thanks to Amos Hillman, Leo Benjamin, Ed Kelley, Professor Burton, and the others. They were all willing to fight for their town if they had to, and that meant Buckskin had become more than just a collection of buildings and people.

It was truly a community now.

With Colonel Starkwell at their head, the militia men marched in from the other end of the settlement and faced the striking miners, with about twenty yards separating the two groups. They carried their rifles slanted across their chests. The miners were all armed too. Tension was thick in the air. All it would take was one reckless act to set off a hell storm of gunfire.

Frank didn't intend to let that happen. He walked into the center of the street, between the two groups. Tip Woodford strode out from the other boardwalk. The mayor's face was pale and drawn from the strain, but he didn't hesitate to place himself between the guns of the two hostile forces.

"All right," Frank began as he and Tip faced the miners. "We're here to lay all our cards on the table and settle this thing—"

"Wait just a damned minute!"

The voice came from the front of the hotel. Hamish Munro marched out into the street, followed by Hammersmith. As the mining magnate came up to Frank and Tip, he continued. "I still think the militia should arrest all these men for their illegal strike, but I can see now you're determined to have mob rule instead of law and order, Morgan. I want the strike against the Alhambra settled as much as you do, though, so—" Munro drew a deep breath and turned toward the miners. "Effective right now, every man who goes back to work for me will have his wages raised fifty cents an hour, and no one will work more than eight hours a day!"

Shocked exclamations came from the assembled miners. Tip Woodford yelped, "Fifty cents an hour! For God's sake, I can't match that! Nobody can! Nobody's gonna want to work for me now."

A smug smile appeared on Munro's face. "That's your

problem, Woodford." He turned back to the miners. "Well, men? What do you say?"

Frank held up a hand to stop them before they could shout their agreement. Into the surprised silence, he said, "We both know why you're doing this, Munro. And you're not going to get away with it." He had spotted the men he was looking for in the crowd of miners, and now he moved toward them. The miners drew aside to make a path for him until Frank was confronting the Fowler brothers, Red Mike and Gib.

"You two are under arrest for murder," Frank said.

Chapter 31

The sound of galloping hoofbeats were loud in the gathering shadows. The men who waited on horseback leaned forward in their saddles. They could tell that only one man was approaching, and since there were about three dozen of them, they weren't worried.

"Hold it right there!" Pool called as the rider loomed up out of the darkness.

"Jory!" Clint Farnum exclaimed. "Thank God I found you. We've got to call it off. The state militia's in town, along with a bunch of well-armed miners who're on strike. Even a lot of the townspeople have got guns and are ready for trouble tonight."

"Call it off?" Pool repeated, as if he were amazed by the idea. "I don't call off a raid once the time's come. We're goin' in there, and we're gonna loot that town from one end to the other and then burn it to the ground, just like we done in a dozen other towns."

"I tell you, you can't!" Clint cried in a ragged voice. "The militia—"

Pool's hand shot out to grab Clint's arm in a cruelly painful grip. "To hell with the militia, and everybody else in Buckskin! They won't know what's hittin' 'em, be-cause they'll be too busy fightin' each other." With his other hand, Pool drew his Colt and jammed the barrel under Clint's jaw. "This is even better than I hoped," the boss outlaw went on. "From what you're tellin' me, that town's like a giant keg o' gunpowder tonight. All it needs is one spark to set it off. Are you gonna go give us that spark, Farnum . . . or do I pull this trigger and blow your head off?"

Clint had no choice. Through clenched teeth, he said, "I'll do it, Jory. Just . . . give me a couple of minutes to get back down there. You'll know it . . . when the ball starts."

Pool let go of Clint's arm, but kept the gun barrel pressed against his neck for a second. "You double-cross me and you'll live to regret it," he said in a low voice. "You just won't live long. Long enough to wish you were dead, though."

He lowered the gun.

Clint took a deep breath and rubbed the spot where the hard metal had bruised the flesh of his neck. Then he wheeled his horse around and rode off, vanishing in the darkness as he headed for town.

Down below in Buckskin, big fires had been kindled at both ends of the main street. By the light of those blazes, the outlaws could see the men who had gathered there. Even at a distance of several hundred yards, the tension could be felt.

As Jory Pool had said, Buckskin was ready to explode.

And when it did, these vicious outlaws would be ready to sweep in and turn the situation to their advantage.

"Murder!" Red Mike Fowler yelped. "Gib and me didn't murder nobody!"

"This is crazy!" Munro cried, a note of panic creeping into his voice. "Colonel, I demand that you put a stop to this! Arrest the marshal so that we can settle the strike."

"I don't believe I have the authority to do that anymore, Mr. Munro," Starkwell replied. "Besides, I sort of want to hear what Morgan has to say."

Frank drew the piece of timber from his pocket and held it up where everybody could see it. "This came from the cave-in at the Lucky Lizard," he said, raising his voice so that it could be heard by all. "If you take a close look at it, you can see that it's been damaged. Practically burned through by sulfuric acid, in fact. Somebody doped those timbers with acid so that the wood was eaten away and the timbers gave out. That's what caused the cave-in."

"You can't blame that on us!" Red Mike said. "Gib and me didn't have nothin' to do with that!"

"You had more reason to do it than anybody else," Frank shot back. "You'd just come over to the Lucky Lizard from the Alhambra."

"We got fired over there!"

"That makes a good story, especially when you were still working for Munro."

"I don't know anything about this," Munro insisted. "You're grasping at straws, Morgan. You're just trying to stir up hard feelings toward me."

Frank shook his head. "I'm just trying to get to the truth." He looked at the miners from the Lucky Lizard. "Did any of you men see either of the Fowler brothers messing with those timbers before the ceiling collapsed?"

The miners muttered among themselves for a second; then one of them spoke up, saying, "Red Mike and Gib were both hangin' around that area not long before the cave-in. I didn't see 'em put anything on the timbers, but that don't mean they didn't. They sure enough *could* have."

"That ain't proof of anything," Gib Fowler said, his voice wavering.

"Then maybe we should search your gear at the mine," Frank suggested. "You might still have some of that acid you used stashed away."

It was a shot in the dark, but it paid off. Red Mike leveled an accusing finger at Gunther Hammersmith and yelled, "It was all his idea. He made us do it!"

Hammersmith, pale and wide eyed with fury, looked like he wanted to lunge at Fowler and snap his neck. He wasn't the only one who wanted to get at Red Mike and Gib. The men from the Lucky Lizard, who had lost a couple of friends in that cave-in, surged forward, their faces twisted in righteous anger.

Frank turned toward Hammersmith and palmed out his gun, covering the big mine superintendent. "Looks like you'll hang too, Hammersmith," he said.

"The hell I will!" Hammersmith responded. "It was all Munro's doing! He's the one who wanted the strike at the Lucky Lizard—"

"Shut up!" Munro screamed. "Lies, all lies!"

"Just like he told me to have the stamp mill at the Crown Royal blown up!" Hammersmith roared. Just as Frank had hoped, the rats couldn't turn on each other fast enough. Threaten one and they would all go down.

Angry shouts filled the air now as the group of miners continued to edge forward like an inexorable tide. Munro turned to Colonel Starkwell and grabbed his uniform, shaking him. "It's a riot!" he screeched. "They're going to kill me! You've got to stop them! The governor would want you to protect me! Order your men to fire, damn you! Fire!"

Frank could tell from the stony look on Starkwell's face that wasn't going to happen. The colonel knew the same thing that everyone else in Buckskin did: Munro and Hammersmith were responsible for all the trouble that had plagued the area.

But then, horribly, a shot rang out. Frank wasn't sure where it came from, but he saw Dave Rogan stagger back a step as the bullet smashed into his body. Rogan clutched his chest, and blood welled between his fingers. He fell heavily in the street.

"One of the soldiers shot Dave!" a miner howled. "Get 'em!"

The militia men jerked their rifles up. The miners surged forward.

And Hammersmith leaped at Frank, slapping the Colt aside and swinging a big fist at the marshal's head.

Curls of smoke still drifted from the muzzle of Clint Farnum's gun as he ducked back into the alley mouth. Lining up the shot through the crowd in the street had been tricky, but he had done it. The miner named Rogan had fallen to Clint's slug, and now more shots rang out and men shouted curses as tight-strung nerves snapped and the two groups opened fire on each other.

Clint had done what he had to do for Jory Pool. Now the gang could sweep into Buckskin and wipe out any resistance before the citizens knew what was going on. Clint's job was over, so he could find a hole and hide until the killing was over. All he had to do was wait it out and collect his share of the loot. It would be easy.

But if it was so easy, why were his guts clenched in a tight ball of sickness? Why did he feel like something had died inside him?

In the darkness of the alley, he pressed his back against the wall of a building and shuddered. Cold sweat beaded on his face. He lifted the gun in his hand and listened to the shots and the cries and the screams.

All that hell unleashed, and all he'd had to do was squeeze a trigger.

Frank ducked under Hammersmith's roundhouse blow as guns began to roar. As Hammersmith stumbled forward, thrown off balance by the missed punch, Frank stepped closer. He had managed to hang on to his gun even though Hammersmith had knocked the barrel aside. Now he slapped the Colt against Hammersmith's head, putting enough power behind the blow to knock the mine superintendent to his knees, stunned.

With Hammersmith out of the fight for the moment, Frank whirled around and shouted at the miners, "Hold your fire! Stop shooting!"

At the same time, Colonel Starkwell was bellowing, "Cease fire! Cease fire!"

But it was too late. Both sides had come here tonight ready to fight. The miners believed that one of the militia men had shot down Dave Rogan, and the soldiers were just fighting back as they were attacked. Already, the street was turning into chaos as the two sides splintered and broke up to do battle in small groups, sometimes firing at each other as they darted for cover, other times grappling hand to hand.

Frank grabbed Tip Woodford's arm and shoved the mayor toward the office of the Lucky Lizard. He saw that Garrett Claiborne had already hustled Diana off the boardwalk and inside the building. Frank was grateful for that, but knew Claiborne and Diana weren't out of danger. With all the lead flying around, some of the slugs might penetrate the walls of the buildings. He hoped everybody in town had enough sense to get down behind something solid and stay there until the shooting was over.

As Frank hurried Tip out of the line of fire, a bitter taste welled up in his mouth. He was supposed to protect the townspeople, and all he had managed to do was start a small-scale war right in the middle of the settlement. This was proof, as if he needed it, that he wasn't cut out to be a lawman. He never should have tried to settle down and give up his drifting ways.

Violence followed him. Always had, and likely always would.

For now, though, all he could do was try to put a stop to this ruckus, once he got Tip to relative safety. He didn't know who had fired the shot that had started the ball, but he hoped he could find out and deal with the damn fool later.

As they reached the boardwalk, a fresh volley of shots broke out, but these came from the edge of town. As a bullet whistled past Frank's ear, so close that he felt it as much as heard it, he twisted his head and saw a totally unexpected sight. Dozens of hard-faced, roughly dressed men on horseback were galloping into town, blazing away with the six-guns in their hands as they thundered down the main street.

Tip yelped in pain, drawing Frank's attention. "How bad are you hit?" Frank asked over the rattle of gunfire.

"Just creased my arm!" Tip replied. "Who the hell are those fellas?"

Frank shook his head. "I don't know. Get inside and look after Claiborne and Diana!"

He gave Tip a shove that sent the burly older man stumbling through the open door of the office, then whirled back to the street, where a three-way battle was now going on. Four-way, if you counted the citizens of Buckskin who had been posted along the street with rifles and shotguns.

They had sought cover behind water troughs, rain barrels, and parked wagons in order to swap lead with the murderous newcomers.

The men on horseback had scattered the battling militia men and miners, riding down some of them and shooting others. As Frank darted along the boardwalk with bullets knocking up splinters from the planks around his feet, he got a look at the big, blond-bearded man who seemed to be the leader of the strangers. A shock of recognition went through him. He hadn't seen Jory Pool in several years, but the big outlaw hadn't changed that much. They had been in some of the same places but had never actually met, which was the way Frank wanted it because he was aware of Pool's reputation as a cunning but brutal and possibly deranged gunman and outlaw. Pool was supposed to be the head of a gang almost as bad as he was.

Frank had no doubt that Buckskin was now under assault from that gang. By busting in and raiding the settlement right now, Pool and the rest of the owlhoots had taken everybody by surprise.

Frank squeezed off a couple of shots, and saw one of the outlaws tumble out of the saddle. Some of the other members of the gang were down too.

But there were too many of them, and even though the militia and the miners would have outnumbered the outlaws by almost two to one if they had been working together, there was no organized defense, and too many of them were still fighting each other, not yet aware that an even greater threat had just galloped into Buckskin.

Frank emptied his Colt at Jory Pool, but the boss outlaw chose that moment to whirl his horse and start charging back the way he had come. The bullets whined past him, all of them missing. Frank sprawled full-length behind a water trough and began reloading, dumping the empty shells from the Peacemaker's cylinder and thumbing fresh cartridges into it.

He hadn't seen Hammersmith or Hamish Munro since the shooting started, he realized, and he wondered what had happened to them.

But he wondered for only a second, because he had bigger worries at the moment. Several of the mounted outlaws charged the water trough where he had taken cover, and a hailstorm of lead scythed through the air around him.

Hamish Munro was shaking with fear as he scrambled up the stairs in the hotel. He had never come so close to death in his life as he just had in the street outside. It was bad enough that everyone was turning on him like that—the Fowler brothers and even Hammersmith—but then to have all that shooting going on around him, with bullets flying through the air so close to his head that he could hear them. . . .

He hadn't thought about it. The instinct for self-preservation had taken over and he had dashed for the boardwalk, getting out of the street as fast as he could, leaving Hammersmith behind—the traitor! If Hammersmith had been more careful . . . if he had hired men who were more dependable than the Fowlers . . . if that damned Morgan hadn't kept pushing and poking his nose in where it didn't belong . . .

Yes, Munro thought, when you got right down to it, everything was Morgan's fault. He would see the man dead. If, of course, Morgan lived through the battle that was going on outside.

Munro became uncomfortably aware that the front of his trousers was wet. Terror had made him lose control of his bladder as he ran for cover. He hated for Jessica to see him this way, but it didn't really matter. It wasn't like she actually loved him. At least, not nearly as much as she loved his money. As long as he had his riches, nothing else really mattered to her.

He paused at the top of the stairs to draw a deep breath and try to collect himself. He had always carried himself with dignity, and there was no reason to change that now. With a furious glare on his face, he stalked along the corridor toward his suite. Jessica had probably heard the shooting and would be scared. She was like a little girl who was easily frightened. Munro would calm her down, and then they would wait out the trouble. He was confident that Colonel Starkwell's militia would suppress the riot going on outside, even though he was still angry at Starkwell for disobeying his orders.

Munro opened the door and stepped into the suite. He didn't see anyone. "Jessica!" he said, raising his voice because even in here, the sound of gunfire was loud. "Jessica, where are you?"

He heard something behind him, the scrape of shoe leather on the floor perhaps, and started to turn, but before he could swing around, something hard and round jabbed against the back of his head and there was a loud noise and a white-hot explosion burst in Hamish Munro's brain. He didn't feel himself falling, wasn't aware of it when he landed facedown on the floor with the back of his head a bullet-shattered ruin. He shouldn't have even been able to think anymore with a bullet in his brain that way, but a few swiftly fading shreds of consciousness remained, just enough for him to think that he couldn't be dying. He was Hamish Munro, damn it. He had money and power. Politicians did his bidding, and a beautiful young woman was his wife. . . .

Jessica.

That was his last thought before oblivion claimed him.

Chapter 32

Jessica lunged at Hammersmith as he came stumbling in the door of the hotel, blood running down his face from the cut that Frank Morgan's gun had opened up on his head. She caught hold of his arm and cried, "Gunther! Gunther, what's going on out there?"

Hammersmith shook his head as if he were still groggy from the blow. "All hell's breakin' loose," he muttered. "Somebody started shootin' . . . then some other bastards came riding in and gunnin' people down . . ."

Impatience gripped Jessica. Hammersmith wasn't telling her anything she didn't already know, nothing she hadn't seen for herself through the hotel's front window. Munro had ordered her to stay upstairs, but she had ignored him, as she always ignored him when it didn't suit her purposes to give the appearance of compliance. She had watched anxiously as the miners and the militia confronted each other, and she had seen the big miner called Rogan fall as he was shot. Jessica didn't know who had pulled the trigger, but Rogan's killing had set off a firestorm in the street.

Even though she knew it was dangerous, she hadn't been

able to tear her eyes away from the spectacle as the battle raged in the street outside the hotel. She had crouched down so that she could peer over the bottom of the window. That was her only concession to caution.

Her hope was that Hamish would be killed in the confusion. That would save her a great deal of trouble later on, and given the circumstances, there was no way anyone could blame her for his death.

But after a few minutes, he had come stumbling out of the melee, seemingly unharmed. As he staggered toward the hotel, Jessica had seen the large dark stain on the front of his trousers, and her nose had wrinkled in distaste. He was such a coward that he had pissed his pants in his fear. How could she have let such a man even touch her, let along some of the things she had allowed him to do to her?

Money, of course. That was the reason. As it always was and always would be. Hamish had the money, and she wanted it.

But she was tired of waiting for it.

She stood up and drew back into the shadows as he came in to the hotel. He never even saw her as he started up the stairs, obviously heading for their suite. She let him go without calling out to him. She had to decide what to do now.

Hammersmith's arrival had helped her make up her mind. Munro could still die. Hammersmith could kill him and bring his body back downstairs. In all the chaos, if Munro's body was found in the hotel lobby or out on the boardwalk, no one would ever question that he had been killing in the fighting.

So as Jessica clutched Hammersmith's arm, she broke through his stunned reverie by saying in an urgent voice, "Gunther, listen to me. It's time."

"Time?" Hammersmith repeated. "Time for what?"

"Time to kill Hamish, so that the two of us can be together from now on, truly together as we were meant to be."

That got through to him, all right. The confusion went out of his eyes as they lit up with lust and avarice.

Jessica reinforced those feelings by saying, "I'll be all yours, Gunther. And we'll have Hamish's money. We can go anywhere we want and always be together, just you and me."

Of course, the time would come when she would have to find a way to get rid of Hammersmith too, because she would tire of him and he would know too much, but she could deal with that when it became necessary. For now, right at this moment, Hammersmith was the most important man in her life.

"Kill Munro?" he muttered.

Jessica nodded. "That's right. He just went upstairs. We can do it, Gunther. We can have everything we ever wanted."

Slowly, Hammersmith nodded too. "Yeah," he said in a heavy voice. "Yeah."

He started for the stairs. Jessica let him go.

But she followed closely behind him, so she would be there if he changed his mind. As long as he could see her and hear her voice, she was confident that he would do whatever she wanted him to. They reached the second floor and started toward the suite.

A shot blasted behind the door before they got there.

Jessica's blue eyes widened in surprise. Had Hamish fired a gun? She couldn't think of any reason why he would. He never handled guns. He always paid other people to do things like that.

Maybe he had killed himself. . . . No, Jessica decided, she couldn't be that lucky.

Hammersmith had stopped at the sound of the shot. He muttered, "What the hell?"

"Get in there, Gunther," Jessica said. "We have to find out what happened."

Hammersmith didn't hesitate. He smashed his shoulder into the door and knocked it open. The crash of the door blended with the sound of gunshots still coming from the street.

Hammersmith went in first, but Jessica was close enough behind him to peer around him and see Nathan Evers whirling around from where Munro's body lay on the floor. Jessica gasped as she saw the bloody ruin that was the back of Munro's head. He had to be dead.

And the smoke curling from the barrel of the gun in Evers's hand made it clear who had killed him.

Evers lifted the gun toward Hammersmith. "Stay back!" he said in a panicky voice.

"Nathan!" Jessica said. "You've killed Hamish!"

She didn't have a chance to tell him that was all right before his lip curled in a sneer and he thrust the gun toward her. "That's right!" he snapped. "And I'll kill you too if you get in my way, you bitch!"

Thunderstruck, Jessica could only stare at him. Beside her, Hammersmith growled as he stood there with his hands balled into malletlike fists.

"Always parading yourself around," Evers went on in a voice trembling with rage and hate. "Munro never saw you for the slut you really are. He was a fool, a blind fool, but not for that reason alone. He never had any idea that I've been bleeding his fortune away from him for years!"

That brought another gasp of horror from Jessica. "You . . . you stole from him?"

"Thousands and thousands of dollars," Evers gloated, "and he never knew. Now he never will. He's dead, and you and Hammersmith soon will be too. All I'll have to do is say that some of those crazy gunmen broke in here and shot the three of you, and no one will ever suspect otherwise. This is the perfect opportunity for me. I can finally stop groveling!"

"You're the one who's crazy," Hammersmith said. "Put that gun down."

Evers shook his head as he swung the pistol back toward Hammersmith. "No. You first, and then the slut."

With a roar of rage, Hammersmith threw himself toward Evers. The gun in the treacherous secretary's hand blasted again and again as Evers jerked the trigger and screamed. Hammersmith stumbled a little as the bullets thudded into him, but they didn't really slow him down. Evers was cut off in mid-shriek as Hammersmith crashed into him and drove him over backward. Hammersmith's sausagelike fingers closed around Evers's neck and twisted hard as both men fell. Jessica heard a loud cracking sound, and then the crash as the two men hit the floor.

A shudder ran through Hammersmith, and then he lay still as he sprawled on top of Evers. Jessica stood there motionless as she stared at them for a long moment. Then, carefully, she moved closer, bending over to take a look at them. Evers had dropped the gun, which was probably empty now anyway. His eyes were open and blankly staring. His head was twisted at an impossible angle on his shoulders. Hammersmith had broken his neck.

Jessica couldn't see the wounds in Hammersmith's chest, but she saw the pool of blood creeping out onto the rug around the two men. Blood ran from Hammersmith's mouth too, and his eyes were as empty and lifeless as Evers's were. Jessica straightened, confident that both men were dead, as was Hamish Munro. She was alone in the hotel room with three corpses.

And as the full implications of that sunk in on her, she began to smile.

* * *

Frank knew he couldn't stop all the outlaws who were charging his position behind the water trough, but he gripped the Colt tightly and steeled himself to take as many of them with him as he could.

At that moment, a shotgun boomed and several shots blasted from a handgun, and as Frank raised himself into firing position, he saw that a couple of the outlaws' horses were now riderless. As a bullet ripped past his head, he triggered the Peacemaker and sent slugs pounding into the other two desperadoes. They somersaulted backward off their mounts.

Tip Woodford and Garrett Claiborne ran toward Frank, reloading as they came. Tip had the scattergun, while Claiborne clutched a Colt revolver in his good hand. As the two men came up to Frank, Tip shouted, "We got to get folks organized! Who the hell are those raiders?"

"An outlaw gang led by a man named Jory Pool," Frank replied. "Pool's the big hombre with the blond beard." He thumbed more cartridges into his Colt as he added, "Come on. We'll form up at the Silver Baron!"

As they ran through chaos and flying lead toward the saloon, Frank spotted Leo Benjamin, Professor Burton, and Ed Kelley, all of whom were armed and trying to mount a defense against the invaders. Frank called to them and waved for them to follow him and Tip and Claiborne.

As they neared the Silver Baron, the group of defenders picked up three more members in Amos Hillman, Claude Langley, and Langley's helper Roy. Frank saw Starkwell and shouted, "Colonel! We're forming up at the saloon!"

Starkwell nodded as he squeezed off a shot from his revolver and sent another outlaw tumbling out of the saddle. The colonel began shouting orders to his men, some of whom were still able to respond. Frank yelled at the miners he saw as well, and they joined the band of fighters headed for the saloon.

Fighting their way along the street, the group of defenders numbered about twenty strong by the time they reached the Silver Baron. Miners and militia men were fighting side by side now instead of battling against each other. Johnny Collyer pushed through the batwings to join them, coughing but determined, the sawed-off Greener he kept under the bar now clutched in his hands.

About a dozen of the outlaws were down, which made the odds roughly even now. The deadly accurate fire of the defenders had drawn Jory Pool's attention. He bellowed orders to his surviving men, gathering them around him for an all-out assault on the Silver Baron. "Kill 'em!" he screamed as he kicked his horse into a run. "Kill 'em all!"

The gang surged forward like a tidal wave of death. As bullets flew, men on both sides dropped. A huge gray cloud of gunsmoke filled the street and stung the noses and mouths of the men who were fighting desperately. A militia man beside Frank grunted and doubled over as he was hit in the belly. He dropped his Winchester as he fell. Frank's Colt had just run dry again, so he jammed it back in its holster and snatched up the fallen rifle. He brought it to his shoulder and began to fire as fast as he could work the weapon's lever.

The huge, mounted figure of Jory Pool suddenly loomed up right in front of him. Frank had to dive to the side as Pool leaped his horse onto the boardwalk. Shouting curses, Pool yanked the animal around in a tight turn and began firing at Frank, who rolled across the planks as the boss outlaw's bullets chewed splinters from them. Frank knew he was only a heartbeat from death.

Then someone leaped past him, gun blazing, and Frank

heard Clint Farnum shouting, "No, damn it, no!" The little gunfighter went right at Pool, firing wildly, but he had taken only a couple of steps before a pair of slugs crashed into his chest and picked him up, driving him backward.

Clint's valiant action had given Frank the chance to come up on his knees and lift the Winchester again. He didn't know how many rounds were left in the rifle, but he prayed at least one still remained. As Clint fell, Pool tried to swing his gun toward Frank again, but he was too late. Frank pressed the Winchester's trigger.

Pool's head practically exploded in a grisly spray of blood, brains, and bone as the rifle bullet smashed through his skull. The outlaw leader toppled out of the saddle, falling to the boardwalk.

Pool's death took the fight out of the remaining outlaws. Some of them whirled their mounts and retreated, trying to get away before they could be cut down. A few made it. The others threw down their guns and thrust their hands in the air, shouting for the defenders not to kill them. Seeing that the back of the attack was broken, Frank surged to his feet and shouted, "Hold your fire! Hold your fire!" He looked along the boardwalk, saw Catamount Jack among the defenders, and told the old-timer, "Jack, start rounding up the prisoners and take them down to the jail."

"Them cells are gonna be crammed plumb full," Jack said with a grin. He had been nicked a couple of times by flying lead, but seemed to be as spry as ever.

Frank turned to Starkwell and asked, "Colonel, will you give my deputy a hand?"

Starkwell glanced at his men, who were now eyeing the miners with suspicion once more, then said, "Of course, Marshal. I think we could use a truce right about now."

Frank nodded in agreement. The last thing he wanted after fighting off this outlaw raid was a resumption of the hostilities that had been going on before Pool and his gang rode in.

He turned toward Clint Farnum and knelt at the little gunfighter's side. The front of Clint's shirt was soaked with blood and more crimson leaked from his mouth, but he was still alive. His eyelids flickered open as Frank put a hand on his shoulder.

"F-Frank . . ." he rasped out. "You're . . . all right?"

"Yeah, thanks to you," Frank told him. He could tell that Clint didn't have much time left. Minutes maybe, or even less. "Thanks to you," Frank went on. "You saved my life, Clint. Pool would have ventilated me in another second."

"That's . . . good . . . I'm sorry I . . ."

Whatever Clint was trying to apologize for, it went unsaid, because at that moment a long sigh came from him and his bloody chest ceased to rise and fall. The light went out of his pale blue eyes.

"You were a good deputy, Clint," Frank said, hoping that somehow Clint could still hear him. Gently, he closed the man's eyes and then stood up.

Dr. Garland had arrived on the scene and was checking over the wounded defenders. Frank walked along the boardwalk, noting that Roy was dead, along with a couple of the miners and one of the militia men. A number of others had wounds of varying seriousness, but Garland seemed to think that all of them would pull through.

The doctor paused in his work long enough to tell Frank, "Considering how badly the town was shot up, we're lucky more people weren't killed."

Frank couldn't bring himself to feel all that lucky at the moment, but he knew what Garland meant. "If there's anything I can do to help, Doc, just let me know."

Tip Woodford and Garrett Claiborne came up to Frank.

"We still got the same mess as before," Tip said. "What're we gonna do about those strikin' miners?"

"Now that the parts Munro and Hammersmith played in everything have come out, maybe we can talk some sense into them," Frank said. "We'll have to have another meeting."

Claiborne looked around and asked, "Where *are* Hammersmith and Munro? I don't see them in the street or anywhere along the boardwalk."

"They must have made it back to the hotel when all hell broke loose." Frank had set the Winchester aside and was reloading his Colt. "I'll go find them."

"Better let us come with you," Tip suggested. "Since they know they're facin' a lot of legal trouble now, they're liable to put up a fight. That bruiser Hammersmith anyway. I ain't sure Munro knows how to fight with anything except money."

Frank considered the offer, but then shook his head. "You fellas have already fought your battle today. This is a job for Buckskin's marshal, and that's who I am, at least for now."

He started toward the hotel. Behind him, Tip called, "Frank? What do you mean by that, Frank? Dadgummit—"

Frank didn't pay any attention. He kept walking until he reached the boardwalk in front of the hotel. As he stepped into the lobby, he stopped short at the sight of Jessica Munro sitting on the stairs leading up to the second floor. Her face was red and streaked with tears, but she was still beautiful despite that.

"Marshal," she said as she looked up and saw Frank. She came to her feet. "It's terrible. They're dead. They're all dead."

She hurried across the lobby to Frank, threw her arms around him, and sobbed.

Chapter 33

"She claims that Hammersmith shot Munro, then Evers shot Hammersmith and Hammersmith broke Evers's neck before he died," Frank told the others gathered in the office of the Lucky Lizard Mining Company.

"You reckon she's tellin' the truth?" Tip Woodford asked.

Frank shrugged. "I can't prove that she's not. My gut says she's lying, at least about part of it, but that doesn't change anything. Munro is dead, so that makes her the owner of the Alhambra. She wants you to settle the strike with all the miners, Tip, and she says she'll go along with whatever agreement you negotiate with them."

Diana said, "What's she going to do? She's not staying here in Buckskin, is she?" Her dislike for Jessica Munro was plain to hear in her voice.

Frank shook his head. "No, Mrs. Munro told me she's going back to San Francisco as soon as she can. She's not interested in having anything to do with running the mine. She's going to hire a new superintendent and leave everything to him."

"All she'll do is collect the money," Diana said.

"Yeah. I reckon she'll do that, all right."

Colonel Starkwell was also at this gathering. He said, "I don't like the way Munro tried to use me and my men, Marshal, but I feel a responsibility to remain here and help maintain order until everything is settled."

"And I appreciate that, Colonel," Frank said with a nod. "All the miners are getting together over at the Silver Baron. Mayor Woodford and I will go talk to them. It might be best to keep your men outside for now, where they'll be handy but the miners won't feel threatened by them."

Starkwell agreed. "But if you need our help, don't hesitate to ask for it."

"I won't," Frank promised, but he hoped above all else right now that the miners' strike could be settled without any more violence.

Buckskin had seen enough bloodshed to last it a long time.

The meeting didn't last long. Fighting a common enemy had rebuilt some of the bonds that had existed between Tip and the men who worked for him, and with Hamish Munro and Gunther Hammersmith both dead, along with Dave Rogan, the miners from the Alhambra had lost some of their anger. Tip's workers knew that the Fowler brothers had been responsible for the cave-in and for stirring up the strike, and since Red Mike and Gib were dead as well, the miners were willing to get back to work with only a few concessions from Tip. The men from the Alhambra were willing to accept the same proposal, and Frank promised on behalf of the Crown Royal's management to go along too, so that the wages and hours and safety conditions would be roughly consistent at all three of the major mines.

"You reckon young Claiborne will go along with that?" Tip asked after the meeting broke up and the workers headed back to the mines.

"I think I can pretty well guarantee it," Frank said.

"Yeah, I forgot you own part o' the Crown Royal."

"But my real job is here in Buckskin." Frank shook his head. "I'm just not sure I ought to be wearing this badge anymore."

"You got to stop talkin' like that," Tip protested as he and Frank walked toward the Silver Baron. "Nobody wants you to turn in your badge. Hell, if you hadn't rallied everybody together when them outlaws come chargin' in, they'd have looted the town and likely burned it to the ground. You said that's what Pool usually did."

"Yes, but I didn't stop Munro and Hammersmith from causing a lot of trouble before that happened. We had a full-scale riot going on, if you remember."

"I remember all right, and I remember you riskin' your neck and doin' everything in your power to head things off before they got that far. It ain't your fault you couldn't."

Frank shrugged. The mayor might be willing to let him off the hook, but he wasn't sure if *he* was.

"I'll think about it," was all he said as they reached the saloon.

Before they could push through the batwings, a man who had just ridden up in front of the Silver Baron said, "Morgan? Frank Morgan?"

Frank stopped, stiffening as he recognized the tone of voice. He had never seen this hombre before, but he knew the man anyway, knew him as well as he knew his own face in the mirror.

"I'm Morgan."

"I got a bone to pick with you, Morgan. Folks say you're mighty fast with a gun, but I think I'm faster." The man dismounted, dropped his reins, and faced Frank in a crouch, his hand hovering over the butt of his Colt, ready to hook and draw. "I aim to prove it," he added.

Before Frank could respond, Tip Woodford said, "Then you're a damned fool, mister. You know who this is?"

The gunfighter sneered. "Yeah, he's Frank Morgan, but he don't scare me. I can beat him to the draw."

"No," Tip said, "he's the marshal of Buckskin, and he's our friend. Even if you do beat him, which I seriously doubt you can, you'll have to shoot me next. And then him—" Tip nodded toward the batwings, where Johnny Collyer had appeared carrying his sawed-off shotgun. "And him." That was Leo Benjamin, stepping out onto the porch of the general store with a rifle in his hands. "And him." Catamount Jack eased along the boardwalk, his gnarled old hand on the butt of the cap-and-ball pistol at his hip.

Tip pointed out half-a-dozen other townspeople whose attention had been attracted by the confrontation between Frank and the would-be fast gun. The stranger looked around, his face growing taut with worry as he realized he was surrounded by hostility.

"So you see, mister," Tip concluded, "when you go up against the marshal o' Buckskin, one way or another you're gonna wind up blowed full o' holes. Don't you reckon the smartest thing to do would be to climb back on that horse and ride outta here while you got the chance?"

The man hesitated, but only for a moment. Then he snarled, "You're the luckiest hombre I ever saw, Morgan." He grabbed his reins, swung up into the saddle, and rode out.

Frank watched him go and said, "Yeah. I reckon I sure am."

Turn the page for an exciting preview of

A TOWN CALLED FURY: JUDGMENT DAY

by William W. Johnstone

with J. A. Johnstone

Coming in November 2007

Wherever Pinnacle Books are sold!

Chapter 1

Jason ducked just in time to avoid catching a slug with his face. As he scurried backward, deeper into the alley, he wiped at his cheek. His hand came away bloody and bearing ragged splinters.

He scowled.

"Damn it, Saul, you nearly got me!" he shouted before he jumped behind a stack of packing crates. For the fourth time, his hand slid toward his holstered gun; for the fourth time, he stopped himself before his fingers could curl around its butt. Saul might have temporarily gone peach orchard crazy, but Jason didn't have to.

For a while anyway.

But if Saul took one more shot at him . . .

"Saul!" A new voice. Doc Morelli? "Saul, it's Dr. Morelli!"

Jason heaved a small sigh of relief despite himself. He'd thought everybody had taken to the hills—or at least, the wagons outside the wall—a while back. At least, he figured the smart ones had.

"Jason? Jason, are you all right?" Morelli called. He was

some distance away, inside the stable and across the square so far as Jason could figure.

"Been better," Jason called back. He touched his cheek again and pulled back fingers dripping with fresh blood. He added, "Might be bleeding to death." That part, he added for Saul's benefit.

It seemed to have no effect, though. Another shot rang out immediately, followed by Morelli's shouted: "Saul! Stop it!"

As deadly as the situation might seem, Jason had more important things on his mind, and Saul's momentary descent into madness was just one more thing to take care of. After all, Saul couldn't help it, he supposed. A man could scarcely be expected to deal with two children being born dead but full-term inside two years. If *he* were Saul, Jason reasoned, he'd probably shoot up a town or two as well.

The street was quiet again, and Jason ventured forward to the alley's mouth, a few tentative feet at a time. He showed his face at the corner, then stepped into full view.

Nothing.

No slugs sang past his ears or pierced his flesh.

Saul's wilding time was over.

He shouted, "Doc? I reckon he's finished."

Dr. Morelli stepped forward through the door of the livery and held up his hand to Jason, waving it. After a moment, he turned to his left, and began walk up the street while calling, "Saul? Saul, where are you, old man?"

Saul must have answered, although too softly for Jason to hear across the street, because Doc Morelli stopped, shook his head, then opened the door of the mercantile and disappeared inside.

Jason let out his breath—a part of which he hadn't known he was holding—and started back toward his office. By the time he reached the northwest corner of the square

and crossed the street to the jail, he glanced back and saw
Doc Morelli guiding a hunched and sobbing Saul Cohen
back up to his hardware store.

Under his breath, Jason muttered, "Hope Doc gives you
a dose of that sleep juice of his, Saul." He opened the door
and let himself into his office. "About two days worth."

Now, he thought as he settled down behind the desk,
thumbed his hat back, and pulled open the top drawer.
Back to the important stuff.

Along about 11:30, Megan MacDonald rode into town
and made her way down the street to the sheriff's office.
She seemed, to anyone watching, as if she rode with a purpose—her face was set with a furrowed brow, her legs
were stiff in the stirrups, and she sat the saddle as if someone had sewn an iron rod into the back of her dress.

She dismounted before the office, tied her horse to the
rail with a quick but decisive twist of the reins, and
marched to the door.

The door was open and Jason was behind the desk, practically buried in papers. Megan let the door slam behind
her and stood there, her posture just as stiff as it had been
all the way into town, just as stiff as it had been since she
woke, once again, to the sound of angry voices.

Jason's head lifted, but the smile didn't stay on his lips
for very long. "Megan. What's wrong?"

Megan pursed her lips, then spat, "As if you didn't
know!"

Jason blinked a couple of times, and looked to be carefully choosing his next words before he spoke. "Megan,
I've been sort of busy this morning, and I—"

But carefully chosen or not, he didn't have much time to
get the thought out, because she cut him off with a toss of

her head. "Oh, no you don't, Jason Fury. We've been over and over this. And don't pretend you don't know exactly what I'm talking about. You've got to do something about Matt and Jenny!"

Jason let out a long sigh. Matt and Jenny must be at it again, as they had been almost continually of late. He shrugged his shoulders and said, "Megan, you know I predicted this from the start. But Jenny's the one who has to decide whether or not she wants out. Either she or Matt. I've told you—and I've told Jenny—that I'm not going to meddle in their business."

He'd told Jenny all right, told her on her wedding day. She'd made her bed, and now she'd have to lie in it. It didn't sound like she was finding it any too comfortable, either.

Megan appeared to relax a bit. At least, part of the starch seemed to go out of her spine, and she sat down in the wooden chair opposite his before her shoulders collapsed into a dejected slouch.

He leaned across the desk, toward her, and said softly, "Megan? Megan, honey, I know it's hard, believe me." He did know, probably better than anyone else. Probably even better than Megan, even though she was Matt's sister, and even though she was living in the same house with them.

But he also knew that Megan didn't believe him. In fact, she pulled back from him with a jolt, spitting out, "Oh, that's so easy for you to say, Jason!" She went to her feet and all the stiffness, all the ramrod straightness, was back in place. "I can see I won't make any progress here. Excuse me. I have errands."

And she left, turning on her heel and leaving a stunned

Jason to suffer the echoes of a slammed door and rattling window glass.

With Saul finally down and sleeping next to his wife upstairs, Doc Morelli quietly let himself out the front door, checking to make sure the CLOSED sign was visible before he locked the door and pocketed the key. He'd give the key back tomorrow, he guessed.

He paused momentarily, then altered his direction. *No,* he thought. *I'll just give it to the sheriff now and be done with it.*

He walked up the street in time to see Megan's dramatic exit from the office, but by the time he reached the door she'd slammed out of, she had remounted and ridden past him at a fast clip. He thought she was going to speed it up into a gallop once she passed the break in the wall that led to town, but instead, she pulled up next to it and tied her horse. She walked around the corner, headed toward the wagons that had parked south of the wall yesterday. *As angry as Megan appeared, she's going shopping?* he wondered as he put his hand on the sheriff's office door. He surely wouldn't want to be a vendor this morning!

He pushed down the door latch and let himself in.

"Now what?" Jason snapped before his head came up and his scowl softened into a smile. "Sorry, Doc," he added, gesturing to the empty chair on the other side of his desk.

Morelli waved one hand and dug into his pocket with the other. "No, can't stay, just had a bit of business to take care of. . . ."

His hand found the key and he stepped forward to place it on the desk. "That's to Cohen's hardware," he said, pointing at it. "I just got Saul put to bed."

Jason nodded. "Medicated?"

Morelli's hand went to the back of his neck and his eyes closed for a moment. "Lord! It took half a bottle to knock him off his feet. Jason, don't hold it against him. What happened this morning, I mean. You've just got to feel sorry—"

Jason stopped him with a wave of his hand. "Don't worry about it, Doc. I forgot about it already."

Morelli nodded. Jason was wise beyond his years, he thought, then said it aloud.

Jason made no remark except to say, "Go on, Doc. Get out of here. Hell, I'll go with you," he added, shoving back his chair and standing.

Morelli smiled despite himself while Jason came around the desk to join him. It was odd, especially with Morelli being Jason's senior, but at times the doctor felt oddly the junior of the two. He supposed this had something to do with Jason's having shepherded him—and all the others in the original wagon train—clear out from Indian Territory after the death of Jason's father.

Still, it was rather strange.

"Hungry yet?" Jason asked. He reached around Morelli to open the door.

Morelli glanced at the office clock. A quarter to twelve. "It's a little early for me," he said, stepping out onto the boardwalk.

"Me too, come to think of it," Jason replied, then tipped his hat. "See you later, Doc," he said. He turned on his heel and started down the street, toward Megan MacDonald's tethered horse and the wagons lined along the wall outside the southern entrance to Fury.

Chapter 2

The town had been in existence only a scant two years, built by the bare hands of pioneers where before there had only been a broad desert prairie sliced vertically by a lonely—and sporadically flowing—creek. Distant, veiled mountains rose to the south, beyond which lay Mexico. To the north, even more distant mountains lined the horizon.

Fury was the name the townsfolk had given the small settlement, in honor of the famous wagon master who had started them westward, and died before they were halfway there. If any man had deserved the honor, it had been Jedediah Fury.

Now, nearly two years since the first walls of the new buildings had risen, since Saul Cohen had begun work on what now served as the town well centering the square, and since the partially built town itself had been attacked and burned by Apaches who rode in from the south, Fury had risen from the ashes.

Men had been lost to them on that day. Others had been wounded, including Jason himself, who had been appointed town sheriff while he lay injured and unable to defend himself from his "friends" in town.

Jason's life took a new path that day, although he could barely know the beginnings of it. He still couldn't possibly guess at the whole of it.

Since the day of the attack, the people of Fury had been busy building it back, and building it bigger and better. In the process, some people had died and others had moved on, but enough had stayed—and been joined by new influxes of people—that the population had nearly doubled in size, the building boom had continued, and an outer wall now completely surrounded the town. Those who wanted to live outside the confines of the town did so more easily than ever, since there had been no more trouble from Apache.

Close to town anyway.

Jason had even taken care of Juan Alba and his *bandidos* last year. At least, he thought he had. Today, the mail had come in, and Prescott had sent out word that a new Juan Alba, taking the place of the old one, was on the prowl. Juan Junior or something like that, he reasoned.

Like father, like son.

Jason gave up on trying to go west to San Francisco, on trying to go anywhere that held anything like a college. He figured to be stuck with sheriffing Fury, trapped forever as surely as a butterfly pinned to a display board.

And he was at least partially right.

He shoved himself away from his desk in disgust. Why wasn't he braver? Why couldn't he just tell the mayor and the citizens to go to hell? Why couldn't he just pack a satchel and leave like other people did? Well, some other people. On the whole, the town was actually growing. Some folks headed back east, some headed further west, but miraculously, more rode into town than rode out.

And they stayed.

He shook his head, and muttering, "Idiots," walked around the desk and toward the door.

He didn't make it outside, though. The mayor nearly broke Jason's nose when he unexpectedly shoved the door open and inward. It hit Jason in the forehead and shoulder and knocked him back a few feet, cursing.

"Oh!" cried Mayor Kendall, and reached out toward the staggering Jason, whose hand was clamped to his suddenly smarting head. "Jason, I'm so very sorry! You all right?"

Jason partially raised his head and glared at Kendall with one eye. "Been better," he growled. "What's your rush this morning?"

"I . . . I just talked to Doc Morelli. Heard about your run-in with Saul Cohen."

Jason brushed the air with his hand. "It was nothing. Doc's got him doped up and at home."

"But your cheek's cut!"

Jason had forgotten. "Probably looks worse than it is." He moved past Kendall and started out the door.

"But still . . ." the mayor said with a painful grimace.

Well, at least someone was feeling his pain, Jason thought, and forced a grin. "I'm fine, Salmon. Just gonna go down and check on our guests."

Kendall followed him out the door. "You mean you haven't been down there yet? Take my advice, boy, and don't take your wallet along. I left with fifteen dollars worth of stuff I'll never use."

"Bet you left with a happy wife, though," Jason added.

"Well . . . true," Salmon replied, then chuckled reluctantly. "True enough, Jason." He scratched at the back of his head. "Come to think of it, most of the haul was woman's stuff. You know, pickle dishes and butter plates and such. And shrimp forks! I ask you, where the hell does Carrie think we're gonna run across any shrimp out here?"

It was Jason's turn to chuckle. "Don't know. There aren't even any crawdads in the creek. When there's water in it, that is. Maybe you can fork yourself up some teensy-tiny little snake eggs?"

They had walked down to the gate by that time, and Jason walked through it, catching sight (without mentioning it) of Megan's horse. Salmon Kendall, however, stopped dead in his tracks. "See you later, funny man. I'm not gonna offer myself up to be robbed blind again."

Jason waved a hand. "All right. See you later, Mayor Shrimpfork."

He didn't look back, but he heard Salmon mutter, "Very funny, very funny . . ." as he turned and walked away, back into town. A smirking Jason made his way down the long line of Conestogas edging the outer wall of the town.

It wasn't easy. It seemed that the entire population of Fury was out here with him; some were clustered in knots around the dropped and propped tailboards of wagons, the children darting in and out between the heavily loaded Conestogas. Some were deeply engaged in conversation with their mates—wives trying to talk their husbands into more shrimp forks, he figured—while others busily bickered with one dusty and harried salesman or another.

Jason had spoken briefly with the wagon master, an affable chap named Fred Barlow, the night before when the wagons pulled in. Barlow was more than content to park his wagons outside the wall, and seemed grateful to have found a town out here, any town. At the moment, Barlow was nowhere in sight.

The citizens of Fury, however, had been out in full force since the crack of dawn. Jason wouldn't be a bit surprised to find the town's well draped in silver tassels and dangling shrimp forks come morning.

"Jason Fury!"

He turned toward the voice and spied Abigail Krimp, already dressed in her spangles, and carting enough loot to stagger a stevedore. She grinned widely. "I got up early to shop," she said, "and I'm so glad that I—"

"Jason!"

He turned around again, because this shout sounded urgent. And it was. Wash Keough, who to the best of Jason's knowledge was supposed to be far out of town working his claim, came barreling toward him in a roil of hoof-raised dust.

"Wash! What are you doing—" Jason began, but Wash cut him off.

"Injuns! Apache, and they're comin' this way!"

Jason jumped out of the way to avoid Wash's lathered horse, and before he knew it, Wash jumped down and was tugging him along and jabbering to beat the band.

"Whoa!" Jason shouted, and Wash stopped to catch his breath, dropping his reins in the process. Jason grabbed them before Wash's horse could skitter off, and Wash hung onto his knees for dear life, as though if he let go he'd fall straight over.

After a moment had passed and Wash seemed to be breathing a little easier, Jason asked, "What's the trouble, Wash? You been sippin' at some of that homemade cactus whiskey of yours?"

Wash wiped at his long mustaches and raised his head again, a look of pure disgust creeping over his craggy face. "You deaf or somethin', boy? I just told you, Apaches! You gotta get these folks inside! You gotta man the turrets! You gotta—"

"Man the turrets?" Jason broke in.

The Reverend Milcher, standing a few feet away, let loose with a guffaw, which he quickly stifled with his fist when Jason shot him a dirty look.

"Well, hell, boy, get some fellers up top on the wall at least! And haul these wagons inside. All they are is Apache ladders!"

As hysterical as Wash appeared, Jason couldn't smell any mescal on him. Quickly, he handed Wash's reins back to him and leapt to the seat of the closest wagon, standing on it to get as high as he could. He stood there a moment, his back to Wash, before he whirled around and jumped to the ground.

"Hey!" he shouted, but it was lost in the crowd noise. He stuck two fingers into his mouth and whistled as loudly as he could. That worked.

Ignoring Wash's whispered "Thank God," Jason began to marshal the crowd, sending families scrambling for the gate in the town wall, sending single men running for their guns, and urging the drivers to hitch their horses in a hurry and instructing them to move with all due haste and circle their wagons around the well, inside the walls.

He hoped Wash was dead wrong, but the truth was that there was a dust cloud to the south, a dust cloud that was fast approaching Fury.

"Come on!" he shouted as he helped a small boy, dusty and crying for his mother, to his feet. "Hurry up, folks! Move it!"

GREAT BOOKS, GREAT SAVINGS!

When You Visit Our Website:
www.kensingtonbooks.com

You Can Save Money Off The Retail Price
Of Any Book You Purchase!

- **All Your Favorite Kensington Authors**
- **New Releases & Timeless Classics**
- **Overnight Shipping Available**
- **eBooks Available For Many Titles**
- **All Major Credit Cards Accepted**

Visit Us Today To Start Saving!
www.kensingtonbooks.com

All Orders Are Subject To Availability.
Shipping and Handling Charges Apply.
Offers and Prices Subject To Change Without Notice.